To the Black girls who make themselves small for love.

Don't.

Acknowledgements

To my parents: Thanks for putting up with all my weirdness, especially when I was having deep, emotional discussions about fictional characters like they were actual people. If it weren't for our endless debates about *Charmed*, *Buffy*, and way too many Hallmark movies, this book probably wouldn't exist. You've always embraced my eccentricities with love (and more than a few eye rolls), and I'm forever grateful for that. You're the real MVPs in this story!

To Victoria, whose bookstore in Manayunk was my personal slice of heaven. You not only run a magical place (even online!), but you also wrote your own series through grief and pain—showing me that even in the toughest

Merry Meet Again

LILY A. LARKSPUR

Self-published by the author through Retrograde Literary

ISBN (eBook): 979-8-9995889-1-3
ISBN (Paperback): 979-8-9995889-0-6

Cover design by *Sam & Mel | Ink & Velvet Designs*
Edited by Bryn Donovan and Nicole Kincaid
Formatted by Nicole Kincaid at Naughty Nook PR

For more information, please visit my Linktr.ee: @anje_thewitchyromantic

First Edition

Printed in USA

times, creativity can flourish. Your messages of encouragement were like little potions that made this story real.

To Dejah and Amara, y'all are my favorite terrible influences (in the best way). Thanks for being the devils on both shoulders at every twist and turn, reminding me that sometimes, chaos and bad ideas are the best kind of fuel for creativity. You're the kind of friends who makes things happen—probably with a lot of caffeine and dubious life choices involved.

To my therapist: Thank you for patiently listening to my rambling. You've been the calm in the havoc, except when I told you my plot twists. This book probably wouldn't exist without you pushing me to stand firm in my passions.

To my unnamed friends—those who love dark lipstick, spooky season, and the kind of chaos that makes people raise an eyebrow—I salute you. You are the reason this book is filled with unpredictable magic, sassy characters, and questionable decisions. You never fail to remind me that normal is overrated.

And lastly, to the readers: Whether you picked this up because you love rom-coms, witches, or just the idea of a romantic disaster wrapped in a cute bow, I hope you enjoyed the ride. If you didn't...well, let's blame that on the planets, shall we?

Thank you for letting my weird little world take over yours, if only for a few hours.

Chapter 1

Cora had a running list of everything that had spectacularly crashed and burned in her life this past year. Relationship: check. Advice column: check. Identity as a witch: double check with an asterisk. Surely, there couldn't possibly be anything else left to fall apart in the span of, what, a few more weeks? The universe couldn't be so cruel as to give her more life lessons at the end of the calendar year. At least she hoped so as she lay in bed, the very picture of existential despair—eyes heavy and shadowed as she stared vacantly at the ceiling.

If only magic could solve all her problems. All Cora needed was a snap of the finger to take away the brokenness she felt inside. Though, there was that one fleeting thought about transforming her ex into a llama. That could've lifted her spirits a bit. For now, she'd have to settle for being a potato in her best friend's guest room. Not the yummy kind of potato either; the kind that had been left in the fridge too long.

She let out a huff as she turned in bed to face away from the blinding sun shining through the window. The December weather had the audacity to be nice since she'd gotten back, Pennsylvania being one of the more fickle states when it came to climate. She had a small hope it would be gloomy, to match her mood, but of course she couldn't have everything. With each inhale she caught the range of scents coming from the cracked window. Cora had almost forgotten how Philly smelled. Not bad, just...different. The nostalgia that came with the mix of old brick, overpriced coffee shops, and the many pretzels she wouldn't admit she missed just made her bitter. Someone might as well have shoved her into a blender set to *high-speed meltdown* after too much time spent hiding away in her Seattle bubble.

Lumi's small apartment, bless her heart, was cozy enough, a soft little cushion in the middle of this urban hurricane. But Cora was still in the delicate stage of pretending she didn't feel like a complete intruder. It'd only been a few days, yet Lumi was persistent in getting Cora out into the world. Would it kill Lumi to let her wallow in peace? Probably. The furthest Cora went was on the sidewalk of the apartment just out of spite.

With an unnatural talent for sensing when Cora was spiraling, Lumi now stood in the doorway of the guest room. Cora was surprised she didn't hear her walk down the hall. This is what she got for being in her head; a plus-sized Latina woman staring down at her with a freshly waxed eyebrow raised in scrutiny. Cora, ever the master of avoidance, pulled the blankets over her head in a last-ditch attempt to disappear from the world. Too bad Lumi didn't take too well to being ignored.

"No, no, no," Lumi said, her voice breezy and light but determined. "We've talked about this. You're not staying here all day and moping."

Cora groaned, muffled by the pillow. "I'm not moping. I'm meditating."

"On your own misery? That's some top-tier witchcraft right there."

Cora peeked one eye out from under the covers, tempted to throw a little jinx her way. Nothing too serious; maybe change her current hair dye attempt to a random color to remind her who was really in charge here. She *liked* her little refuge of a blanket fortress, tucked away and shielded from the world. Though the walls were starting to make her antsy, painted in some warm cream shade that reminded her of the hazy morning spent watching her father cook. Cora mentally added "forever alone" to her list and checked it off. This was getting a little long. If she added any more items she may consider talking to a therapist, but she wasn't that bad yet. As long as you didn't consider losing your job because you didn't handle your breakup well so then you move back home 'that bad.'

While she still had her mom, she was sick of the trailing reminder that everything used to feel just right, instead of the cruel joke her life was now. She could practically hear her mother's voice echoing throughout Lumi's in her head, nagging at her to get up and do something. But honestly? Cora wasn't ready for that level of responsibility.

"I don't need to go out," Cora muttered. "I'm fine here."

"You're not fine." Lumi stepped into the room, honey-kissed skin and a cascade of espresso-colored curls glowing from the sunlight. She looked so radiant, so vibrant with her eccentric holiday outfit of an oversized sweater shaped like a giant tree. So freaking annoying. Even the foil at the tips of her hair for her latest dye project sparkled more than Cora's current mood, just itching for a jinx. She felt invisible in comparison, bundled in her sweats, a jade necklace from an old friend tucked inside, with her bonnet slipping a little and letting a few pesky thick curls escape for breath. Cora snapped her fingers, but instead of gently drawing the curtains closed, they jerked violently, ripping down from the rod in a tangled mess.

She cursed under her breath, once again imagining her mother's nagging. A witch's magic tended to be unpredictable when overwhelmed by strong emotions like doubt or fear for long periods of time. Cora was two for two so far. Just another thing for Lumi to be on her ass about.

"See?" Lumi chastised further. "My point exactly. Even your magic is acting up! I'm not letting you turn into a sad, hermit witch who only talks to the plants in her room. You have me. And you're going out. Whether you like it or not."

Why wouldn't anyone just let Cora curl up and hide? Though she had to admit, Lumi's words had a familiar sting of someone who knew exactly how to break through the walls she'd spent weeks building, brick by brick. She scowled, pulling the covers tighter around her shoulders. "I don't feel like seeing anyone, Lumi. I just want to sleep and be. Okay?" What was it about Lumi's determination that made everything feel like too much?

She shouldn't have been surprised by the almost re-hearsed conversation they'd had since Cora's return, Lumi's attempts at making her a person again increasing by the day. They spent the first night drinking cider, eating chicken noodle soup, and wiping the traitorous tears that ran down Cora's cheeks. Day two and three were nearly the same, except less tears, more bitterness, and even more of Lumi trying to physically drag her from bed. Now, they were on day five and Cora was very committed to having her current routine on repeat.

Lumi's lips curled into a grin. "Yeah? You totally *want* to be miserable. But I'm not gonna let you. No more of this self-pity crap. I wouldn't be doing my job as your best friend if I didn't force you out of this state." Her grin dropped into a pout. "Where'd all your spark go?"

Cora's words felt like stones in her mouth. "It died."

"Well, that's unfortunate since Sparks is your last name."

Cora threw a pillow at her, and Lumi dodged it with the skill of someone who had lived through enough of Cora's tantrums to know how to avoid getting hit. Considering they were college roommates, she was well-versed in dodging.

"Are you seriously throwing pillows at me? That's your big rebellion?"

"No," Cora said, voice flat, "that's me throwing a pillow at you for not leaving me alone like I've been saying."

Lumi flopped down on the edge of the bed, throwing a dramatic huff into the air. "I swear you're like a toddler in a thirty-year-old's body. Looks like I'm gonna have to do something drastic."

Cora's eyebrows furrowed. "What? You're already chastising me like my mother. I would've just Ubered home if I knew I'd get the same treatment."

"I meaaaan if I really wanna sound like your mom I could pull out the go-to 'stop crying or I'll give you something to cry about.' But I won't stop you there. You *should* go home. You used to love coming back to celebrate Yule with your mom. Some chick shouldn't ruin that."

Cora winced, taking that quip like a slap to the face. Her ex, Avery, wasn't just 'some chick,' but in Lumi's world, anyone who hurt her friend got demoted to being called some something or other. If she knew about the cheating, she'd come up with a name much worse.

"If you don't get that butt up and start being the bad witch I know you are," Lumi's smile turned wicked, "I will sit on you."

Cora's eyes flicked to Lumi's hips, her brain briefly imagining the sheer force of that attempt. "You think that'll work? And don't you have a lingerie business to attend to? I think I hear your mannequins calling."

"I have plenty of time to spare when it comes to forcing you to be a person. I'm just saying. My body is powerful. You've been warned."

Cora just stared. "I have enough core strength to survive it."

"Oh really?" Lumi leaned forward, making a show of rubbing her palms together as if preparing for a wrestling match. "You sure about that? Because I'm about to do it."

Cora, not one to back down from a challenge, pushed herself up onto her elbows. "Do your worst, Lumi. I'll survive."

Lumi quirked an eyebrow, then slowly moved to hover over Cora, looking ready to pounce. Lumi's energy was so bright, so unapologetically vibrant, that Cora almost looked away. Cora couldn't shake off her haze, body stiff from the endless plane ride and hours of lying around, avoiding everything she left behind. If a reader had written to her asking for advice about navigating a breakup or some kind of lifestyle change, she'd tell them to go back to the things that brought them joy or spend time with loved ones. But since Cora sucked at following her own advice, her version of this involved having a month-long breakdown, breaking her lease, and leaving the state to return home.

She tried to forget the pieces of her life that shattered. Tried to ignore the silence that clung to her like a second skin. But Lumi was someone who often forced her out of her cocoon. And right now, she *hated* it. Just as Lumi was about to lower herself onto the bed with her full weight, her phone buzzed in her pocket.

"Saved by the bell," Cora muttered, flopping back onto the bed with a dramatic sigh. "Your move, Lumi."

"Don't get cocky. I actually have a huge favor to ask. It's low stakes and will briefly get you out for some fresh air."

Cora was tempted to refuse outright, to stay cocooned in her self-imposed prison. But she couldn't. She wasn't that rude, even if she was currently a hot mess. "Depends on the favor."

Lumi quickly got up and slid down the hall in her fuzzy turquoise socks, returning at a much slower speed a few moments later carrying a heavy bag filled with books. "Can you take these to Sticks and Stones bookstore for me? Up in Valley Creek Hollow? I've been meaning to donate them but keep forgetting, and I won't have time to head up there like I thought."

Cora sat up in confusion. Valley Creek Hollow was her hometown. "Why don't you just donate them somewhere here? There's plenty of bookstores around."

"Cause it has all the best witchy literature! And I know they take those kinds of donations."

Lumi wasn't wrong, but that didn't help Cora's confusion. "So, you're using your poor planning to get me out of the house to be a person?"

"Pretty please? With cinnamon sugar on top and drizzled with butterscotch." Lumi even gave her the puppy dog eyes for flourish.

Cora mentally swore. That line somehow always got her. "Fine! Since you want to get rid of me so badly. But this is all I'm committing to."

"It's for your own good! Plus, it's Yuletide season. Don't you wanna be home for the stuff you do with your mom?"

The question brought an ache to Cora's heart. She swallowed hard, trying to push down the tightness in her throat. Of course she wanted to, but going home also meant facing her failures in the most important parts of her life. She didn't want to see her mom until she pulled herself together a little more. But if that were the case, she may never do it.

"I do," Cora muttered, unable to look at her friend. She missed the comfort of old traditions and the warmth of their holiday routines. She hasn't had them since entering a relationship back in Seattle two years ago, and now she was back in her home state, single. She knew as soon as she returned home, with every twinkling light and every phone call, the painful truth would crush her; all the years she chose her ex over her own family, the years she missed, the years she could never get back. And it wasn't the festive cheer that was stifling—it was the grief.

"But?"

"But...I feel like I haven't *done* anything. Haven't figured things out. I can't face Mom until I'm at least a little less gloomy. And let's face it, I'm pretty much Eeyore."

Lumi huffed. "But you also haven't genuinely tried. You can't pull yourself together if you're too busy moping to give yourself a chance. If you keep telling yourself 'I'll go when..' then you might never get there. And your mom misses you! Doesn't missing her override this...whatever you're feeling?"

Guilt. Shame. Grief. Exhaustion. Too many words Cora could rattle off, and all the reasons she'd rather stay in bed. Cora's lip trembled slightly, but she held back the tears that wanted to come. Instead, those emotions sat on her chest, pushing her further down. It was so much easier said than done, but Lumi was right; she did miss her mom. And that mattered more than hiding away.

Cora took a long deep breath, picturing her mother's excited face as she exhaled. "I'll donate the books first," Cora said finally, her voice steadier now, but still uncertain. She lifted her head to meet Lumi's encouraging gaze. "Then I'll see how I feel. It's just...hard to stop running."

"You've been running for a while, Cora," Lumi stated, placing a hand on Cora's. "You're sad, I get it. Breakups are tough. But you used to tell me how much you loved this holiday season. Why not find that love for it again?"

Her breakup wasn't just tough, it was traumatic. But Lumi didn't know that yet. Cora thought back to her previous Yuletide festivities. Singing off-key carols. Helping her mom build altars of questionable design. The warmth and comfort of their home wrapping around her. The scent of cinnamon and pine lingering on her clothes when she'd go out. Maybe this is what she needed to be on the mend again. A little Yuletide creativity, a sprinkle of nostalgia, and a dash of her mom's questionable decorating skills. First, the bookstore. Then she'd find the courage to face her home turf. Baby steps. She could do baby steps.

Chapter 2

L umi shoved her out of the apartment.

Cora deserved it, really. She took her good old time sifting through her wardrobe once Lumi rejected anything resembling sweats. Apparently, being a person meant looking like one too. So instead of delivering the books and getting the hell out, Cora had left close enough to the bookstore's closing time that it would be considered impolite to linger there. At least she had time to zone out on her Septa ride.

Nestled in the rolling hills of Southeastern Pennsylvania sat Valley Creek Hollow. The name of the town was fairly unoriginal, sharing a portion of it with a creek, park, and preserve. That's King of Prussia for you. Still, there was something stubborn and ancient about this place; something you didn't notice until you'd left and came crawling back. Valley Creek Hollow had been around since the early 1800s, founded by pioneers who were probably tired of the noise and nonsense of bigger cities after William Penn's grand tour. They came looking for quiet—and maybe found more than they bargained for.

The land here had a pulse, a kind of memory baked into the rocks and trees. Magic didn't come from fancy schools or secret books, it was older than that. Passed down like a family recipe, rooted in blood, belief, and the occasional whispering breeze that knew your name. Of course, it didn't take long for people to start gossiping about the Hollow's unusual residents and the unique way their gardens always thrived a little too well.

When Cora begrudgingly arrived, she inhaled deeply as if the familiar scent of pine and rain-soaked earth would undo all the reasons she'd left. The air was sharp with winter's bite, filling her lungs with a crispness that stung slightly, leaving a lingering chill in the back of her throat. The breeze, cold and whispering, tugged at the loose coils that framed her face. It almost felt like a hand brushing against her skin—playful, urging her to let go of the past. The evergreens and oak trees around her stood like sentinels, their branches heavy with frost, their stillness sharp against the restless wind.

Seattle had been perfect for her once upon a time; it had all the nature she appreciated without the emotional baggage. It worked for the most part when she started grad school, the easiest way to get to know people and have somewhat of a social life. Then, after school, came her tiny bubble of work friends, though they were more like associates than anything else. She had a bad streak of keeping surface level relationships. Despite Seattle itself not having baggage, Cora seemed to bring her own with her. Avoidance for the win. At least, up until she met her now ex-partner. *Doesn't matter now*, she mused.

The sound of dead leaves crunching under her boots played as the soundtrack to her childhood. She could practically hear her mom's voice, cheering her on as she spent hours attempting to make wreaths from twigs she wasn't exactly talented at weaving. But of course her mom acted like each creation was a masterpiece. The memory made something tighten in Cora's chest—a mixture of longing and guilt, and a reminder of all the love she'd left behind. Her throat felt a little tight as she inhaled again, the cold air seeming to press deeper into her lungs. She couldn't help but think, *How did I even stay away from this for so long?* All the reasons she'd turned her back on her home were suddenly distant and fragile.

When she finally arrived at the bookstore, she noticed its renovation since her last visit home two years prior. Previously a quaint, dark-wood building, it now stood as a sturdy stone structure. Sure, it still had that old-world charm, with ivy creeping up the walls and winter sunlight spilling through the windows like a scene out of some cozy holiday movie. Flower beds of holly and thistle lined the area, and Cora could almost picture them bursting with lilacs come spring. She paused for a moment, just standing there, staring at the door as memories came rushing back. Summer afternoons spent among books and laughter, getting lost in worlds that seemed to promise a future far grander than the reality her adult self had walked into. It warmed her slightly, but the sadness lingered.

Remembering the weight of books she was lugging around, Cora took a deep breath and shoved the door open. The air inside was cool and musty—classic old bookstore vibes—with the comforting scent of aged paper and the faint hint of dust settling in forgotten corners. Rows upon rows of shelves stretched out before her, crammed with stories just waiting to be unearthed. The tables were all decked out with electric candles and fairy lights, clearly going for a mystical feel, with holiday-themed tablecloths that screamed *I'm festive but still serious about my books.* Over by the windows sat little ceramic snowmen, all painted with ever-cheerful smiles. Though their noses had seen better days, each slightly crooked with one too many curious hands probably poking at them. Tinsel swirled in and out of the spaces between them, along with a stack of festive bookmarks with various winter designs.

But what truly caught Cora off guard was how much bigger the place appeared on the inside. It appeared much smaller from the outside than the labyrinthine maze of shelves and nooks within. She blinked, her eyes sweeping the high ceilings that seemed to stretch far beyond what she'd expected. The air hummed, too. Subtle, yet unmistakable to her magic. She could sense it more clearly now—the magic, faint but ever-present, lingering along the bookshelves, curling in the corners like wisps of smoke.

It's charmed, she realized with a start, her hand brushing lightly against the doorframe, feeling a slight tingling sensation run up her fingers. It wasn't exactly surprising, but it was her first time experiencing it firsthand.

She didn't see anyone at the counter, but she was *done* carrying the bag, so she made her way over anyway to unload her burden. "I'd like to make a donation," Cora called out, huffing as she dumped the bag of books onto the counter. She flexed her fingers, sore from holding it for far too long, her gold rings digging into her skin. As she waited for someone to appear, the sound of books clattering to the floor followed by a few choice curses echoed through the room. Well, at least she wasn't breaking and entering.

"Be there in a minute!" came a soothing baritone voice. It was meant to be reassuring, but after hearing more things fall and the extensive swearing, Cora started to wonder if she'd walked into some kind of disaster zone.

Her eyes darted to the back stacks, where all the commotion seemed to be coming from.

Finally, the person emerged, dusting himself off and leaving Cora's breath caught in her throat. *Oh my Hekate.* Her mouth definitely dropped open, but she couldn't bring herself to care. The man who appeared was tall, Black, and *good grief*—sexy didn't even cover it. He wore a beige cardigan, just worn enough to suggest he had a real love for his work and that particular article of clothing, and his coffee-brown hair hung loosely around his shoulders, a half-bun pulled to the back keeping it somewhat in check.

I must have a thing for people with hair I can run my hands through, Cora thought as her ex's features vaguely came to mind. But the long onyx tresses didn't begin to compare. She blushed once she realized she was staring. He didn't seem to notice though, too busy wiping his glasses with his shirt before placing them back on his face. When he finally looked up, his gaze lingered on her, blinking once, twice, then settling. Cora held his stare, the awkwardness slipping away as something tugged at her chest. There was something familiarly magnetic about him—the warmth in his brown eyes, the mischievous twinkle that tugged at her memories. He tilted his head, mirroring her own movement, both of them frowning as she tried to figure out why his face was so damn familiar.

Then, his eyes trailed down, widening in surprise when they landed on her chest. Her cheeks heated as she almost called him out on it, until she remembered the jade shell-shaped necklace she wore.

"Cordelia?" he whispered. A pleasurable shiver ran down her spine at the sound of her name from his husky voice. Only two other people called her by her full name, her ex being one of them, and it surprised her that it didn't feel so...*wrong*. "Is that really you?"

"Theo," Cora replied, the recognition hitting. Her eyes immediately fell to his chest, trying to focus on the jasper turtle hanging from his neck instead of the, um, very noticeable shape of his pectorals. "I didn't expect to see you here."

A younger version of the witch always kept her company at this very bookstore in its previous state. The boy with chubby cheeks, crooked square glasses, and a shy smile who had once shared her secrets and dreams, her curiosity and magic, was now a man with strong shoulders that could probably carry the weight of all her lingering feelings. She couldn't believe he stood before her, having not seen him since he moved away after her thirteenth birthday. He exuded the confident air of someone who had found his place in the world. She wished she could exude the same confidence.

"It's been a while," Theo commented, stepping out from behind the counter, looking both hesitant and way too eager for her poor heart at the same time. He paused, like he was weighing something in his head, then a smirk tugged at his lips. "Loser."

Cora couldn't help it—she snickered at the old nickname, one that hadn't been used in two decades. "Oh please, you're one to talk, dork." She tried to smile, but it came off as more of a twitch that didn't quite reach her eyes. "What can I say? I needed a change in pace." She glanced around the bookstore, seeing it in a whole new light now that an old friend had appeared in the middle of it. "So, you went from playing hide and seek in the stacks to running the show here?"

"Yeah, well, it's not what we used to talk about as kids, but I love it," he admitted, rubbing the back of his neck. Cora found his humility oddly endearing. "I took over the bookstore about two years ago, after Mr. Hargrove retired. What about you? I heard you moved across the country."

Theo leaned against the counter, genuinely curious. "Not that I'm stalking you or anything, but I didn't expect you back because your mom always talked about how great you were doing. How's Seattle treating you?"

The mention of Seattle made her stomach drop—crowded streets, endless emails, and a mountain of heartache. "When do you even see my mother?" she shot back, the words tumbling from her mouth before she could stop them.

Theo didn't miss the dodge, but he just shrugged. "She attends a book club here. And if you don't tell me, I'll just start using her as my personal gossip source about your life. Looks like she still adores me like she did back in the day."

Cora groaned, because of course her mother would spill every little detail to Theo just to get her nose into something. She tried to force her smile to look more real, but it felt like an attempt at being someone she wasn't quite yet. "Not so great, to be honest. Decided to come back for a breather. I needed to...recalibrate I guess." She looked down, trying to avoid his gaze as a sudden wave of shame washed over her, wishing her coils could just cover her entire face. Compared to what her mom probably said, this most likely wasn't the answer he was anticipating. "Things didn't go quite as planned in Seattle."

Theo tilted his head, brow raised in that way that made it clear he was curious but didn't want to push. Yet. "If you ever need someone to talk to, I'm here. The bookstore's a good place to escape, and I don't mind the company." Noticing her hesitation, he shot her a grin that was more charming than it had any right to be. "It can be nice to come home and have a place to heal. I would know." He gestured to a cozy armchair tucked away in a quiet corner toward the back. "Can I get you a cup of tea?"

"You sure? Isn't it practically closing time?"

"All the more reason to catch up. I'll just lock the doors."

Cora nodded, grateful for the offer and momentarily forgetting about the bag of books she was supposed to donate. Theo disappeared into the back, and Cora—being totally *not* obvious—caught a glimpse of his backside, muscles taut in his worn denim. She quickly pinched herself for staring. *Hot damn.* Then she patted her messy space buns, making sure they were still mostly in place and presentable. Cora initially regretted not putting them in a protective style for the winter, and now she regretted not doing so because it was hard to look like a hot mess with braided hair. Though she was pretty sure Lumi wouldn't have allowed her to leave if she didn't look decent.

To avoid her brain turning into a puddle of goo, she focused on the familiar ambiance of the bookstore. The same comforting silence enveloped her, the kind that invited deep, introspective thinking. It wasn't hard to remember the afternoons spent debating the greatness of Roald Dahl versus E.B. White, throwing out random theories about utopian societies and laughing until the sun sank behind the tall windows. They'd stay until dinner, unwilling to leave their little haven. Ah, the days when life felt a bit——a lot——less complicated.

Theo returned with two steaming mugs, setting one down on the table before her. "I've been working to turn this place into more than just a bookstore," he explained with an enthusiastic smile. "The first year I focused on giving it a makeover, which was *not* easy. Would not recommend. This year I've focused on making it more integrated in the community. There are book clubs, poetry readings, sabbat celebrations. I want it to be a real community hub."

Cora smiled as she took a sip, the warmth of cinnamon and cloves spreading through her. *He remembered.* "You've always known how to bring people together."

That brought a soft smile to Theo's lips as they fell into easy conversation. They strolled the aisles of memory lane, reminiscing about their childhood—building forts from books, hosting secret two-person book clubs, and hiding away from the world, lost in their imagination. It felt good to talk about the simpler times. Cora almost felt bad; with each passing moment she started easing up a little. Theo's mere presence did that, compared to poor Lumi's days of pestering.

Though, she fought the restless urge to hide, unable to meet Theo's eager gaze for long without feeling exposed. Each time he asked about Seattle she crossed her arms instinctively, as if the gesture could somehow shield her thoughts. Thank Hekate he couldn't read minds, but he *was* perceptive to body language. Cora couldn't hide her ping pong of ease and unease even if she tried.

She wanted to kick herself. How was she so awkward around him now? He'd only changed physically, but his personality was *exactly* the same. This should've been easy. But no, instead, he was seeing her after her life had fallen apart, even though he didn't know it. She just wanted to pretend she was still that awkward witch from their youth—the one he remembered before all the...well, the *mess* that came after.

"So, back to my mother. She never told me you came back!"

Theo chuckled awkwardly. "She said you hadn't come back home in a while, so I told her not to say anything. I didn't want to interrupt the life you created over there."

Cora pouted, disliking the answer the more he talked. Theo would've been a welcomed interruption, even back when things were going well with her and Avery. *Then again, maybe not.* The longer she stayed quiet, the more he stared at her, waiting for the opportunity to ask her the laundry list of questions just waiting to spill out.

Better get on with it. Cora swallowed as they returned back to the quiet corner. "Okay, go ahead. Start the interrogation."

Theo sulked. "So you're not interested at all about my life since we lost touch. Just here ready to talk about your extravagant West Coast life?"

She appreciated him trying to make light of the situation, but still felt guilty for how it came off. So she joked back. "How interesting can your stories of Missouri be?"

"I'll have you know I was in the very important city of St. Louis. Plenty to do, and that's not including the excitement of tornado warnings."

"There must've been some allure. I never saw you all the times I came back here to visit."

Theo winced, taking his glasses off to rub the bridge of his nose. Cora hated how attractive she found the action. Did she prefer him with glasses or without? She wasn't sure yet. *Focus, Cora.* "Didn't exactly have many opportunities. Money was tight on my end, and I wasn't in the position to come back until a couple of years ago. When I came back I started working for Mr. Hargrove, and when I found out he wanted to retire and close the bookstore, I just couldn't let it happen."

That lined up with when Cora stopped coming home once she entered a relationship. She found herself wondering why her mother never mentioned Theo's return. If she had known, maybe it would've given her more of an incentive to come back at least once. Giving into a yearning for a piece of her past that she long missed.

She shook her head. No, even that wouldn't have brought her back with how enraptured she became with Avery. "Okay then. Tell me some wild stories about living out in the Midwest."

"Hmm." Theo took a moment, prompting Cora to pause in sipping her drink. She leaned forward onto the table with her elbows, signaling that she was both patient and eager to hear. "Okay, here's one. I ended up living next to this retired guy named Mr. Jenkins. He taught me how to drive a riding lawnmower."

Cora snorted, picturing a younger Theo trying to handle a lawnmower in St. Louis. "A lawnmower? Seriously?"

Theo grinned back, still holding his glasses in one hand as his hair fell in front of his eyes. They were golden from the light spilling in from the windows. "Nearly ran it into the bushes the first time I tried. But I picked it up quickly. Actually ended up really liking it. Mr. Jenkins had this huge backyard he manicured based on the gardening magazines he'd read, and we spent weekends trimming the hedges and planting tomatoes. You'd be surprised how much I learned about lawn care."

"I asked for a wild story, not a wholesome one," Cora chided, but she looked at Theo with warmth. "That sounds amazing."

"It was a lot quieter than I expected." He shrugged, putting his glasses back on as if re-arming himself. "But my parents loved it, still do. I took a job at a local bookstore on a whim, needing something to fill my time. I didn't think I'd truly enjoy it, but I read more in those years than I ever did before." He paused, eyes looking glazed over as he delved into his memories. "Sometimes I'd read stories to kids during a weekly storytime hour they had. It was...fulfilling. Reminded me of how we used to make up stories on rainy days."

"You always had a vivid imagination. I remember when we created that world of talking animals. You made up the best characters."

"You flatter me. You're the one that made Oswald the wise old owl and Rita the feisty raccoon. I still think about those stories sometimes."

"What was it like being away from everyone?" Cora asked the question she wasn't sure she wanted the answer to. "Away from me?"

"I could ask you the same." Theo looked down at the table, fingers tracing the ceramic edge of his mug. "It was lonely for a long while, like a part of me was missing. I missed our adventures, but I think I had to find my way in a new place. Grow up a little." Then he looked her right in the eyes, her heart quickening at his gaze. "I'd be lying if I said I didn't think about you."

Cora didn't know how she found her voice with how dry her throat became. She licked her lips subconsciously. "I can definitely relate. In both aspects. I just decided to go further out west than you." She poked his nose, attempting to dissipate the serious tone. "I wrote you letters for a while. And I tried to look you up sometimes, but you know how Mom was about social media. I didn't even get a cell phone until sophomore year of high school."

"Ah, so I didn't get replaced right away."

"Dork." Cora lightly kicked him under the table. Theo's face wincing in mock pain. "There's no replacing you, 'cause you're *you*. I mean, there's my friend, Lumi, I met in high school, but she's still not you, just like you're not her."

"So it's not too late to reconnect?"

Cora didn't miss the apprehension in Theo's voice. He wasn't the type to have doubts about their friendship, but years apart can change things. This, though, the thing between them, was something she didn't want to change. Even if his good looks were admittedly somewhat distracting.

"Never too late," she beamed. "We may have lost our awkward teenage years and disastrous twenties, but we still have our memories. And I'd love to make new ones with this cooler version of you."

"You're *such* a loser." Theo glanced outside to see the sun dipped on the horizon. "I think it's past time to officially close up shop. Are you staying at your mom's? I'll walk you there."

Cora hesitated. She didn't plan to see her mom until later in the week and used this excursion to test the waters. But she was enjoying their conversation too much, and a walk could extend their time together.

He caught her hesitation and dramatically placed a hand on his forehead like he might faint. "I guess I'll wait another decade or so."

Cora shoved him, but paused before pulling her hand back. The shame made her want to run, to avoid officially returning home with the wounds and bitterness from her breakup still fresh. But as she looked into his warm, earnest eyes, she remembered how safe he always made her feel, how genuine he'd been. She shoved her anxiety down.

"Okay," she finally said. "Why not?"

His grin stretched ear to ear, filling Cora with a joy that surprised her. Going to the front door and facing the whole building, with a flick of the wrist he got to work.

The books shimmered, their spines glowing with a soft light. Tendrils of silken rays wrapped around them as they floated toward their shelves with an almost peaceful sigh. The lights dimmed like fireflies at dusk. The books she'd brought with her rose from their bags, finding their rightful places among the shelves, while the tea mugs floated out of sight. The once chaotic room transformed into a serene sanctuary, everything neatly falling into place as if it had always been that way.

Cora stood there, mouth agape once again. She must've looked ridiculous, but the sight of him so effortlessly using his magic in front of her filled her with awe and a longing she hadn't expected. Avery wasn't a witch, and neither were the acquaintances she made in Seattle. It stirred an unanticipated longing. Her own magic tingled at the edges

33

of her awareness, wanting to join in. How could Theo be so calm, so sure of his magic? It felt pure, untouched by the fear and self-doubt that had gnawed at her since being with Avery.

"Hey. Want to help me with the wards?" he asked.

Cora's cheeks flushed. "Wards?"

"Yeah. Just a little protection spell to keep the bookstore extra safe."

Her nervousness traveled up her spine, knowing how on the fritz her magic had been as of late. But the idea of magic together sparked a flicker of excitement. "I've never done wards with anyone before."

"Well, you have me now," he encouraged, pulling out shimmering crystals from his pocket. "Here, hold this." He passed her black tourmaline and citrine, while he palmed obsidian and clear quartz. As Cora wrapped her fingers around them, she was surprised by the warmth they emanated and the immediate calm that settled on her.

With his guidance, they stood side by side, weaving their intentions into the air. Cora could feel the vibrant dance of magic as it swirled and twirled around them. The energy thrummed, and she allowed herself to let go of fear.

As the last of the magic settled, Theo turned to her with a wicked grin. "And there you have it—closing time, courtesy of a little magic."

Chapter 3

It was ridiculous, really, being so anxious to go home to see your loving parent. Cora mentally kicked herself with every step she took. *It's just Mom*, she told herself. *She knows what happened and hasn't treated me any different.* She felt like shaking some sense into herself. Theo's presence didn't help as much as she wished it did; not because they fell into awkward silence or anything, but because she still couldn't get over how attractive he'd become. That alone was its own problem that she didn't have the mental space to address. Her heart wouldn't stop pounding as they made their walk to her childhood home.

It was all fun and games at first, Cora thought, reflecting back on her brilliant decision to move to Seattle. Nine years ago it felt like the boldest choice she could make—new city, new life, where the rain never stopped and coffee was practically sacred. She'd been fresh out of undergrad with a couple of short story prizes tucked under her belt, and her fiction professor had practically begged her to take the leap for a master's program. In hindsight, it wasn't the worst decision. But now, in the middle of a casual career crisis and a relationship train wreck, she found herself wondering if winging it had been overrated. The petty side of her thought it would've been nice to make it to ten years there, if Avery hadn't ruined everything.

Once, she thought she was thriving—a somewhat successful witch in a city full of potential. Now? Now, she was back in her hometown and on the search for a personal refresh, while the bitter reality settled in that maybe she'd walked straight into a midlife crisis at thirty years-old.

In an effort to prolong their walk, Cora suggested they meander about the town's square since so much was settled in one place. Not that it could make much of a difference; it was a blessing and a curse that everything within Valley Creek Hollow was within walking distance. Its original settlers were her kind of people; building a town with everything you'll need so there's no reason to travel far. Theo happily agreed, completely oblivious to her inner turmoil——bless his pure heart——as he chatted away about the various food spots they used to frequent as children. Marigold Café was one of them, closed at that hour, but the lingering smell of fresh pastries remained. A smile tugged at her lips when she remembered how she used to grab a chocolate chip croissant from the owner, back when her biggest problem was forgetting her homework. Then there was Valley Creek Hollow Diner, which supposedly still had the best peppermint mocha hot chocolate that she might have to grab sometime.

But all too soon they found themselves in the residential area and at the edge of the familiar gravel driveway. Cora placed a hand on her chest, her heart hammering like it was trying to escape her chest. She thought Theo might just leave her there, but in a show of some chivalry he accompanied her to the door. They walked up the heart-shaped stones that lined the path to the thick wooden door framed by ivy. Icicles hung from the eaves like crystal chandeliers, the sucker punch of nostalgia causing more anxiety. Though she needed a breather from the bitter emotions that resurfaced, she ended up walking into a whole different kind.

"Don't be a stranger now," Theo demanded as he turned to her. "I know where you live."

"Well, I was staying at Lumi's, but this might've been the push I needed to come back up here."

"Good, 'cause I still have questions about your life, too, ya know. You can't get off that easily."

If only. "Idle threats."

His gaze dropped to her necklace again, lingering in a way that ignited a sudden heat in her that made her frustrated and embarrassed. "I can't believe you still have it."

Nodding was all she could muster. Cora fingered the stone delicately in her hand, remembering how he gave it to her through hiccups and tears before moving away. She had long moved on from the painful goodbye and the lost contact between them, but she still wasn't prepared for the rush of seeing him still wearing his as well. At one point the necklace bothered her ex, but that was one of the few areas where Cora refused to bend.

Theo smiled—a familiar smile that took Cora back to when she was a skinny girl, and he had the embarrassing glasses. Full of optimism, dimples on full display. Had he always had such cute dimples? Before she could turn to leave, he grabbed her wrist and pulled her into a tight hug. Cora froze in shock for a moment, then slowly melted into the embrace and returned it. His chin rested easily on top of her head, allowing her to bury her face in his chest. He smelled of vanilla and must, and she tried to ignore how sturdy his chest felt against hers or how natural it all seemed. They simply stood there, breathing together in the quiet of the evening.

When they finally separated, Theo's hands lingered around her waist a moment too long before stepping back and waving goodbye as he headed back down the path. She suddenly felt colder without him by her side, though it could've just been the winter breeze. Either way, she swallowed hard and adjusted the bottom of her flowing, forest-green dress and reached for the key buried deep in her tote. No turning back now.

Once she managed to unlock the door and shuffle inside, warmth immediately engulfed her, thawing out all her anxieties. The scent of cinnamon and cloves, her mom's signature move to make the house smell cozy, clung to the air. The living room to her left hadn't changed in the slightest. The beige leather couches, bought just before Cora left for grad school, like her mom was anticipating her absence, still sat in their same exact position. The walls were lined with pictures of various family members from Yuletide's past, none of them able to make a serious facial expression or pose.

The stairs in front of her were carpeted in burgundy, freshly cleaned, with that faint smell of cleaning product still clinging to the fibers like it wasn't quite ready to let go of its last-minute touch-up. Boxes of decorations were spread out on the glass dining room table, reminding her of the inevitable fate of coming home: decorating duty. Cora mentally prepared herself to spend the next few days elbow-deep in tinsel.

"Cora!" A voice rang out, filled with the kind of joy that could almost make her forget why she was so nervous in the first place. Cora's mother, Nicole, emerged from the kitchen in a plush lavender robe and matching slippers.

41

Her short, graying curls were clipped back in a tiny pony-tail, not a strand out of place, though Cora knew better than to underestimate the amount of hair product it took to achieve that effortless look. And that smile, *that smile*, full of enough whimsy to send you running for the hills, or into a hug depending on the kind of person you were. Right now, Cora was decidedly the latter.

The spritely woman practically bounced over to her with the energy of someone half her age, though Cora had a sneaking suspicion that was mostly due to the pinch of magic she added to her morning tea. If anyone could convince you that the chaos of the holidays was worth it, it was Nicole, with her endless enthusiasm and a gift for making every holiday feel like it came from a movie.

"Mom!" Cora exclaimed, dropping her bag and rushing into her mother's embrace. The tension in Cora's body immediately dissolved. It wasn't lost on Cora that her mother was so short, she could practically rest her head on Cora's chest without even trying. Of course, Nicole was too busy squeezing the life out of her to notice, as if she could somehow absorb all of Cora's Seattle-induced exhaustion with just one hug.

"Oh, look at you! Our video calls didn't do you justice!" her mother gushed, stepping back to take her in. Nicole's pride for her radiated from her gaze, eyes scanning every inch of her. Cora giggled, doing a dramatic turn to help. It assisted in ignoring how, of course, her mother would be so excited when she hadn't seen her only child in person for two years. Nicole reached out to smooth back a stubborn coil of Cora's thick, dark hair, trying to tame the wildness that no longer wanted to be contained by her hair ties.

"You're even more radiant than last time. You should've told me what time you were coming! Let me brew your favorite spiced cider," Nicole added, as if the entire house wasn't already glowing from her enthusiasm.

While Nicole disappeared back into the kitchen, Cora took those few moments to examine the pictures surrounding the dining room. The silver frames gleamed as if they'd been polished just an hour ago—classic Mom move, getting ahead of herself on the housework. Most of the pictures featured Cora and her parents, all neatly arranged by year: awkward middle school speech contests, the volleyball games in high school where she barely kept the ball from hitting the floor, and then her college graduation, a rare bright spot in the blur of everything else. But after her father left the world, the pictures started to dwindle.

Suddenly, it was just Cora or her mother's phone holding onto those moments, and the shelves were left to hold a frozen, outdated timeline—stuck in some earlier version of their lives where it was just the three of them, before yet another thing in her life had fallen apart.

"Cora you won't believe what happened at the shop today," Nicole started as she ushered her into the living room, two mugs of spiced cider in hand. "You know how I said I've been getting more tourists lately, right? Well, there was this one woman who came in, all boho chic, saying she was searching for 'authenticity' or whatever that means."

Cora could feel her eye twitch at the thought of where this story was headed. Her mother's metaphysical shop was the go-to place in Valley Creek Hollow if you wanted candles, oils, and pottery. It often attracted tourists who were into the metaphysical for fun, while also offering services to local witches. It was perfect for her mother's specialty—a hearth witch who blended magic with an overly generous helping of meddling.

"Mmm, sounds like someone who'd be drawn to a place like Moonlight Magnolias."

Nicole laughed. "Exactly! So she asks me about the oils and I'm giving her my whole spiel, talking about lavender for peace and rosemary for clarity, when—wait for it—she spots the pottery."

"Oh dear."

"But not just any pottery. She picks up this little terra-cotta bowl, and I swear, her eyes go wide. She says, 'This bowl has a story, doesn't it? It calls to me.' So, naturally, I lean in, all serious-like, and I say, 'Ah, yes. This bowl was crafted by an artist who channels the energy of the full moon, imbuing each piece with...' and I'm totally making this up as I go, Cora—"

"Naturally." Cora was starting to remember just how much of a human glitter bomb her mother was, her sparkly personality clashing with Cora's more subdued and sarcastic one.

"I know, I know, but she ate it up! She was hanging on every word, nodding like she was getting the secret to the universe. And then—get this—she buys the bowl and asks if I can charge it with a bit of lunar magic."

Cora chuckled. "Charged pottery. That's a new one."

"I couldn't help myself! I told her, 'Absolutely, I'll take it under the next full moon and let the energies flow through it.' I'm sure it was all nonsense, but hey, she left happy, and that's what matters. No harm, no foul."

"Moonlit Magnolias," Cora took another sip of her cider, "where the pottery's magical, and the storytelling's even more so."

"Speaking of storytelling." *Uh oh*. "Do you think you'll take this break to start writing fiction again?"

Cora bit her lip, not knowing how to answer. Their weekly calls had fizzled over the last two months, Cora feeling too embarrassed and hurt with how the end of her relationship spilled into her career. She didn't have a plan of how to get back on her feet let alone explore writing for herself again.

"I'm not sure," she answered slowly. "I haven't thought about it. I mean, I already hate feeling like I'm imposing on you, suddenly coming home." But deep down, she just wasn't ready to face her yet.

Her mother waved the comment away, the arm of her lavender robe practically swallowed her hand whole. "Nonsense, you're my daughter. I just feel bad I didn't get your room properly set up yet."

"I'm a big girl," Cora replied, flexing her small biceps. "I can handle it."

She received a disbelieving look. "You told me almost exactly the same thing when you called crying about Avery."

Cora winced, sinking deeper into the couch, hoping it could swallow her up like a black hole. They'd broken up at the end of October, and she'd been tight lipped about the details to everyone but her mother. Not that there were many people to tell. In the aftermath of the emotional wreckage, Cora went from being cold and distant toward Avery in an attempt to display being unaffected by the turn of events, to a blubbering mess on a phone call with Nicole. Her mom tried to comfort her, saying 'You two wanted different things,' in the same breath as offering to send cookies that could bother Avery's stomach for at least a week. Cora wasn't having it then.

"Mom, I don't know what I'm doing anymore," Cora's voice cracked, the familiar ache of uncertainty heavy in her tone. It was so much easier sulking, feigning indifference, or avoiding how she truly felt, but she couldn't hide her true feelings around her own mother.

Her mother, ever the optimist, reached across the couch and squeezed her hand with the kind of warmth that only came from years of dealing with this exact breakdown.

"Honey, you're not the first, and certainly won't be the last, to feel lost in her thirties."

Cora let out a shaky breath. "But everyone else seems to have their life figured out. Have stability. I thought I did, and look how that turned out: no relationship, no inspiration, no joy. I'm a walking Pinterest fail."

"Don't believe that for a second. Everyone's grappling with something, even if they don't show it. You're just being honest with yourself, which is a good thing."

"But it's been so long since I've written anything! What if I never figure it out?" It was the same disastrous thought loop she'd been spiraling through for weeks. What if all the years of writing, of striving, of pretending she had a clue, were for nothing? What if, without her pen in hand, she was just a regular person with a job and a paycheck and a sad, pathetic life? She couldn't imagine it. Writing wasn't just a passion—it was basically her oxygen. What did people even do if they didn't have that?

Nicole leaned closer, her cinnamon eyes sparkling with that *I'm about to drop some wisdom on you* look. "First of all, it hasn't been that long since your relationship ended. You need to give yourself actual time to grieve, not just shove it all down with work like you've been doing. And second, you don't need to have every single thing in your life figured out right now. I know you think you do, with your 'big girl age' and all, but honey, you're still in the process of figuring out who you are and what you want."

Cora shot her a look. "Uh, yeah, Mom, I'm fully aware. It's called living in existential dread." She sighed, slumping further into the couch. "Since when did you get all wise?"

"Always, you just don't like listening to me."

"As an only child I can't help myself."

The two sat in silence for a few moments, Cora stewing over her mom's pearls of wisdom. The fire crackled in the background, offering up a faint warmth, but even that wasn't enough to drown out the anxiety of not knowing what she should do next.

Finally, Cora admitted what truly bothered her. "I don't even know who I am anymore, Mom. I've spent so many years just drifting along, and now I feel like I've completely lost myself. Like everything I thought made me me, doesn't even matter anymore. And now I'm back here, in this town that somehow feels even more foreign than Seattle. It's a lot, Mom. A lot. Too much, actually."

Nicole sighed. "You're not running away, Cora. You're just hitting pause. Everyone needs to stop and let the world catch up to them eventually. This town, this weird little bubble, it's all part of the process. If you actually let yourself, you can find your way back to who you are. I know you can, even if you'd rather sulk about it."

"You always know how to make things sound easier than they are."

"Well, life's a bit easier when you've already survived it all," Nicole replied with a grin, then quickly sobered. "But seriously, it's okay to be lost for a while. Sometimes, being lost is the only way to find yourself again. Or at least that's what I tell myself when I lose my keys for the third time in a week."

Cora remembered how her mother was a wreck after her father's death, barely holding herself together. Her own breakup was tragic, but not nearly as much. "You make yourself sound ancient."

"Shut up! But really honey, there's nothing you can't get through. You're strong, capable, and intelligent. Just remember, you're not alone. We're always here for you, no matter what." Nicole pulled her daughter into a warm embrace. "Now, how about I make you some of your favorite chicken noodle soup? You know, the one that makes you feel better, right?"

Cora smiled, not having the heart to tell her she'd already had some with Lumi this week. A mother's home cooking hits different. "Perfect pairing to my cider. Honestly, you should charge for that soup. Other people though, not me."

After engulfing Nicole's cooking, Cora was released to her childhood room, a time capsule of her teenage self. The door groaned in protest as she stepped inside, making her wish she'd at least made a few upgrades when she made her monthly visits back in undergrad. The lilac walls that she once begged for in her youth now seemed out of place, a relic of someone she used to be. The boxes of her things from her previous apartment were piled high atop of the carefully drawn sigil that helped transport them there. She remembered she still had some of her things at Lumi's, and almost considered using that as an excuse to go back and stay there.

She shook her head at the thought. No, she couldn't just spend the night with her mom and say *thanks, but I'll go back to staying with my friend who actually peer pressured me into going home in the first place.* It was nice being home again, even if it forced her to feel those icky feelings. She'd go back for her things and thank Lumi for being a menace.

Plus...Cora blushed as her thoughts trailed to Theo. *I need some girl talk.*

Chapter 4

Cora wished she was better with portal magic, wanting to use it for herself as she dashed through the busy city streets toward Lumi's apartment. But with her magic still being as unpredictable as her mood, she couldn't chance it. She still had a fear that she'd try to portal somewhere and end up inside a wall. Instead, she tried to ignore that she wore the same outfit as yesterday due to being too lazy to fish for something in her unpacked boxes, anxiety and excitement swirled within her from the previous day's events.

When she finally reached Lumi's building, Cora paused, her hand pressed to her chest as she tried to calm her frantic heart. Then, with a deep breath, she knocked furiously on the door.

Lumi must've been waiting just behind it, because on the third knock, she swung it open, grinning like a cat that got the cream. "You're later than you said you'd be."

Cora stepped inside, the scent of vanilla candles and freshly popped popcorn greeting her. She kicked off her boots, a welcome relief after the rush. Lumi was already lounging cross-legged on the couch, pulling her oversized baby-blue striped sweater over her legs. Her playful grin remained as she snatched a handful of popcorn from the bowl.

Cora shuffled through her purse, her fingers brushing over the small rocks she'd picked up earlier. She pulled out four smooth stones—two typical gray ones, one grayish-pink, and a dull tan one—and held them out for Lumi to see. "I saw pretty rocks and couldn't help myself!"

"Girl, if you don't put those away!" Lumi laughed, shaking her head, but there was a gleam of curiosity in her eyes as she waited for Cora to stow the rocks and toss her purse aside before starting her questioning. "Okay, spill! What has you huffing and puffing like the big bad wolf just blew your house down?"

"Well, first, aren't you impressed I actually stayed at my house last night instead of putting it off?"

"Oh, yes, I'm so impressed that you listened to me and came back here in yesterday's fit." *Dammit.* "Does it have anything to do with why you ran over here?"

Cora sank onto the couch beside her, practically vibrating with excitement. She dug her hand into the popcorn bowl, trying to calm herself before she spilled everything. "I do need to pack my stuff and bring it back so I can officially stay with Mom. But anyway, you won't believe who I ran into yesterday! You remember that childhood friend I used to talk about, the one who moved away before high school?"

"Kind of? You were pretty cagey about it."

"It wasn't something I dealt with well," Cora winced, trying to pretend the popcorn wasn't suddenly turning into sawdust in her mouth. Once she befriended Lumi and

55

completely lost contact with Theo, bringing him up felt like dusting off a haunted attic. "He's the owner of Sticks and Stones!"

Lumi almost fell off the couch in shock.. "GIRL, WHAT? *He's* your childhood friend? He's so hot! I can't even focus when I go there. Like, do I want books or do I want to stare at him?"

"I know! Imagine how I felt seeing him after twenty years. He used to be this short kid with nerdy glasses and chubby cheeks. Now he's...he's..."

"Scrumptious," Lumi finished for her. "Tall, lean, tousled hair when he lets it down, and don't even get me started on that smile. It could melt the polar ice caps."

Cora squinted at her friend. "Have you two ever...?"

"No!" Lumi explained, shaking her head vigorously. Cora let out a breath she didn't realize she held. "No, no. Trust me, you would've known if I ever involved myself with that fine specimen of a man."

Cora sighed as she mentally replayed the moment she'd seen Theo again. The warmth and mischief in his eyes, his monochromatic wardrobe perfectly contrasting his skin, and oh, his arms. It was all too much. She didn't know how she managed to keep it together. "We ended up staying there and talking past closing time. It was like no time had passed at all. And then he walked me home."

"Ahh, so that's why you went home. You were bamboozled."

"Hoodwinked I'd say," Cora chuckled. "But I figured you were right, of course, and I should see Mom. And when he hugged me goodbye..." she trailed off, blushing just thinking about how warm and safe his arms felt wrapped around her. Like he could easily hold her together. "His awkward, nerdy self? Definitely behind him."

"It's behind you too, girl! I'm sure you've filled out since the last time he saw you. He was probably just as stunned as you were!"

"I don't know. He seemed way more composed than me."

"He's a guy," Lumi rolled her eyes, clearly unimpressed. "And if he hugged you he must've felt something. Did you get his number? Are you gonna see him again?"

Cora's face fell as she realized she'd somehow forgotten that, you know, they weren't twelve anymore. They had phones, they had texting, they had *modern communication*. She hid her face in her hands and groaned in frustration. "I didn't even think about it! I'm not even sure if I can keep my cool around him."

"Well, now you know where he works, so you can drop by whenever you want! Maybe even start writing for fun?" Lumi nudged her knee. "This is the perfect opportunity. Use his bookstore as inspiration while also casually checking him out."

"That sounds pretty stalker-ish."

"If it were *me* it'd be stalker-ish. But you know each other so it's fine. Listen, Cora, you're not that meek pre-teen anymore. You're vibrant, funny, *single*, and just as stunning as ever. You could totally be the hot girl in his life. Show him your Black girl magic!"

Cora felt her cheeks heat up at the compliment, the idea of actively seeing Theo more both thrilling and terrifying. She didn't come home to entertain something new with someone, but Theo was like a piece of her puzzle that had been missing for so long. "But what if he doesn't think I'm as cool anymore? What if that...spark? Whatever it was, what if it was just in that moment?"

"Then you move on! But how will you know unless you give it a try? More importantly, I wanna be a witness to these possible adorable awkward moments!"

Cora grinned as a laugh spilled out of Lumi, easing the anxiety she felt just a little. Perhaps running into Theo was a sign that life was steering her toward something good and new. She'd almost forgotten about her troubles while in his presence.

"And while you're here," Lumi started in a tone that alerted Cora to being roped into something, "how about you thank me by helping me decorate the apartment? It needs some holiday spirit."

"Well, if you oh so insist. Let me pack up my clothes to bring home first before I'm uninspired to do it later."

Half hour later, Cora was glad she decided to pack first as she stood precariously on a stepladder, sticking snowflake wall decals around Lumi's floor-to-ceiling windows. The apartment hummed with the faint buzz of holiday lights being plugged in, and the sweet scent of baked sugar cookies drifted from the kitchen. For a moment, it reminded her of the simple joy of baking with Lumi in their dorm kitchen at 2 a.m. back in the day when they were both avoiding class assignments.

The thought of those little joys made her heart flicker, less steady once again. Last night she'd reunited with two important people in her life, but now she was reminded of her reality. She was only a week into unemployment, and without the distraction of work, she didn't know what to do with herself. She took a moment to try pinning the snowflake decals with her magic, but it ended in the poor design being torn in half. Her thoughts were as scattered as the half-finished stories stuffed in her bedroom closet.

"What do you think?" Lumi asked, pulling back on her tree decorating task to admire it from a distance. Her hair was dyed a soft pink at the ends——which wasn't as adventurous as she'd claimed—and tied back in a high ponytail as they worked. Cora turned just in time to see her gesture dramatically as if a hostess on a game show. "Too gaudy, or just enough sparkle?"

"Is there such a thing as 'too gaudy' in your world?" Cora mumbled, immediately regretting it and adjusting her tone. "Just enough sparkle," she corrected, throwing in a halfhearted smile and some spirit fingers for extra flair. Her eyes lingered on the mannequins Lumi had placed around the room. One was wearing a Santa hat, and another was decked out in festive lingerie. Lumi's lingerie business had gone from a cute little hobby to a full-fledged success while Cora was away. They thankfully looked a lot less creepy in broad daylight than when the apartment was cloaked in darkness. "You're turning this place into a festive wonderland. I should've flown you out to decorate my apartment when I was still in Seattle."

Lumi clicked her tongue. "You really should've. I didn't even get to have any adventures with you!" She paused, absentmindedly adjusting a garland on the mantel. "Sometimes I wonder what it'd be like to just pick up and go. No deadlines, no orders to fill, just the freedom to do whatever. But the business kinda took over." She glanced up at Cora with a half smile that didn't quite reach her eyes. "Guess we all get stuck in our own little worlds sometimes."

"Sorry about that," Cora chuckled guiltily. She was starting to regret bringing up Seattle at all. "Too bad you'll never get the chance now."

"Are you not going back? And don't try to deflect; I'll pester you to no end."

Cora sighed, stepping down from the ladder and tucking a stray curl behind her headband, the clink of her bangles reminding her of an overly enthusiastic bell choir. "Honestly, I don't think I will. But, this first week has got me thinking a lot about my job as an advice columnist at that newspaper. I kind of fell into it to get by in grad school. At first it was thrilling, like a fun challenge. People treated me like some kind of all-knowing sage." She thought about the heartbroken lovers, the aimless dreamers, the confused teens. "But now, after everything, I'm starting to wonder if it's all I'm really good at."

Lumi fell onto the sofa, arms stretched across the back. "And you don't know what else you'd do?"

"No. I just know it doesn't give me that same spark," Cora muttered, her frustration creeping in. "I used to write stories—*real* stories, whole worlds I put my heart into." She hesitated, almost unsure of where to take it next. "Even with being a TA, I poured myself into students' work during office hours. It was great for them, but I totally neglected my own. Now, every time I sit down to write, I feel like a fraud." How did she help other students with the art of storytelling if she, herself, couldn't even figure it out? She felt like a hypocrite.

"You always tell the best tales," Lumi encouraged. "Remember that Halloween story you wrote about the haunted bookstore? I still think about it!"

Cora let herself smile at the memory. It had been one of her favorite pieces, filled with clumsy characters and playful ghosts. "Yeah, but it's been so long since I felt that spark. When my relationship started going south, it felt like I was just delivering packaged advice, like some emotional vending machine," Cora mused, her voice teetering on frustration. "It became more of a distraction than a passion, and I never quite shook that mindset as things got worse." A distraction from all forms of grief that followed her like a lost puppy, begging for the attention she refused to give. If she addressed what lingered, she feared it would shatter her, and she didn't know if she could put herself back together.

"Vending machine? Come on, that's harsh! Imagine pressing B1 for advice and it just gets stuck in that ring thing." They both chuckled at the image, their laughter quickly dying down before returning to a more serious tone. "But I get it. You want your writing to mean something, not to just be a means to an end."

Cora nodded slowly, looking around at Lumi's apartment filled with cheerful gold trinkets and hand-knitted garlands. "Exactly. Every time I try to write, I just stare at the blank page. I don't think coming back here is going to fix anything. It's almost like I've forgotten how to play."

Lumi stood and approached Cora, cocking her hip as she leaned against her mantel. "Playing isn't something you just lose, Cora. Maybe you need new context. How often are you spontaneous? Explore new ideas without the pressure of making them perfect? Since when did you give up before you could try?"

"You sound like my mother." Cora flinched at the thought, her ex and their life together creeping into her mind. Lumi's patient gaze grounded her, and she gathered herself before answering. "Maybe I just need to remember what joy feels like in writing. It's been ages since I embraced that kind of freedom."

"There's no pressure in writing for yourself. It's about what speaks to you. Look around! The holidays are full of stories—magic, nostalgia, even the odd mishap. What about that time we got lost on the way to the Yuletide market?"

Cora snickered at the memory. The snowy evening after getting off the train, wandering unfamiliar streets in search of the market. "You think I could write something out of that?"

"Of course! It's all about the little moments that resonate. Just write what you feel, boo. You might surprise yourself," Lumi urged, giving Cora's butt a little slap as she moved to adjust the garland on the mantelpiece.

Cora considered her words, gazing at the snow-frosted windows. She remembered making paper snowflakes in school, how each one was unique, different from the others. Even something as simple as that felt magical—maybe her writing could be again, too.

"Maybe I will," Cora said, reaching to help with the garland. "You've inspired me."

"I'll hold you to it! Especially because a certain bookstore with a certain hot owner could provide plenty of inspiration."

Cora blushed and shook her head. "You're terrible," she teased, but the warmth of the suggestion lingered in her chest.

Lumi only grinned. "What? I'm just saying, the setting is practically begging for romance. Hot owner, cozy bookstore, maybe a rainy day. Don't tell me that doesn't spark ideas."

Cora rolled her eyes. She'd always loved the charm of that bookstore growing up, and it had gotten even more charming with Theo's spin on it. The creaky wood floors, the smell of old paper, the cozy furniture, and...yes, *Theo*. Her stomach twisted in a pleasant way at the thought of him. He had this quiet intensity, a way of making every-thing feel a little more meaningful, even if he didn't try.

"Alright, alright. Maybe I'll figure something out while I'm there. Just don't expect any steamy scenes. I'll leave that to the experts."

"Pfft," Lumi scoffed. "As if you *couldn't.*"

Chapter 5

As the first snowflakes of December started drifting down, Cora bundled herself up in a thick scarf, preparing to brave the brittle air outside. Her mother had been on full holiday mode all week, mainly when it came to her media consumption. Cora was somehow dragged into watching copious amounts of holiday movies with her, all featuring either some small town charm or a big city that needed a little magical reminder. At first, it was a nice distraction, like a fuzzy little blanket around her grief. But then, as the days passed, the reality of spending her first holidays without Avery came crashing in like a freight train. Not to mention many of the movies had a main character navigating their holiday alone.

Nicole, of course, took it upon herself to *fix* things by keeping Cora busy with errands for their holiday celebrations. "This will be good for you," her mother insisted, as if running around gathering supplies would erase the emotional wreckage inside. Cora tried to tell herself she should be thankful, that she had family to come back to that cared about her. It was over between her and Avery, but her thoughts would trail to spending time immersed in Avery's traditions and never receiving the same openness. It was time to get her priorities in order.

Before heading out, Cora decided to pull a tarot card for the day. It used to be a regular practice, but after the card that changed her relationship, she hadn't bothered with a pull in weeks. This was definitely the time to get back into the routine. Reclaim her witch identity and all that. She shuffled the deck with a quiet, almost reverent energy, letting the familiar cards settle in her hands. As she cut the deck, a thought popped into her head—something about needing *clarity*, or maybe just a little reassurance that everything wasn't a total dumpster fire. With a deep breath, she drew a card and flipped it over. The Fool.

Her heart stuttered as she stared at the image—a carefree figure standing on the edge of a cliff, a knapsack slung over his shoulder like he was about to go on some whimsical adventure, a tiny dog at his feet, casually gazing into the void. Because, of course, that was exactly what she needed to see right now. Here she was, a week back in town, drowning in fears, regrets, and the burden of everything. Meanwhile, this guy with his tiny dog was just out there, staring into the abyss like it was no big deal. But hey, The Fool was all about new beginnings, right? Embracing the unknown, taking a leap of faith without worrying about the inevitable crash landing. Clearly, the universe had a sense of humor. Still, it was exactly the jolt she didn't know she was looking for.

She slipped the card back into her deck, feeling a flicker of something that might've been hope—or maybe just mild optimism—stir in her chest. Could it be that simple? Probably not. But it was a start.

"Cora, dear, could you please grab a few more boxes of ornaments and present boxes from the shop?" Nicole called from the living room, her voice rising over the sound of holiday music. They didn't celebrate Christmas, but Cora's mother loved listening to the songs every year. "And don't forget the cinnamon sticks!"

"Sure, Mom!" Cora called back, zipping her coat with a little force when the zipper struggled to contain her scarf. She stepped outside, feeling the cold air immediately slapping her in the face. For a second, it felt like the guilt she'd been carrying around just evaporated into the frost. Maybe it was the crispness of the morning, or maybe just the fact that her brain had finally turned off for a minute. As she closed her eyes and let the chill bite at her skin, she felt more awake than she had in weeks.

"A new start," Cora muttered, giving her cheeks a little slap—because, apparently, that was what one did when trying to shake off the remnants of her past life.

The scent of pine and burning firewood clung to the air, wrapping around the neighborhood like a cozy cashmere blanket that only appeared around the holidays. Cora used to be fond of this time of year and its over-the-top festive cheer, but this season had a few extra weights strapped to it. The smells were an old punch to the gut, dragging up memories of her childhood—running wild between bushes and trees, like a miniature woodland creature. She pinched herself, bringing herself back to the present. *I'm gonna get emotional whiplash at this rate.*

The small town glowed with holiday spirit: twinkling lights draped over shop windows, families giggling as they fought over pinecone decor, window stickers plastered with wreaths and snowflakes, and armies of kids on a mission, dragging snow sleds. Cora strolled through the square, feeling the faintest lift in her heart as she watched the chaos of joy around her. Laughter echoed in the streets, jingle bells rang through the air, and posters for yule log cake and altar decorating workshops plastered every storefront. Way better than Seattle and its lack of cheery witches.

But as she wandered down the cobblestone streets, she couldn't help but think that Valley Creek Hollow was just as charming as the big city in winter. Only, this place had a nostalgic grip on her that Washington could never touch. She inhaled deeply, steadying herself again, the sweet scent of fresh pastries wafting from Marigold Café. If it weren't for the line out the door, she'd march right in, soak up the warmth, and pretend she wasn't going to purchase one of everything. And speaking of warmth...

Cora spotted Theo by the bakery—navy jacket, cozy plaid knitted scarf snugly wrapped around his neck. Snowflakes clung to the edges of his dark hair not quite covered by his hat, giving him that almost too-perfect, ethereal look. If she didn't know better, she might've assumed he was part of some winter wonderland dream. Their reunion at the bookstore replayed in her mind, the years apart seeming to do nothing to the old habits they fell back into—except for her awkwardness, of course. He was still the same charming troublemaker, and honestly, that mix of endearing and infuriating never got old with him. Cora felt comfortable with him, sure, but also on edge, wondering what exactly this one little meeting was stirring up inside her.

"Hey, Cordelia!" He waved when he spotted her. "Out spreading holiday cheer, loser?"

Cora hesitated, her cheeks warming against the cold. She tried but failed to ignore the flutter in her stomach. Something about him being so excited to see her kept the flutter burning. "Just picking up a few things for my mom, dork."

"Need a hand?" he offered, waggling his eyebrows mischievously.

Cora bit her lip, weighing her options. Part of her wanted to say no because, you know, *emotions*—a lovely tidal wave of them since she got back. Another part of her—a small, sexually deprived part—entertained the idea of some adult fun with him, but that thought quickly fluttered away. "I don't know...I'm pretty much halfway done," she said, already feeling the guilt of the obvious lie. She hadn't even picked up a single thing. Honestly, at this point, she was just pretending to be productive. "I'm really nailing these errands."

"Come on! It's Yuletide," Theo said with a grin that showed off his damn cute dimples, making her blood pressure go up for reasons she wasn't ready to unpack. "I can't just let you trudge around alone, can I? It's against my holiday code of conduct."

Those dimples. Why did they have to be so effective? "Fine, but just for the errands."

"Great!" He stepped close beside her, matching her pace. "Where to first?"

They weaved through the shops, grabbing an assortment of ornaments, and the cloves and cinnamon sticks

Nicole needed. Theo purchased a few holiday cards, then picked up some tea bags that Cora didn't fail to notice were her favorite. They wanted to swing by Thistle and Thorn for some plants, but quickly left to avoid being in the crossfire of some arguing herbal and hearth witches. She almost forgot how East Coast folks had mastered the art of being *kind* but not *nice*—sure, they'll help you pick up your dropped items, but don't even think about taking their spot in line.

They dropped their things off at her house, and her mother nearly trapped them inside with the smell of fresh-baked gingerbread cookies. They escaped—barely—and made their way into the city for the Christmas market at Dilworth Park. The stalls, overflowing with handmade crafts and treats, radiated unmistakable holiday cheer. The mix of subway smells and the relentless honking of cars almost triggered a flashback to the life she left behind, but Cora fought through it.

That was, until she spotted a father helping his daughter pick out a snow globe, her high-pitched laughter echoing as she pointed at the twinkling lights. Cora felt a pang of sadness, but she quickly looked away, not ready to confront it. Instead, she discreetly pulled out her phone, snapped a selfie with Theo, and sent it to Lumi with the caption, *Look who I ran into.* After hitting send, Cora put her phone away and crossed her arms as she glanced over at a booth filled with hand-carved wooden figurines, hardly able to suppress a smile at a clumsy little snowman.

"Do you like it?" Theo asked, eyeing her expression. "You look like you're about to burst into a fit of giggles."

"I just—" Cora started, then let the laugh escape her. "I can't help it! That snowman looks like it fell face first into a snowdrift."

"You're right! It's not every day you find a snowman with a commitment issue."

Ouch, burn. Cordelia's smile faltered for a brief moment. The words weren't directed at her, but they still stung, reminding her of Avery once again. The thought lingered, an ache she tried to ignore but couldn't fully shake. She cleared her throat, pushing it aside.

Theo noticed her prolonged silence. "You know, the holidays can be tough. Especially when you've been away for so long."

His tone made her turn to him, catching a more personal meaning behind just trying to empathize. As Cora looked into his eyes, that boyish grin she usually brushed off started to seem endearing. Suddenly, there was a warmth sparking within her.

Cora swallowed the lump in her throat. "You're not wrong."

"What were you doing out there anyway?" he asked as if it were a simple question, turning to look at more trinkets as she took her time to respond. "Lemme guess, you were a handy-woman?"

Cora snorted at the absurdity of that guess. She could just picture herself as some sort of DIY wizard. "Close, but no cigar. I was an advice columnist."

"What kinds of advice were you offering the poor souls of Washington?" Theo didn't even flinch. He continued to inspect a tiny seven-inch-tall Santa gnome like it held the secrets to the universe. That would've been nice.

"Romantic endeavors," she responded with a shrug, taking a discrete deep breath to calm her beating heart. "It was a gig I picked up during grad school, and I ended up sticking with it even after graduation. Made me put my story writing to the side."

Theo finally turned to face her, his frown deepening. "Why not both? You loved making stories as a kid."

Cora sighed, her gaze shifting to the ornaments Theo had skipped over. The silver glitter reminded her of her mom's never-ending Yuletide cheer she was slowly warming up to again. "I don't know, things just changed too quickly. Giving advice was easier, safer, less risky than throwing myself into stories that might go nowhere. Everyone I knew kept telling me I was great at it. I guess I just never stopped to listen to myself." *Everyone, including Avery.*

A stampede of unsupervised children barreled toward her, halting the conversation. Cora started to sidestep to avoid them, and felt Theo's presence before she even saw him. He moved with purpose, his hand grazing her back, nudging her gently but firmly out of the way. The heat from his touch seeped through her jacket, and for a split second, Cora could've sworn she felt his hands through all the layers. It was almost *too* much—this unexpected intimacy that made her heart skip a beat. Too much and too nice of a feeling.

Just as she was recovering from the sensory overload, Theo spotted a garish elf hat on a nearby table. Without missing a beat he snatched it up, his grin widening as he shoved it playfully on top of her head. Cora froze, blinking at him in stunned silence as he erupted into laughter, clearly enjoying his little victory. She couldn't decide if she wanted to punch him or laugh along with him. The serious conversation they had been having just moments before vanished in an instant, replaced by the infectious sound of Theo's laughter soothing her. She couldn't help it as the corner of her mouth twitched upward despite herself.

"You should see your face!" he got out between laughs, holding his stomach. "You look like you just got off Santa's longest work shift and you're ready to unionize."

"Hardy har har." Cora poked her tongue out at him, swiping the hat off and putting it back on the table. The seller witnessed the series of events, shaking his head at Theo's antics. "I bare my troubles to you and you make a joke out of it."

"Not much has changed about you, loser, especially how you talk about heavy things. You looked like you wanted to run, so I thought I'd lighten you up a little."

She hated how he was right, but still melted at his attentiveness to her. "Thank you, dork."

He waved off her gratitude. "Don't worry about it." He continued walking along the lines of tables not facing her, but not looking at the merchandise either. "I know what it's like for things not to work out. You get stuck, or you feel like you're missing something or...someone. I hope while you're here you can fall in love with the things that brought you joy again."

Cora stopped in her tracks, watching Theo ahead of her as she processed his words. He had this annoying ability to make things seem so much simpler when her mind was caught in knots. Back in Seattle, she'd buried herself in her routine, not even considering picking up a pen again. Theo's advice mirrored what Lumi had been saying to her, and she was starting to pick up on the signals from the universe of a necessary change in direction. And that look in his eyes, the quiet understanding swirling in the depths of brown, as though he wasn't just talking about her, but about himself, too. She began to wonder what Theo had gone through in life as well.

Pulling out her phone, she saw Lumi's response, accompanied by a picture of her pulling a kissy face with the caption *meant to beeeee*. Cora snorted and rolled her eyes. She wasn't even going to dignify that with a response.

With that thought bouncing around in her head, Cora quickened her pace to catch up with Theo, who was eyeing a festive bag that probably contained a gift for someone. As she jogged, she picked up a flat rock that begged to be added to her collection, and appeared beside him just in time to catch his easy smile as he thanked the seller.

"How about this? I'm hosting a fairy tale reading event at the bookstore on December 23rd, and I could use some help. Want to do a good deed while getting a distraction from...whatever happened in Seattle?"

The offer tempted her. She still didn't have a concrete plan for being back home. So far, it was just her mother's attention and being on call for whatever Lumi needed help with. Having something to do sounded like a decent escape. "Do I have to participate?"

"Nooooo," he drawled, clearly trying to make the offer sound casual but not quite pulling it off. "But it'd be great if you did. You could share something old if you're not up to writing, or even do a dramatic reading of someone else's work."

Now that was a little more enticing. "Sure, count me in."

He sighed in relief, making her squint at him. "Thank goodness. There's a lot to do before the big day." Theo continued, raising his fingers to count off his to-dos. "I have plans for storytelling, activities for the kids, cookies to bake... It's all a bit chaotic right now."

"Theo," Cora droned. "Do you not have anyone else you hired to help you out at the bookstore?"

"I do! It's just... they're a college kid and already went home out of state for the holidays."

"So you're really just using me, huh?"

"I mean, I guess I could do it all myself. I have before. But maybe I want an excuse to see you more in case you decide to whisk back away to your West Coast livin'."

Cora's stomach tightened—thank you, traitorous insides. She wasn't supposed to be flattered. But of course, Theo had to go and look even better than when they were kids and say cute things. "I'm not going back."

The words slipped out before she could stop them, and she immediately regretted them. Her mom and Lumi knew, but the more she said it aloud the more real it became. Her gaze flickered toward the ground, unwilling to meet his eyes.

Theo was quiet for a beat, before he gently lifted her chin with a finger, coaxing her to meet his gaze. "Not going back, huh?" His voice softened, not a hint of judgment there.

"I...there's nothing there for me anymore," she stuttered, the truth tasting bitter on her tongue. She hadn't expected this conversation to go in such a direction, but now that it had, she realized just how much it hurt. And the way he touched her so gently, so carefully, her blush had to be obvious to him. Hopefully he'd take it as embarrassment and not longing.

Theo's eyes lingered on her, understanding flickering in them, but instead of pushing her further, he simply nodded as he dropped his hand. "I get it," he said, offering her a small, reassuring smile. "I'm glad you're here, Cordelia. Really. Hey, how about we go walk around Rittenhouse for a bit? I bet you've missed how dead it looks compared to summer."

Cora snickered and nodded, appreciating the subject change as she adjusted her scarf against the crisp winter wind. The light snowfall of the morning already faded, the light dusting on the sidewalks revealing the shoe prints of busy shoppers. As they changed course, the cold nipped at her cheeks, and she couldn't help but steal a glance at Theo. He looked effortlessly cool, hands shoved into the pockets of his navy coat and a calm expression on his face. What kind of mess was she walking into?

They wound their way through the thinning crowd, the cobblestones echoing with memories long embedded in their childhood. They passed pigeons pecking for crumbs, couples nestled on benches, fragments of their younger selves resurfacing with each step.

"Remember those afternoons at the bookstore?" Cora asked, a playful smile creeping onto her lips. "Playing around with our whispered spells."

Theo chuckled, leading them to sit at the fountain. "How could I forget? We spent so many hours pouring over those dusty tomes when we weren't supposed to, thinking we'd be like the sorcerers on TV."

"Or at least make that book float," Cora replied, laughing as a warm wave of nostalgia washed over her. "I remember the first time we tried to lift that giant encyclopedia. It hovered maybe a centimeter off the ground before I ended up toppling over in exhaustion, and you had to cover for me by pretending you were demonstrating gravity."

"Only for half the kids in the bookstore to witness your magical disaster. But you know, I think we actually did conjure something special, didn't we?"

Cora tilted her head, looking into the distance where the outlines of City Hall loomed against the late afternoon sky. "What do you mean?"

"Well, we might not have had the greatest control over our magic, and experimented without adult supervision, but we created our own world. The hours we spent there were magic. Our imaginations could outshine any spell."

They began to walk again, lives interwoven yet diverging, a testament to their youthful bond. The square was quiet with only a few people dwindling for pictures, punctuated only by the rustle of leaves and distant laughter. Squirrels darted about fighting over acorns, oblivious to the memories unfolding between the two friends.

"Do you think that kind of magic still exists?" Cora asked, her voice becoming contemplative. "Not the obvious kind we can clearly use, but the wonder we felt? The everyday things?"

Theo paused, glancing at her. "I think it especially exists in those moments where we feel truly alive. Like today—sharing stories and laughter. Or even while reading a good book. It's not always flashy or grand, but it's still there. Like an invisible thread connecting us to our childhood."

Cora smiled, remembering how their youthful persistence had led them to try ridiculous endeavors—turning their backyard into a makeshift potion lab they'd seen on television, gathering ingredients from the pantry and woods. "Like the time we made that game-changing potion with grape juice and my mom's lavender."

"Yes! It smelled awful. We ended up getting in trouble for leaving a sticky mess everywhere."

"What about that time we tried to make that potion to summon the bookstore ghost?"

Theo grimaced, feigning horror. "Don't remind me! I still can't believe we nearly turned Mr. Hargrove into a toad. All because we thought cinnamon was an 'essential' ingredient. What were we thinking?"

"We were eight! All we knew was that it sounded cool," she chuckled, brushing a stray curl behind her ear. Their laughter faded into a companionable silence as they ambled on. As they wandered over to their favorite spot near the statue of the poet, Cora sat down on the cool bench while Theo leaned against the stone pedestal, his arms crossed casually. "You know, those afternoons spent in the bookstore felt like magic themselves. Not just because we were experimenting with spells, but the stories, the adventures swirling around us..."

"We weren't just casting spells; we were discovering who we were—who we wanted to be. What was your favorite? The story of the Wandering Prince?"

Cora's eyes widened as she reminisced. "I loved that one! He had to unravel the riddles of a thousand lakes to find his heart's desire! Like us trying to figure out how to create that storm spell without ruining our birthday cake."

"Speaking of cakes, remember your thirteenth birthday? We accidentally turned it into a chocolate volcano?" Theo snorted.

"Oh, the horror on my mother's face!" Cora doubled over, clutching her stomach. "And we acted like it was all part of the plan!"

"You were always the better liar. I was just the accomplice who couldn't stop giggling."

Cora took a few breaths to settle herself again, the memory of their adventures floating warmly in her heart. "I miss those days," she said, her tone shifting to a more reflective one. "We were so carefree, so curious. It wasn't the same after you left." It wasn't long after that birthday that Theo moved away for his father's new job. It seemed bittersweet that she got to spend that special day with him just for him to leave. "Sometimes, especially after everything that's happened to me this year, I feel like I've lost that wonder."

Theo stepped closer, the twilight casting a gentle glow around them, and touched his necklace fondly. "Cordelia, the magic isn't just in spells and potions. It's in our friendship, in the way we look at the world. We can still find that wonder. Those years apart didn't change anything between us, not for me anyway."

Cora nodded, her fingers playing with her necklace. Words? Nah, she didn't have those right now. Sure, their friendship was still fine, but without him around, she'd apparently forgotten just how *simple* life could be. Her little stroll down memory lane with Theo led her to bouncing between the amazing times she had growing up, and the times the universe had sent as a curveball her way. Like the park where her first college boyfriend decided to dump her for no apparent reason, sending her running back to her dorm in tears like a bad rom-com. Then there was the whole high school bullying fiasco where she was too much of a doormat to stand up for herself until Lumi swooped in and taught her how to not be a walking target. Oh, and can't forget her dad's unexpected death in a car accident after college graduation, giving her the final reason to leave Valley Creek Hollow and all her swirling sadness. By that point she thought her own character development involved adding more grief to her already sparkling collection. Theo and her had already lost touch then. And while she adored Lumi, Theo had been the one person who actually *saw* her.

Years went by, and somehow he could still see her. It was sweet and all, but after everything she'd been through, Cora wasn't exactly sure she was ready to handle that much emotional exposure again. She wasn't quite a gaping wound, but the scabs were still fresh enough to bleed. Not exactly the kind of thing you jump back into when just starting your vacation from all the feels.

Theo poked her nose to bring her back to reality. "Hey, since the sun is setting, let's make a new tradition. Let's go grab cocoa and then explore, see the lights around the Christmas village—just the two of us."

Cora could feel her resistance starting to crumble. It could just be the magic of Yuletide, or maybe it was just Theo's painfully earnest face, but those feelings she'd shoved down for so long were starting to bubble up like the first snowflakes in a winter storm. Oh great, maybe she could let him in. Just a tiny bit. A smidge.

Cora nodded, feeling herself enter cheesy rom-com mode as she remembered what Lumi said and took out her phone. "Only if I get your number."

Theo, clearly embracing the role of charming man-of-the-hour, gave a dramatic bow. His rough hands brushed against hers, sending a shiver up her arm. She could tell he felt it too. He quickly typed his number, sending a text to himself for good measure. *Nice touch, Theo.* With a grin, he offered his elbow. Cora couldn't help but giggle as she took it, letting him lead the way.

Chapter 6

"Why don't you come help me decorate a little?"

Cora rolled over to her back, pushing her bonnet from her eyes. "We'll have plenty of time later."

"And there's plenty to do." Nicole marched over, grabbing Cora's wrist with a smile that meant business, and started dragging her out of bed. "Just do this one thing for your poor, ailing mother."

"You're literally neither of those things." But she relented, allowing herself to be dragged downstairs. Since she hadn't spent the holidays home during her relationship with Avery, this could be her way of slowly making it up to her mother.

But Nicole's festive nature was on a completely different level than Cora's, even pre-Avery. Cora was all about the quiet moments—sitting by the fireplace drinking cider, laughing with loved ones, snuggling in blankets. Nicole needed everything to be an event. She wanted to blame it on her hearth witch abilities, bringing protection, energy, and cleansing to their home, but Cora knew it was just an innate energy her mother contained. Nicole always had the talent for turning their home into the biggest exemplification of what they were celebrating at the time, wanting to outdo whatever she organized the previous year. As much as Cora admired her mother's energy, her enthusiasm was quite hard to match.

Nicole was in full-on holiday mode, ready to transform their home into a winter wonderland. She didn't require much to get into the spirit, she was more of a year-round festival and solstice enthusiast, really. This Yuletide, her grand plan was to have as much cookie baking, gift wrapping, pine decorating, and booze drinking that she could muster. Cora wondered if she was overdoing it a little now that her daughter was back.

Her mother's gaze zeroed in on her, and Cora gulped, knowing she was about to be trapped. "Come on, honey! Just because you're out of practice doesn't mean you can just sit there!" She waved a garland of colored lights draped over one arm, and a basket full of ornaments hung on the other.

"We can literally use our magic for this."

Nicole's eyes narrowed. "Can *we*, or can *I*?"

"You can." She was caught, but it didn't look like her mother was going to make her feel guilty about her possible magical faux pas for the foreseeable future.

"Exactly. You know it's not the same. This is when we act like everyday mundanes and enjoy the process of decorating together."

"What exactly do you want me to do?" Cora glanced longingly at the stairs to her room, wishing she stayed in bed, curled up with a book and blankets.

"Help me decorate! I can't do this all alone! Plus, I want to run the color scheme by you. I'm going for 'elegant winter' this year," her mother exclaimed, shuffling over to grab her reluctant form up from the floor.

Cora's eye twitched. They still had two weeks until Yuletide even began. "How did you get along without me these past couple years?"

"It was much more painfully boring."

Cora sighed but obliged, taking the lights and moving to the dining room. As she worked, she couldn't help but be transported back to past Yuletides. Particularly, the carefree moments with her father. Once, when she was younger, they decided to put a star atop the tree for fun. But as her father lifted her smaller self up toward the top of the tree, the star went careening off and crashed onto the floor, a dust cloud of glitter in its wake. Her mother laughed so hard she nearly dropped a batch of gingerbread cookies at the scene.

Cora realized how much she had pushed away memories of her father and other events that caused her grief. Part of her move across the country was for graduate school, that was true, but it also presented an opportunity to escape the scene of her childhood friend leaving, her father's sudden death, and a small list of inconsequential grievances she found as perfect excuses. It was so much easier to run away from her emotions than face them.

"Do you remember the year we made our own ornaments?" her mother asked, startling her from her thoughts. "You insisted on using glitter for everything."

Cora shuddered at the memory as she opened a box of artificial cotton snow, thinking back to the chaos of colored glue, ribbons, and construction paper. "I don't know why you let me do that. We couldn't get the glitter glue off the couch for *weeks* after that!"

"You almost turned me into a glitter explosion by accident with the magic you were using."

Cora puffed her cheeks in slight annoyance, taking care not to cut the current ribbon in her hands too short. "I thought I could add a little sparkle to our counter tops."

Nicole's eyes turned to her, hazel irises twinkling. "I still find it in very unfortunate places."

With the ribbons cut to perfection and tied into perfectly symmetrical crimson bows, Cora stepped back to admire her work. Back in Seattle, her decorating consisted of a tablecloth and a couple of disposable cups—real top-tier stuff. Now, she enjoyed the dining room decked out in silver and red, with electric candles flickering on the long, glass table in the middle. She carefully taped and clipped garlands of holly and dried herb charms along the wall shelving, still giving space for the picture frames to be seen. Green garland hung along the banister of the stairs, yellow lights—because subtlety is overrated—twisted around them for flare.

The living room on her left dipped three stairs down, beige leather couches shuffled around to make space for the impending Yuletide tree. The glow from the fireplace highlighted Cora's homemade twig wreath, a tradition her mother started eons ago, perched proudly on the fireplace ledge, practically begging for attention. As she looked at it, she almost teared up—because clearly, this whole elaborate setup was *just* for her. She wouldn't have mushy feelings, not at all.

"You did great, Mom," Cora said with a whimsical sigh, practically glowing at the thought of what the place would look like once they shoved that massive tree in here. "Okay, fine, maybe I grumbled a bit, but I guess it was kind of fun to help...in the most begrudging way possible."

Her mother beamed, thrilled with the praise, and pulled Cora into a warm, forced hug as they both stared into the space. "I'm glad, too. This is what Yuletide is all about—not just the decorations, but the memories we've created all coming together." *Sure, Mom, sure. It's not like the tree, or the garlands, or any of this endless prep matter more than the memories.*

Cora let her mother's words linger, *really* letting the flood of cheerful holiday memories wash over her. The last time she was here was two years ago, when she was living her best 'single and thriving' life while finishing up her master's degree. She spent the entire month of December here. But this time, heartache lurked. Back then, she mourned her father, but also managed to glow with this whole confident future vibe. Who wouldn't be thrilled when their side hustle advice column became a surprise hit and editing a book was more fulfilling than torturous? But she survived. Coming home then was more about recharging her batteries—not that she needed it, because her time in Seattle was all about success and progress. But even then she couldn't shake that nagging feeling that something was missing.

She flopped onto the couch and melted into the cushions, staring at the ceiling as she wished for clarity. The only thing it offered was a warm golden glow. You'd think the coziness of the living room would be a hug for her soul, but no. Turns out, the memories she'd conveniently suppressed were coming back for an uninvited encore.

It'd been so long since that day Cora and her mother sat by her father's hospital bed, hearts shattering into a million pieces. While she was thankful he at least got to see her walk the stage for her undergrad graduation, she never stopped wishing he could've been there for all her other milestones. Cora fiddled with her t-shirt, the ache from her father's death hovering around, an energy she couldn't shake. Funny how you think you've moved on from something, only to be confronted by it and realize you were horribly wrong.

Nicole pulled Cora from her marinating thoughts. "Have you talked to Theo today? You two looked like you were having fun yesterday."

She sighed, rubbing her temple. "I don't even know where to start. He asked me to help plan an event at his bookstore though, so it'll give me something to do. It's a fairy tale reading."

"Now that's exciting! Are you gonna write something?"

Cora froze. "I was considering it. But do you think I should? I'm not kidding when I say I'm really outta practice."

"Cora, I shouldn't have to lecture you, but here it is, for the umpteenth time. You've got *story magic,* okay? You pull people in with your words and vision—*that's* your gift. But you...you lost yourself when you were with Avery." Cora flinched like she'd just been slapped. "Sure you were 'thriving' as you say with your column, but writing stories came much easier to you. And when you stopped doing it for yourself, it just spilled into everything else."

Cora looked away in embarrassment, being called out by her mother. All the distractions she'd hid behind were now thrown in her face, and she had no idea how to shake them off and actually start fresh. The Fool card said she'd figure it out, but *how* was still a mystery—one she had no idea how to begin solving.

"Okay," Cora started, still not facing Nicole. "I'll try a little something."

"And use your magic more."

Another wince. "And use my magic more."

Her mother tsked, flicking her forehead lightly. Cora rubbed the spot in mock pain. "And you're way overdue for cord cutting. Sever that leftover energy from that ex-fiancé of yours. Remember, you're not alone in this, darling."

You have me, you have your friends. You can make this your true home again."

Ex-fiancé. A term Cora had been ignoring since coming back. It was easier to dub Avery her ex-partner or just an ex, but fiancé held a completely different weight to it. A testimonial to how serious things had gotten between them, and why she'd been so broken in the end.

"I couldn't possibly..." Cora trailed off. When she moved for grad school she built a life for herself—well, until that life crumbled into dust thanks to her relationship. She had nothing left in Seattle, especially not a place to call her own. Cora bought a one-way ticket without a single thought of what she'd do after, just knowing she had to get the hell out. It was just supposed to be a long, extended layover until she figured things out. She couldn't possibly consider moving back home now, could she?

Nicole's gaze became distant for a moment. "You know, Cora, I've seen the way you've been since your father died. You're holding onto all that grief like it's some kind of prize, and it's eating you up from the inside out. I get it. I've buried my own feelings, too. Us Black women are practically *trained* to hide our grief, push through, work ourselves into the ground, and pretend nothing hurts. But you don't have to do that anymore. You can lean on people, let them help. You've carried enough."

Her mother was trying to make her cry, that had to be it. In so many ways, Cora had watched Nicole throw herself into her work at the shop after her father's death, as though keeping busy could erase the pain. Her mother seemed to be moving forward now—more at ease, or at least pretending to be—but Cora could see that sadness still lingered in her eyes, the kind of sorrow that would never completely go away.

"You know there's always a place for you here," Nicole reminded her with a more upbeat tone. "Well...your room certainly needs some redecorating to fit your adult tastes. But Valley Creek Hollow will always be your home if you want it to be."

Cora couldn't help but laugh at her mom's attempt to make things less awkward. "I appreciate it. Really. But I already feel self-conscious enough that I ran home at my big girl age."

"Sometimes, going back to where things made sense can help you gain a fresh perspective. There's nothing wrong with that. Just because you're thirty doesn't mean you can't make mistakes and learn from them."

"You've been watching *way* too many Hallmark movies, haven't you?" Cora raised an eyebrow, slightly dreading the answer.

"You know I can't help it!" Nicole laughed. Nicole pulled her daughter into a warm, unnecessary embrace. "Now that we've done some decorating down here, why don't you do some work on your room while I cook?"

Cora followed suit, trudging upstairs like she'd just run a marathon; such an emotional conversation. As she stepped inside the reminder of her past life, she looked at it with new eyes, finally noticing just how *different* her taste was and how much she had evolved.

The walls, painted a soft lilac that her younger self had practically demanded, felt like something from a time capsule. Butterflies still covered the white bedspread. Her childhood books were piled haphazardly on the desk, as if she was still twelve and expected to read them for homework. The drawings on the walls? Pure nostalgia. She cringed, a little horrified she hadn't noticed how outdated everything looked. She must've still been jet-lagged and caught up in the emotions of her return. Her mom was definitely right; this room could definitely use some magic—preferably of the grown-up variety.

Cora decided that if she was going to do this starting fresh thing, she might as well begin with her room. After all, what better way to embrace the new her than by transforming the space that still screamed awkward teenage phase? And if she could transform her room, with time she could transform herself. She took a deep breath, grounded herself, and focused. She said she'd use her magic more, right?

Grasping the edges of her bedspread, she gave a strong flick and watched as the ripple transformed the old, tired bedspread into a flowing tapestry of deep greens. Specks of gold shimmered across the fabric, like drops of morning dew caught in the first light. Satisfied, she thought back to the vibrant colors she adored as a kid, the ones that reminded her of wildflowers she'd spend hours collecting. With that whimsical thought, she walked to the wall and gave it three taps, the dull lilac walls shimmering and shifting into a calming, sage green that matched her necklace. *Nope, not gonna read into that right now.*

A little thrilled with herself, Cora twirled around the room, waves of energy trailing behind her and leaving the air smelling suspiciously like lavender and chamomile. She thanked Hekate that home improvement could be this easy. The dust vanished, revealing a pristine dark hard-wood floor beneath her feet. Everything else poofed away, neatly tucked back into place, as if the room had never been abandoned. She snapped her fingers and vintage fairy lights appeared from her closet, twinkling merrily along the window's edges, casting soft, flickering shadows that danced like memories she couldn't quite shake.

This'll do for now. Cora didn't want to rush into any decisions—not when she'd just rolled back into town like a lost tourist. Sure, the cozy room gave her a fleeting sense of comfort, but the thought of moving back in with her mom and having absolutely zero direction in life made her feel like a character straight out of a Jane Austen or Brontë novel—minus the corset, of course. Better to sleep on it, let her brain reboot overnight.

Except, sleep? Yeah, that wasn't happening.

Cora let out a huff. She'd done everything she could to make the room her own—revamped the space, and even let the full moon flood her window with its light. Yet there she was, bonnet on and dressed in her trusty hedgehog spaghetti strap nightgown, staring at the glow-in-the-dark stars she added to the ceiling.

The town was dead quiet, but the house? It was alive with its usual squeaks and creaks, mixed with the cricket symphony outside. She thought she'd feel comforted, like coming back to an old pair of jeans. But instead, anxiety wrapped itself around her chest like a vine, its grip tightening with each passing minute. Sure, there was some sweet nostalgia, but there were also the complicated ones that had a way of sneaking in.

During her last week in Seattle, Cora had taken a match to the remnants of her relationship with Avery, watching as framed photos from their road trips to California went up in flames—postcards from each stop, mementos of their laughter, and all those sweet promises of a future that was clearly never meant to be. She told herself it was cathartic, a necessary purge of what no longer fit. But in reality, it was just burning the last bits of what had once been her "perfect" life. The relationship had crumbled under unmet expectations, as they all tend to do. Even now, weeks later, she couldn't wrap her head around how fast her bright future had dimmed, how joy could flip to sorrow in the time it took to blink.

Cora rolled over, the sheets cool against her skin but offering none of the comfort she'd hoped for. The adrenaline that had propelled her here—whether by choice or by force—finally drained away. Memories of Avery flickered in her mind like an old movie reel—dinner dates, holding hands in art galleries, running barefoot in the grass at their favorite park, the way Avery used to gently brush her hair. Each one gave the sting of a paper cut, a reminder of what never was—the wedding dress still gathering dust on the vision board, the vows that would remain unspoken.

Cora sat up, pulling her knees to her chest to self-soothe. She waved her hand for her magic to turn on a soft light to the room, but the light flickered from her emotional distress. She replayed their last encounter, Avery standing there with tears in her eyes, while Cora—being the picture of empathy—stood there stone-faced. Sure, she still stood by her decision to end things, but never wanted to revert back into that version of herself again—cold, sharp, and uncaring.

In desperate need of something, anything, to distract herself, Cora shuffled off her bed and wandered over to her closet. Feeling nostalgic and oh-so-vulnerable, she pulled out a box that immediately made her heart do that annoying little squeeze thing.

Her fingers brushed against a dusty photo of her and Theo. They'd snapped a picture during a beach trip the summer before he moved away. Matching pineapple-shaped sunglasses stared back at her like a pair of overly cheerful reminders of a simpler time. Their smiles were all carefree, despite knowing full well their days together were numbered. She sighed, hoping the simplicity of that photo would bring her some solace as she clutched the necklace Theo gave her.

Theo, the little witch who was chasing frogs in her yard and trying to turn them into classy, bow-tied gentlemen. The day ended with him chasing her with one. But somehow, even after that weird start, she found him fascinating enough to become friends. She could still remember the loneliness she'd felt before—no other witches to talk to, too quiet to approach anyone. But with Theo? Every day was an adventure, whether they were chasing frogs or just talking nonsense.

And then he left her. Fast forward, and here he was, back in Valley Creek Hollow. And here she was, too. Was it serendipity? She wasn't entirely sure, but what she was sure of was that the moment she saw him, it was the first time since returning home that she actually felt...well, at home. And let's be real, it didn't exactly hurt that he had turned into a total heartthrob softy either.

With a sigh, which was basically her personal soundtrack at this point, Cora decided to leave her self-pity party and head to the kitchen. The last thing she needed was to continue marinating in her own thoughts, so off she went. As she made her way down the stairs, her knees gave the loudest crack—thank you, years of volleyball—making sure her body still remembered how to sound like a broken machine. She hobbled her way to the fridge, grabbed some milk, and put it in the microwave. She set the time just right, not wanting to wake her mom. Turns out, it didn't matter anyway.

"Can't sleep?" a gentle voice broke her from her movements. She nearly poured honey onto the counter instead of into her steaming mug. "Do you wanna talk?"

"What's there to talk about?" Cora murmured, eyes focused on her sweetened milk. "It would just be more of the same."

Her mother wrapped an arm around her shoulder, drawing her close and causing Cora to lean into her. There they were, in the kitchen, embracing the kind of love that reminded her that, despite the train wreck her engagement had become, there were still people who didn't seem to mind her existence.

"Can we just sit here a while?"

Her mother easily caught her wavering voice. "Of course."

They sat there at the kitchen counter, sipping warm milk in an oddly comforting silence. Staring at absolutely nothing, Cora reflected on how change was basically the worst thing ever, especially when there were new beginnings supposedly on the horizon. But she didn't have the energy to even think about that right now. *I wonder*, Cora thought, *if I'll find my peace again.*

And of course, because her brain had a love affair with tormenting her, her thoughts flickered right back to Avery.

Cora winced, her body reacting involuntarily while still leaning into her mother's embrace, and she really wasn't here for it. She didn't want to deal with that right now. So, she did the only thing she could do; She enjoyed this rare, fleeting moment of calm.

Chapter 7

T heo must've forgotten Cora wasn't a morning person, because he excitedly demanded she come over bright and early Monday morning when the bookstore was closed. He mentioned something about doing his best planning early in the day, and Cora tried to refute him by saying Mondays are for intuition. He countered with

Mondays also being good for creative ideas. He had her there.

Cora subconsciously fluffed her low afro puff she pulled back that morning as Theo described his vision. He aimed for something cozy and intimate—a storytelling corner with oversized pillows and blankets, where children and parents could gather around like one big happy community. He envisioned all the fairy tale books from the children's section, plus adult reimaginings, neatly lined up on tables at the front with a special holiday discount. Snacks and beverages would be available on the other side, because naturally, you need to keep the audience well-fed.

"I want every child to experience the wonder of these stories like we did," Theo declared, practically oozing passion. It was obvious that this event was about a lot more than just a holiday gathering for him; he checked his list every time they brainstormed. "I have books for a lot of age ranges here, but wanna do something for kids this season."

Cora gave a thoughtful nod, easily getting swept up in Theo's energy the more he talked. "What if we add some interactive elements? Like a create your own fairy tale station, with printouts so kids can design their own characters and plots. And we could even toss in some coloring pages of different tales."

Theo hummed in agreement, furiously jotting down everything she said. "That's brilliant! They'll get to express their creativity, and we can even read their stories aloud during the event."

Cora volunteered to dig through the mountain of storybooks to find the perfect ones for the event, while Theo took on the task of hunting down printouts. After a little nudge from her, he reluctantly agreed to the idea of making some simple ones on Canva—because luckily, getting crafty with her was something he was willing to try.

She smiled as she chose another book, an updated edition of one she read as a child. Theo's voice caught her attention, and she realized he was muttering to himself. She caught his hazelnut eyes as he tucked a stray hair behind his ear, his grin pulling at the corners of his mouth showing off those dimples.

"I was thinking of tying silver ribbon around some books. Or would that be too much?"

"Well if you're going for royal vibes then it's not enough," Cora joked.

His chuckle, light and familiar, loosened a knot in her chest. She hadn't realized how much she missed this easy banter, the way his enthusiasm made even the simplest task feel like an adventure between them. She set the book down on the table and scanned the shelves for another, images of trees and snowflakes along the spine of one caught her eye. Cora went to grab it for a closer look just as Theo's hand reached for it at the same time. His hand brushed gently against hers as her breath hitched, not even noticing when he'd gotten so close to her. Their fingers lingered for a second before he pulled away, but the spark was unmistakable. So much so, that the book she sought, and a few others, tumbled off the shelf as her magic spiked.

Theo chuckled, kneeling down to help her pick them up. "You know, I've always thought you had a special way with stories. Have you given any more thought to doing a reading?"

Cora grimaced as she stood back up, putting the books back into place. The idea of speaking to a crowd made her stomach do somersaults, but for some reason, Theo's suggestion poked at something she hadn't felt in ages—like excitement, maybe? "I actually think I might. Maybe I could redo *The Snow Queen*. It's one of my favorites."

"In a *Frozen* kind of way?"

"Uh, I have no idea yet, but definitely not that. Mom and Lumi have been super encouraging about getting me to write again, though."

"You know what might help? There's some storage upstairs in the attic that I have left over from when I remodeled the place. Maybe there's something we could use there."

Cora shrugged "Lead the way."

Theo took her through his office and guided them through a back door. He led the way up the narrow staircase, his footsteps heavy on the creaky wooden steps. The dim light from the hall barely reached the top of the stairs, leaving the attic door in shadows. The door to the attic was an old wooden thing, worn at the edges, with a small brass handle that gleamed faintly in the dim light. Theo pulled it open with a grunt, and as it creaked, Cora was hit with a wave of musty air.

The room was exactly what Cora imagined, cramped, a little chaotic, but undeniably full of potential. The musty smell gave a testament to the mix of old books, forgotten furniture, and time itself. The attic, like so many parts of the bookstore, had that cozy, forgotten charm that only seemed to come with age. It also seemed to be the only place that wasn't charmed to be more spacious on the inside. Cramped, with just enough space to maneuver between the mismatched shelves that lined the walls, each one a patchwork of old oak and cedar, some worn and sagging under the weight of their contents.

Cora started to step inside, too distracted with reading the items on the shelves that she didn't notice a small box in her path until she tripped over it. She closed her eyes, bracing for the impact as she fell, until a strong arm wrapped around her waist and pulled her back. Her heart fluttered for reasons not related to almost ending up on her ass as she became very aware of the strong chest she leaned against.

"You okay?" Theo asked. His breath tickled right against her ear and she had to swallow a moan that threatened to burst forth.

"Y-yeah. Sorry about that."

"No need to apologize. I should've made sure there was nothing in the way."

She definitely didn't imagine the way his arm tightened around her waist, the arm that no longer had a reason to still be there. But it was. And it was steady and warm and made her feel safe. Cora thought someone must've glued her feet to the floor because she couldn't move an inch.

But Theo did, finally releasing her after a few short moments. His arm slid away from her painfully slowly, hand lingering on her hip before letting go and stepping into the room. Cora's hand flew to her chest, heart racing beneath her palm as she gazed around the room to look anywhere but Theo's direction. The shelves caught her attention again, most of them holding boxes labeled in Theo's meticulous handwriting, while others were cluttered with odd items—a collection of old stamps, stacks of novels with cracked spines, and an old rocking chair sitting in a small patch of sun. A few boxes had little notes taped to the side, each scribbled in different handwriting, marking their contents: "Out of Print," "Unopened Stock," "To be Repaired." Piles of old hardcover books leaned precariously against one another, their pages seemingly bursting with secrets.

Cora sneezed as she approached the shelves, sending a cloud of dust flying into the air. The sun that filtered through the small windows caught the dust motes floating around her. She wiped her nose with the sleeve of her cardigan and scowled at the dusty, forgotten stacks of books around her. Theo, crouched beside a small rickety old shelf, raised an eyebrow.

"You okay over there?" he asked with a warm voice and the same dry humor that always made her feel irritated and oddly charmed.

She waved her hand in the air in an attempt to clear the lingering dust. "I'm fine. It's just, how is it even possible for a room this small to contain this much dust?"

Theo chuckled, rising to his feet to stretch his arms above his head. The motion lifted his sweater slightly and revealed a small portion of his waistline, and Cora had to look away before she started staring. The sunlight shone across his eyes, causing her to tilt her head as the hazelnut melted into amber in the natural light.

"Well, if you're done attacking the air," he started as he motioned to the piles of old books and papers strewn across the floor, "we can get back to sorting through this stuff." Some of it looked like it hadn't seen daylight in years, white pages faded to a slight beige and book covers torn at the spines. He pulled out a large wooden crate from a corner shelf, the wood rough to the touch, and dust swirled in the air like a faint mist. The crate creaked as he set it down, the sound somehow fitting for a place that had witnessed so many years of history. "Why don't you use your magic to help with the dust?"

"I'm going through something."

Cora bit her lip, afraid he'd question her about it. Instead he winced. "Ugh, that's the worst. Like, can I just have a breakdown in peace without things falling around me?"

Cora's response came out a little too high-pitched as she picked up an old ledger, pretending to examine it. But really, she wasn't entirely paying attention to the books. Cora wasn't ready for the *my ex cheated, I lost my job, and now my magic's a mess* conversation, but his understanding warmed her.

The attic felt too quiet, too intimate with Theo in such close proximity. She didn't like how it made her so self-conscious. They'd been working together for barely an hour, shuffling around each other to look for what could be used for his event while better organizing the space. She started a mental running tally of how many times they bumped into each other, chuckling at their awkwardness, and the higher the number went, the more frazzled she got around him.

"I could write my story for the reading here," Cora joked. "Just give me a quill pen and a shadowy corner."

Theo laughed lightly, pulling open a box to reveal a collection of vintage books. "You could totally be a Victorian writer. Until you're taken away to the seaside."

She shut the ledger, putting it down to rummage through a stack of yellowed papers in a cardboard box. As she took them out something caught her eye at the bottom—a red ribbon tied neatly around a thick bundle of old letters. The ribbon had a familiar gold trim on the edges, making her heart do a strange little flip. It was the same ribbon she used as a child when helping her mother wrap presents. Her fingers trembled slightly as she lifted the bundle, the familiar handwriting of her younger self with "To Theo" scrawled across the envelope.

A nervous laugh tumbled out. "I didn't know you got these."

Theo, who had been a few feet away sorting through another pile of books and old decorations, was now beside her, his gaze fixed on the bundle in her hand. He didn't speak at first, leaning down to take the letters from her and carefully untangling the ribbon. His touch was so gentle—almost reverent—that it made her chest tighten.

"You wrote these to me, back when I'd moved away," Theo said softly, his voice becoming quieter as he unfolded an envelope and scanned the pages. Cora's cheeks burned as he did so right in front of her.

"I—yeah. I wanted to keep you updated and all that."

Theo raised an eyebrow teasingly. "You wanted to update me on a rock you found?"

Cora flushed, not knowing what to say. It was silly, wanting him to know every nonsensical thing that happened when he was gone, but she found it comforting at first, like Theo had never left. She shifted uncomfortably, suddenly too aware of how close they were when she finally stood from her spot. She could feel the heat of his body, smell the faint scent of cedarwood on his shirt, and her pulse quickened.

Clearing her throat, she tried to ease the tension. "So, you kept them. That's...uh, nice."

Theo's expression softened as he looked at her. "When I'm having a bad day, it's nice to look back at them. Like you were with me through it even if you weren't physically there."

"But why didn't you ever write back? I mean, I thought you'd at least say something after I'd sent so many."

He hesitated, eyes lowering to the floor as his fingers stilled on the letter in his hand. "My parents. They took them, hid them before I even knew they'd been delivered. I didn't know this until later, too much later. They told me you'd forgotten about me, and it was best to move on. They didn't want me to be too attached anymore."

Anger surged on his behalf. "They kept them from you?" She'd met his parents, always greeting them with kindness albeit a little shy. She would've never thought they'd tried to separate Theo from her.

"Yeah. I didn't find out until I was going to college I think. By then it felt awkward, ya know? Like too much time had passed and maybe you wouldn't write back." He looked at her then, determined to make sure what he said next would get through. "But I never forgot about you, Cordelia. I just didn't know how to bring it up. Thought it'd be too late."

Cora bit her lip as her mind spun. She'd wondered for so long why he never responded, why he could move away and just forget about their friendship. And now that she knew it wasn't his fault, a different wave of grief hit her. All the years they spent apart that could've been bridged, nothing could bring that back.

"I wish you found them sooner," she whispered. For a moment she wondered if it would've changed anything. If it would've affected her previous relationship at all. "Did you...did you ever wonder what happened?"

"I used to argue with my parents a lot about it. That you'd never just forget about me and we were friends. But after a while..." he trailed off. For a moment, Cora considered that he gave up on her, that he actually believed what they said. She wouldn't blame him, but something inside her twisted at that. "After a while, I just didn't want to keep hoping if there wasn't a chance."

Theo took a small step closer so they were almost chest to chest, and for a moment, everything seemed to slow. But neither of them moved further. "I'm glad you found them now at least."

Cora swallowed, her heart racing. "I—I didn't know you were so sentimental."

"Guess we all have our things. And here we are, after all this time."

The silence stretched on, awkward now, and Cora glanced down to distance herself from the intensity of Theo's gaze. She shuffled her feet, unsure of whether she wanted to pull away or...she didn't know what.

Finally, Theo cleared his throat. "We should probably get back to sorting. For the event."

"R-right," Cora stuttered. She kneeled back to the open box, trying to focus on the task at hand. But she could feel the tension lingering, thick and unspoken, as they each turned back to the piles of old books and letters, the air in the attic suddenly too heavy with words they hadn't said. It wasn't just the stuff in the attic they were still sorting, but the remnants of their pasts.

"Ya know," she started, still finding doing these mindless tasks easier than looking at him. "It's all in the past now. We can sort ourselves out just like these books. One page at a time."

As the silence went on, she was beginning to think what she said was so painfully cheesy that Theo was too embarrassed to respond. But eventually he did, a smile in his voice. "Yeah. One page at a time."

As they continued to sort through the attic's clutter, Cora found herself absentmindedly flipping through the yellowed papers in a dusty box. But as she pulled out the final stack, something caught her eye. Tucked beneath the papers was a thick envelope with the familiar logo of a local bank stamped on it. She pulled it out, frowning at the several unopened letters piled inside. It was clear from the marks and creases that they had been ignored for some time. Her stomach churned as she scanned the names on the letters—*Theo Mercer* clearly stamped at the top of each one.

Curious, she began to flip through the contents, her hands trembling as she flipped through the letters. Each one made her stomach twist tighter. There were notices of past-due loan balances and urgent reminders of unpaid bills, the same desperate language urging immediate payment. Cora's stomach dropped. Her eyes scanned the letters faster, growing more frantic with each word. She pulled out another, and then another, until they spilled out onto the floor in front of her like an avalanche of hidden trouble. Most had the name of Mr. Hargrove on them, but more recent ones had Theo's name. He mentioned taking over because he didn't want the bookstore to close, but never would she have thought it was due to financial turmoil.

Theo was drowning.

Her heart sank as she realized that behind the cheery façade of the cozy bookstore and Theo's passion for the fairy tale event, something else was pushing him. He was desperately trying to keep the store afloat from financial ruin.

She quickly shoved the letters back into the envelope, a cold knot forming in her stomach. She could hear Theo moving around the room, unaware of what she had just discovered. She wanted to confront him—ask him about these bills, ask him why he hadn't said anything—but she couldn't. Not yet. It wasn't really her business, and she had no clue what to even offer him when she could barely handle her own crap. She folded her arms, trying to suppress the unease building in her chest and turned back to the piles of books. Hopefully, with time, he'd tell her himself.

Chapter 8

In the days that followed, Cora itched to confront Theo about the bills. In a way, she was impressed he hadn't said a word. Instead, excitedly going all in with the event preparations. Every time Theo handed her a new receipt for his records with the same easy grin, she bit her tongue. And maybe that's what made it harder—watching him get excited over glittery banners and snack lists, like they had all the time and money in the world.

But somewhere between the late-night laminating sessions and the quiet debates over which picture books would draw the biggest crowd, other emotions began to manifest. She felt it in the way their hands brushed over the same roll of tape, in the way his gaze would linger longer on her, how she caught him each time she looked up from a spreadsheet to find him already staring. An old familiar flicker stirred, once innocent from their youth, but now matured. Each of these moments, spent side by side with Theo, filled her with a warmth she couldn't quite explain.

Somehow, these moments with Theo had started to eclipse her usual afternoons at Lumi's. Not that her friend even minded. Every time Cora sent a picture of her and Theo mid-prep, she'd get a string of commentary like *'Get it girl!'* and *'Just take him already!'* The comments made Cora smother her laughter behind a halfhearted cough when Theo would glance over, one brow arched in playful suspicion, never pressing for details. If he did, she'd just deny, deny, deny. Because there was no possible way she could explain to him the *'just take him'* text.

They spent entire afternoons like that for a week straight—browsing cookie trays at Marigold Café as if they were seasoned pastry critics, trading overly serious judgments on texture and icing before inevitably walking out with more sweets than they needed. The gingerbread versus snickerdoodle debate had become something of a ritual, a running bit neither of them seemed willing to let go.

Even the smallest tasks took on a certain weight when they did them together. Crafting invitations turned into an hours-long affair, Theo obsessing over fonts and gold foil like the fate of the event depended on it. He tied each ribbon bow with maddening precision, and though Cora rolled her eyes at the effort, she found herself memorizing the way his fingers moved. How focused he looked when he thought she wasn't watching. Once in a while, she would get a stray thought of what else his fingers could do. What they would feel like tracing along her arms, her waist, her most intimate places. Then she'd pinch herself and let the thoughts go. Absolutely no way to think of a friend.

Cora had her own quirks when it came to prep, finding herself lost in the bookstore's shelves for hours as she chased the feeling of getting it just right—the perfect mix of fairy tales, picture books, and read-aloud favorites. There was something oddly grounding in it, like brushing the dust off a part of herself she hadn't seen in years. She let her fingers trail the spines as if the stories might whisper back, offering little bits of childhood magic tucked between the pages. It was a feeling she hadn't gotten since undergrad, the wistfulness and joy of exploring worlds.

It was during one of those afternoons that she noticed her, a frequent visitor, somewhere in her twenties, with long braids and a worn paperback in her hands. The girl glanced up just long enough to catch Cora's eye and nodded toward the display Theo had just finished rearranging for the third time that week.

"Pretty sure Theo's trying to turn this place into a book-themed amusement park," she said, deadpan. "I'm bracing for a roller coaster to pop out of the nonfiction aisle."

Cora snorted. "The 'Librarian's Coaster.' Thrilling, disorienting, and ends in a paper cut."

The girl's smirk deepened. "That's how you know it's authentic."

Cora hadn't planned on making a new friend, but Tessa—she learned her name a few visits later—was hard to ignore. Her humor was bone-dry, always delivered without looking up from her book, but somehow landed with perfect timing. It became part of the rhythm of things. Cora browsing new arrivals, Theo immersed in another over-the-top display concept between customers, and Tessa, watching it all unfold from her usual spot like a self-appointed bookstore critic.

She never interrupted, never inserted herself, just existed there with a kind of ease, folding into the atmosphere like she'd always been part of it. But every now and then, Cora would catch her eyes flicking toward Theo, following his meticulous reordering of the donations shelf, and she'd swear there was the faintest glint of amusement there—like Tessa knew exactly what kind of chaos he was.

"You know," Tessa said, not looking up from her book, "I'm starting to think Theo's organization system is really just an elaborate cry for help. No one arranges books by spine color unless they've given up."

Cora smirked. "He calls it 'aesthetic balance.' You've seen his Pinterest boards, right?"

"Aesthetic balance?" Tessa snorted. "More like chaotic bookstore chic."

Cora's laugh slipped out before she could stop it. But beneath it, something unsettling stirred. There was an ease to Tessa's teasing, the kind that didn't ask permission. Like she'd been around long enough to earn the right to poke fun. Like she belonged here—with him.

Theo, oblivious as ever, was hunched over a stack of mystery novels, humming softly as he alphabetized them for the third time that week. Cora's eyes drifted back to Tessa just in time to catch a flicker of something—barely perceptible—as her gaze landed on him. It wasn't fondness, exactly. Not quite disinterest either. Whatever it was, it made Cora's chest tighten, that same old ache winding its way in again.

She forced her voice into something breezy. "So...you and Theo go way back or something?"

Tessa's grin was faint but sharp, like she knew exactly what Cora was fishing for. "We've had our moments. Mostly me mocking his overly sincere energy. He takes everything way too seriously. It's kind of endearing, in a painful sort of way."

Cora tried to read her, but Tessa was already reclining again, attention drifting back to her book like the moment hadn't meant anything at all.

"So…" Cora's voice came out more tentative this time, "…no interest, then?"

"Ew." The response was automatic. "Nope. He's like the slightly neurotic older brother I never asked for. I only started talking to him when he took over here. The timing just lined up with me blowing past my annual reading goal."

The way she said it—so casual, so final—caught Cora off guard. She wasn't even sure why. Maybe she'd been bracing for something else, something messier. But Tessa's indifference made her own feelings feel unavoidably real, like they couldn't be explained away by convenience or nostalgia. Great, she was being ridiculous with her fishing. Theo was allowed to have friends, other people in his life. Before she knew it, she thought, *But I want to be his person.*

"Relax," Tessa added, dry as ever. "It's cute. Honestly. You should just kiss him already. Or do whatever people do when they're pretending they don't have a crush."

Cora choked on nothing, blinking fast as she tried to recover. "I don't—what? That's not— I don't know what you're talking about."

"Mmhmm." Tessa didn't even glance up. "Just don't expect me to play matchmaker when you finally come to terms with it. I've got reading to do."

Cora glanced over toward Theo to see if he'd heard, but he was ringing up an order for a customer. Cora wasn't sure if she wanted to laugh or disappear into the nearest shelf. Tessa had a knack for saying the exact thing Cora was trying not to think about, and doing it with the volume turned all the way up. It was like someone reading her texts out loud in a silent café. And the worst part? She wasn't wrong. Cora did feel like a giddy schoolgirl every time Theo smiled that crooked smile or said something in that soft, offhand way that made her think he felt it too.

Meanwhile, Tessa watched it all like she was in on some private joke, tossing in the occasional wink or nudge that made Cora feel like her internal monologue had been leaked to the entire building. She was probably loving every second of it.

Theo, for his part, was buried in promotion mode, typing away with single-minded determination. He'd been reaching out to community centers, school boards, local businesses, probably even someone's grandma in line at the post office. The man could've taught a masterclass in email etiquette: warm, polished, relentlessly polite. Cora admired the hell out of it, even if it made her feel like she should be doing more. Like, say, figuring out how to keep the bookstore. Theo was clearly too proud to ask for help, but Cora wasn't. At least, not when it came to this. She'd have to brainstorm when she had the chance.

While he worked, she turned her attention back to her own contribution: the story she'd volunteered to read aloud. Cora dug through her closet, unearthing an old notebook filled with childhood scribbles and melodramatic prose. It was...a lot. Every sentence made her cringe just a little more than the last. She'd once treated every piece of critique like an insult, all raw nerves and literary ego. Those years made her sharper, more measured,m but flipping through her old words still felt like opening a time capsule sealed with secondhand embarrassment.

Still, there was something there. A kernel worth reworking.

Wrapped in a burgundy sweater dress and boots that made her feel more put together than she was, Cora headed to Sticks and Stones, texting Theo a quick heads-up. His response came almost immediately; *Praise Hekate*. She laughed into her scarf. Of course he'd say that. This whole thing may have started as a shared project, but it had quickly become his baby, just like her stories were hers.

Theo's obsession with detail had reached new heights. Wrong ribbon shade? Tragedy. Misaligned coloring pages? End of days. He'd dubbed the event 'the day of reckoning,' and honestly, she didn't doubt he meant it. But there was something oddly sweet about how much he cared. Like he wanted to give people more than just a fun afternoon; he wanted to give them something magical.

While he made a few calls, she let herself drift through the shelves, breathing in the familiar scent of paper and possibility. Normally, this was where the stories would start whispering to her. But today, they were quiet. Stubborn. Like her ideas had curled up in the corner and refused to come out.

Then—footsteps. Soft, steady. She glanced up to see Theo approaching, rubbing a hand over his face like he was trying to wake himself up. The dark circles were showing through his glasses, but his smile was still there—tired, but real.

"Need some help?" he asked, leaning against the shelf like he had nothing but time.

She eyed him. "You look like you need help. How many coffees deep are we today?"

He shrugged. "Let's just call this a much-needed distraction. What's going on?"

Cora sighed, knowing he was probably sneaking in some finance related calls during all this. Instead, she stared at the shelf like it might offer a solution if she just squinted hard enough. "I was hoping something would jump out at me, a spark, a sign, anything. I want to rewrite my story, make it lighter. Something about a woman who finds her people through her love of winter. But it's all kind of... stuck."

Theo nodded thoughtfully, scanning the shelves before pulling out a slim, icy-blue book: The Psychology of Fairy Tales.

"This digs into character motivations, especially figures like the Snow Queen. Might help you get into her head a little."

Cora took the book, magic humming gently beneath her fingers as she flipped through the pages with a light spell. Images bloomed in her mind—frostbitten landscapes, glittering silence, loneliness masked as power. At least she didn't accidentally tear the book to pieces.

"I want people to see her differently," she murmured. "Not as a villain, but as someone just... trying to be understood."

Theo's grin widened. "I'm just here for the deep psychological drama. You've clearly got the magic part handled."

"No evil cackling this time, promise."

"Shame. I was looking forward to it."

Their rhythm was so easy, so them. As she skimmed, Theo stayed close, arms folded, head tilted, like this was his favorite show. She could feel his gaze more than see it—steady, warm, focused. It made her forget entire lines and have to reread the same paragraph three times just to remember where she was.

"What if the Snow Queen meets a child?" she asks suddenly. "Someone lost. Maybe helping them helps her reconnect to herself."

Theo's eyes lit up. "That's something. There's a book over there—Winter's Heart. Not fairy tale exactly, but it hits that theme. Lonely landscapes, connection, redemption. Could give you a vibe to work from."

She nodded, reaching for it, but Theo beat her to it. His shoulder brushed hers, nothing dramatic, just a simple touch that somehow sent a pleasant shiver down her spine. She hadn't even noticed him move closer, but there he was, right next to her, reaching up to pull the book from the shelf. Cora's breath caught, her mind suddenly less interested in fairy tales and more in how close he was. Close enough that she could smell the hint of cedar on his sweater, see the strands of hair that had slipped loose over his forehead.

"Here, let me," he murmured, his voice low and annoyingly smooth as he focused on the task at hand. Cora watched him, because, well, how could she not? The way his brow furrowed in concentration, the soft curve of his lips—she couldn't help but wonder how those lips might feel. His eyes flicked to her lips—once, twice. At least she wasn't the only one thinking it. Cora's heart rate picked up, the warmth of his hand practically consuming hers, even if it was for a second.

"Cordelia..." he started, voice low, barely there. She couldn't help but start imagining all the possible scenarios—the bookstore, the shelves, the undeniable pull between them. But of course, reality was always way more intoxicating than whatever her mind could cook up. She knew that if she leaned in just a little, if she allowed herself that one tiny slip into the "what could be," everything would change.

Ping.

The universe is a buzzkill. Cora flinched at the sudden interruption. Pulling away like she'd been burned, she checked her phone to see a message from her mom. *Dinner at 6?*

"Right," she muttered, the moment cracking and vanishing. She felt shy now, like the almost-kiss was some heavy weight she couldn't shake off.

Theo stepped back, his usual calm slipping into place like armor. "Damn phones."

Cora forced a breath, gathering the books like that would ease the tension still humming in her chest. "Thanks for the help. I'll give these a read."

As she turned to go, she risked one last glance over her shoulder—only to find him watching her, eyes steady, expression unreadable. But something unspoken hung there between them, a thread neither of them seemed ready to cut.

What narrative are we even building here? she wondered.

And more importantly—how much longer could they pretend it was nothing?

Chapter 9

Cora stood at Lumi's kitchen counter, sleeves pushed up, fingers dusted with flour, the scent of vanilla and melting chocolate wrapping around her like a blanket she hadn't realized she needed. The oven clicked softly in the background, and somewhere between measuring out sugar and cracking eggs, the tension of Theo's financial woes she'd been carrying started to loosen—if only slightly.

Across from her, Lumi was focused on chopping a dark chocolate bar into uneven, rustic shards, her movements precise but casual. The two of them were covered in a fine constellation of flour and cookie dough, the kind of mess that didn't ask to be cleaned up right away. It was the kind of afternoon that had quietly slipped into evening without anyone noticing—music humming low, utensils clinking in a kind of rhythm, laughter threading between old stories and knowing looks.

It wasn't lost on Cora that she always seemed to end up here—Lumi's place, Lumi's kitchen—after a particularly *charged* moment with Theo. Like she needed neutral ground. Like her body instinctively sought out familiarity after walking through something more uncertain. This time, it had been *that* moment in the bookstore. The not-quite brush of his lips, the way their fingers had lingered, the way her name had sounded when he said it like that.

She shook her head, trying to focus on the recipe, but her thoughts kept drifting back to the exact angle of his smile, the brush of his sleeve against hers, how close they'd been—close enough to count eyelashes. It was maddening. Sweet, dizzying, infuriating.

"You've got that look again," Lumi said without glancing up, voice light but knowing.

Cora raised an eyebrow. "What look?"

"The one that says you were just mentally somewhere else—probably stuck between Theo and a bookshelf, trying to pretend it didn't mean something."

Cora groaned, leaning against the counter. "I hate how well you know me. But it's not just that."

"Then what is it exactly?"

"Fear of starting over, I guess," Cora mumbled, her spoon scraping the bowl with just a little too much force. The batter clung stubbornly to the sides, much like the thoughts she was trying—and failing—to stir away. "Letting someone in again. Letting *him* in."

She kept mixing, shoulders tense, eyes fixed on the swirl of flour and eggs like they might offer an answer. They didn't.

"I can't stop thinking about him, Lumi. We had... some kind of moment in the bookstore when he was helping me. But of course, I'm terrified it's going to end up exactly like it did with Avery."

"Moment, you say? Should I light a candle or...?"

"Focus, Lumi."

"I am focusing, particularly on making sure I don't slice my finger off," Lumi huffed, a hint of sarcasm in her voice as she put the knife down. She turned her full attention to Cora, her expression one part concern, one part amused. "And you're the one being stingy with the details." Cora shot her a look, but Lumi didn't back down. "But Theo's not Avery. He's—"

"I know!" Cora snapped. She stopped stirring, gripping the edges of the countertop like it was her lifeline. "But Avery was supposed to be different too, you know? She proposed to me and everything."

She bit her lip, cutting herself off before she said anything else. She was one word away from dumping the whole cheating story over cookie dough. The words pressed against her throat, aching to spill out—the lies, the betrayal, the moment it all cracked open and collapsed. But she swallowed them down like she always did.

It wasn't that she didn't trust Lumi. It was just...hard. To say it out loud. To admit how fast it had all happened, how deep it had cut, how much she still blamed herself for not seeing it coming.

Lumi's eyes softened, but her voice remained steady. "You can't keep letting Avery haunt the rooms she walked out of, Cora. I know it's not easy, but you're not doing yourself any favors by staying stuck. You can't keep letting her keep write the script for your future." Her voice dropped a little, becoming quieter, more thoughtful. "I've been there. It's easy to get stuck in the what ifs, especially after a mess like Avery. When I was with Michelle—"

She hesitated, her eyes flicking away as she picked up the knife again, resuming her chocolate chopping. They rarely talked about Michelle. It was the kind of shared understanding that didn't need to be dissected—too many quiet nights after it ended, too many glasses of wine and half-spoken sentences that led nowhere.

"We made all these plans. Thought we were doing everything right. And then one day, it just wasn't there anymore." She exhaled softly, the memory clearly weighing on her. "I had to let go of what I thought we were, because it wasn't real. We were just going through the motions of a perfect life we were never actually living."

Cora stopped stirring. Her hand hovered over the bowl, spoon still half-buried in the batter. She wasn't expecting Lumi to go there—not tonight, not over cookies. But maybe that was the point. Truth always seemed to show up when the kitchen was warm and the walls weren't listen-

144

ing. Cora had been messier with her grief, dramatic even. Lumi had just gone quiet. Both of them had been stuck in their own ways of mourning what wasn't meant to last.

Her thoughts drifted to the trail of exes that read more like footnotes than chapters. Every man she'd dated had treated her like an idea; the clever girl, the artistic one, the mysterious type who would eventually become wife material if they just waited long enough. They never really *saw* her—just a version of her that fit the narrative they'd already written.

The women were different. Softer, more honest. But even those connections had faded before they ever fully bloomed. Like they all carried some invisible expiration date no one wanted to talk about.

But Avery? Avery had felt like a spark hitting dry kindling. Immediate. Consuming. She'd made Cora believe they were the real thing—that this time, the story would stick.

And when it didn't?

Now, all that was left was the echo of that failure. This dull ache that whispered, maybe it wasn't about who she chose, maybe it was her. That no matter how carefully she loved, she always seemed to fall short of the kind of love she thought she'd one day deserve.

The kitchen went still, save for the low hum of the oven and the soft ticking of the wall clock—small sounds that somehow made the silence louder. Cora stood frozen, arms wrapped tightly around herself, blinking hard against the burn behind her eyes.

"It used to be easier," Cora said, finally. "When I was mad. When I trashed her apartment and felt like fire instead of...whatever this is." She let out a shaky laugh that didn't quite land. "Now it's just this... ache. I hate that it still hurts."

Lumi didn't say anything at first, just kept chopping chocolate with slow, deliberate movements. The pieces clinked into the glass bowl one after another, like punctuation marks in a conversation Cora hadn't finished starting.

"I keep thinking I'm walking into the same story again," Cora murmured, her eyes fixed on the counter. "Different cover, same ending. What if Theo's not interested? What if it's all in my head?"

Lumi scoffed lightly, setting the knife down with a soft thunk. She leaned one hip against the counter, crossing her arms as she gave Cora that look—equal parts exasperation and love. "You know what your problem is?"

Cora blinked, caught off guard. "Wow, subtle."

"I'm serious. You're so afraid of being wrong again, you're not even giving yourself the chance to be right."

Cora looked away, guilt creeping up her spine.

Lumi pushed off the counter and stepped closer, pulling the bowl out of Cora's grasp and starting to scoop messy dollops of dough onto the baking tray with practiced ease. "You can hide behind what ifs forever, but none of them will protect you. They'll just build a wall so tall you forget what it's like to be seen on the other side."

Cora swallowed hard, the lump in her throat pressing higher. "It just feels safer this way. Distant. Detached. Like if I don't let myself hope, I won't have anything to lose."

Lumi let out a quiet, almost tired sigh. "Safer doesn't mean better. And it definitely doesn't mean honest."

The cookies were lined up unevenly on the tray now, imperfect little things that somehow made the room feel more human. Lumi glanced over her shoulder, her voice softening. "Cora. You're allowed to want something good. To believe that this—whatever it is with Theo—might be worth the risk."

"But what if he doesn't get it? What if he thinks I'm too much? Or not enough?"

Lumi turned, her expression softening completely now, the teasing edge gone. "Then he's not the right one. But you'll never know unless you let him see you for real. Not the guarded version. Not the edited draft. What would you say to a reader in the same situation?"

Cora's voice trembled. "He isn't Avery. I know that."

"Then stop treating him like he might become her," Lumi said, setting the tray aside. "Stop waiting for someone to disappoint you. Let him surprise you."

"And if he doesn't understand?"

"First of all, Theo is a cinnamon roll," Lumi said, punctuating the declaration with a pointed look. "You've said it yourself. If he cares about you—and come on, he does—he'll get it. But you can't expect him to read your mind. You two have history. Trust it a little, yeah?"

"There's a twenty-year gap in that history," Cora muttered, her tone edging toward skeptical.

Lumi waved her off. "Irrelevant. He's clearly still Theo, just with better hair and jawline definition."

"That's not the point we're making here," Cora said, trying and failing to ignore the blush creeping up her neck. Lumi's words unlocked a door in her brain she really didn't want to open. Because, sure, "hotter" didn't even begin to cover it. Her mind betrayed her instantly—cue image of Theo on his knees, her fingers tangled in his hair, that soft spot behind his ear—

Cora blinked hard, furiously shaking her head as if that could erase the very *inappropriate* reel now playing in her mental cinema. *God, what is wrong with me?* She gripped the mixing spoon like it might anchor her back to earth.

Trying to recover, she focused back on the dough. "What if I get hurt again?" she ventured, trying to inject seriousness back into her tone, but her voice came out a little breathless, still catching on the heat of that spiraling thought.

Lumi didn't bite. Instead, she muttered something under her breath, too quiet for Cora to catch, which only deepened the crease between Cora's brows.

"You okay?" she asked, pausing mid-stir. "You're kind of...snippy today."

Lumi didn't answer right away. Instead, she flicked the last of the chocolate into the bowl and wiped her hands on a kitchen towel with a little more force than necessary.

"There's just a *lot* of 'what if' happening for someone who hasn't even tried yet," Lumi said, not quite looking at her. "You're the same person who once packed her whole life into a car and moved across the country without knowing a single soul. You've done scary things before, Cora. This isn't new."

There was something in her voice, something a little too sharp to be just about Theo. Cora caught it immediately.

"The difference now is you *know* your worth," Lumi continued, scooping batter onto a tray with uncharacteristic precision. "And honestly? If one of your readers sent you a letter with this exact dilemma, you'd probably write back, 'What if it works out? What if it's actually everything you hoped for?' So?"

Cora sighed loudly, giving in. "Yeah, yeah. 'Don't let fear steal your joy.' I get it."

"Exactly!" Lumi threw her hands in the air like a victorious coach. "Now, if we could please return to the matter at hand—cookies. No one's allowed to ruin dessert, not even fear itself."

Cora smiled at that, but the moment didn't settle like it usually did. Instead, she found herself watching Lumi more closely—noticed how her shoulders hadn't quite re-laxed, how her smile didn't quite reach her eyes.

"But are you okay?" she asked again. "Is something go-ing on?"

Lumi froze for just a second—so small it could've gone unnoticed if Cora didn't know her like she did. Then, just as quickly, Lumi shrugged and flashed a breezy smile. "I'm fine. Just a long day."

But Cora wasn't convinced. The answer came too fast. Too rehearsed. Lumi wasn't the type to hide—at least not from her. Yet, now, something was tucked behind that casual tone, hidden in the cracks of her voice.

"If you're sure..."

"I'm sure," Lumi said, already turning back to the bak-ing tray.

Cora followed suit, shaping the last bit of dough into uneven little balls, filling the silence with idle chatter about Lumi's partner overseas. But her mind kept circling back to the shift—the too-quick brush-off, the brittle humor, the silence that hummed underneath.

What if it's me? she wondered. *What if she's tired of hearing about Theo? What if I've pushed her too far without even realizing?*

She placed the tray in the oven with care, but even the blast of warm air didn't cut through the sudden chill in her stomach. There was something unspoken between them now, and it wasn't just her unresolved feelings for Theo.

Maybe it *was* just a bad day. Or maybe they were both carrying things they weren't ready to say.

Cora glanced back at Lumi, who was still fussing with the placement of cookies. *Tell me what's going on,* she wanted to say. *Let me in.*

But she didn't. She stayed quiet.

And Lumi didn't offer.

And the space between them—like the tray cooling on the counter—stayed warm on the outside, but cold in the center.

Chapter 10

Cora sat cross-legged on her bedroom rug, surrounded by a sprawl of scribbled notes, open books, and half-finished drafts that curled at the edges like fallen leaves. A pecan waffle-scented candle flickered on the windowsill, its warm aroma threading through the air like a quiet reminder to breathe. Her mug of tea had long since gone cold, forgotten in the flurry of ideas she kept chasing but couldn't quite catch.

She'd carefully constructed the scene; cozy lighting, scattered inspiration, her favorite fountain pen uncapped beside her like it had something important to say. All in service of diving back into something she hadn't touched in months—writing.

At the center of the storm, *The Snow Queen*. Or at least, a version of her. Cora had always felt oddly drawn to the character, not as a villain, but as someone no one ever tried to understand. A woman made of sharp edges and layered silences. The more she sifted through old fairytales and notes—many of which Theo had dropped off with a shrug and that secretly-pleased look he tried to hide—the more the queen started to feel like a stand-in for something deeper. Loneliness. Reinvention. Protection disguised as coldness.

She wasn't aiming for a neat, sweet retelling. No, Cora wanted spark and bite. Something that looked like magic on the outside, but pulsed with something heartbreakingly human underneath.

In Cora's version, the icy monarch wasn't some villain draped in malice—she was simply a woman craving solitude, someone whose vibe just didn't match the world's noise. Cora imagined her gliding through winter like a secret no one had the patience to unravel, her frostbitten fingers sketching delicate patterns into pine needles and frozen windowpanes. She didn't freeze things out of cruelty, she just found beauty in cold clarity.

But every time the Snow Queen tried to connect, the world retreated. People locked their doors, built fires, and whispered about her like she was a walking blizzard. No one ever asked *why* she was cold. No one stayed long enough to learn.

Cora's pen tapped rhythmically against the edge of her notebook, thoughts swirling like snowflakes—elegant, chaotic, and threatening to melt before she could catch them. The old habit returned easily, hoarding stray ideas like precious trinkets, each one a possible puzzle piece for something not-yet-written. That familiar thrill buzzed beneath her skin—the moment right before a story truly takes shape.

And then it hit her, the Snow Queen didn't need a prince or a savior. She needed a companion. A child, maybe—someone small enough to still believe in magic, someone curious enough not to fear the cold. Cora saw her clearly now, a little girl spinning through snowdrifts, unbothered by the chill, singing into the wind just to see her breath. This girl didn't want to fix the Queen, she just wanted to play. That was the difference.

As Cora scribbled the first lines of their meeting, the story began to crack open like ice underfoot. The girl wasn't melting the Queen's heart with dramatic gestures—she was simply showing up, moment by moment, with joy and wonder. Together, they built impossible things: a castle of light and frost, a garden where snow bloomed in intricate petals. The Queen didn't even realize she was thawing—until she laughed. Really laughed. And the silence she'd wrapped herself in for centuries broke apart like icicles in spring.

The more Cora wrote, the more the story shifted beneath her pen. It wasn't just about magic anymore. It was about rediscovery—of self, of connection, of what it means to let someone in after being cold for so long.

Cora paused, pen hovering mid-air. That familiar ache bloomed low in her chest. The kind of ache that usually came with memories, with names she tried not to say out loud too often. Avery. Theo. And even earlier, the girl she used to be before heartbreak turned her soft edges sharp.

She stared down at the page, the icy landscape she'd created, the lonely queen who never asked to be feared. It wasn't subtle anymore, was it? This wasn't just a fairytale. It was a mirror. Maybe it had been all along.

Because wasn't that her? Quietly guarding the parts of herself that had once been wide open? She wasn't out here building ice castles, sure, but she had walls. Whole cities made of them. Her cool detachment at parties. Her perfected smile when someone brought up Avery's name. The way she laughed off anything too tender, too sincere.

The Snow Queen didn't mean to be alone—she just got used to the quiet.

Cora let out a breath she hadn't realized she was holding, her pen finally moving again, slower this time. The little girl in the story—brave and curious—kept showing up, thawing things word by word. And maybe, if she let her, that girl could thaw something in Cora, too.

Not literally. There'd be no magical moment where everything cracked open and made sense.

But maybe the point wasn't to melt all the ice. Maybe it was to let enough of it soften that someone could step closer.

Maybe that's why Theo still haunted the corners of her mind the way he did. Not because he was her fairytale ending, but because he'd been the first person in a long time to see through the cold. Not afraid. Just...patient. Still standing there, even after all this time, waiting for her to stop flinching every time warmth showed up at her door.

Knock, knock.

Of course, just as she was on the verge, reality decided to show up, interrupting her literary exploration.

"Cora?" came her mother's voice behind the door. "Just checking in if you still wanted to eat together."

"In a bit, Mom," Cora nearly gritted out, trying to keep her thoughts in place before it disappeared. "Just getting some writing in."

There was a long pause from the other side. "I'll let you know when it's ready and bring it up for you."

Cora chuckled softly, appreciating her mother's understanding. She knew all too well the dangers of an interrupted writer—and a witch. Her mom had learned that the hard way in the past, having been on the unfortunate receiving end of more than one of Cora's groove disruptions.

The story still felt half-formed—like a blurry Polaroid waiting to sharpen into focus—but the emotion behind it was crystal clear. Every stroke of the pen released something inside her: the ache of being misunderstood, the quiet desperation for connection, the long, tangled history of learning to survive by staying guarded. The Snow Queen's world, cold and glittering, was starting to feel less like fiction and more like an echo of her own.

She leaned back onto her hands, her body finally relaxing into the stillness around her. For once, the noise in her head had settled into something close to clarity. In her story, the Snow Queen wasn't just searching for a companion anymore—she was standing at the edge of a frozen lake, staring at her own reflection for the first time in years. A woman not just awakening, but choosing to unfreeze.

Cora traced her fingers along the margin of the page, a slow smile tugging at her lips. It had been a while since she'd made something for herself. Not for school, not for work, not because someone else expected it, but because something inside her had insisted. It didn't matter that the idea was stitched together from bits of her own heartache, from the town that had swallowed her whole, and from conversations she pretended not to replay at night. This was hers. And that made it matter.

Pages of notes fluttered beside her, all part of the other project—the fundraiser, the messy half-sketched plans that felt a little too big and a little too brave. Funny, how the energy from one story fed the other. Both were about rebuilding. Both were about choosing not to vanish.

On impulse, she reached for her phone, ready to text Lumi about the breakthrough. She needed to share this; someone had to know what it meant to feel herself cracking open like this.

But as her thumb hovered over Lumi's name, her eyes flicked one line down.

Theo.

Of course.

Like some cosmic nudge—or maybe just her own subconscious being annoying—she found herself tapping his thread instead. No message. Just scrolling. Re-reading old texts. Not even the deep ones. Just the casual check-ins, the occasional jokes, that one dumb GIF he sent that still made her smile. She didn't even realize she was holding her breath until it escaped in a sigh.

Maybe it was time to stop backing away too.

"Guess who finished her story for the reading." she sent, trying really hard not to overthink why she texted Theo instead of Lumi. She gathered up her papers, pretending to be productive and organizing them for later, typing to distract herself from the fact that she was now waiting for his reply. Definitely not desperate or overly excited about it. Nope.

The ping that jolted through her spine and sent her bolting to her phone? Yeah, that showed otherwise. *"Your mother? I knew she'd finally listen to my begging!"* was his response.

"Hardy har," she typed back, grateful he couldn't hear the inner eye roll she was doing at his typical joking. Her face scrunched in annoyance; he could've said something like "Good job, you talented being, you." But no, apparently sarcasm was the default setting. *"Just for that, I'm not giving you a sneak peek. You'll have to wait like everyone else."* That'll show him. Maybe.

A few minutes later, Cora received a "boooo" followed by a sad face emoji, which made her smirk in satisfaction. Victory. She decided on a whim to call him just out of spite. He picked up before the first ring even ended. Of course he did. "You're incorrigible," she said, knowing full well he'd just keep being his usual, charmingly annoying self.

"I know, right?" he chuckled, and unfortunately that chuckle made her shiver in spite of herself. "But I'm impressed. I can't wait to hear it."

Cora's smirk faded just a little as something stirred inside her—a tiny flicker of curiosity she couldn't ignore. She hesitated, her fingers lightly tapping the phone, stalling. "Theo, can I ask you something?" she finally asked, hoping this wouldn't lead to more teasing.

"Of course." The way he said it made her wonder if he was already bracing himself for some weird, Cora-level question. And maybe he was right to.

"Why did you come back to Valley Creek Hollow? I mean, I know you took over the bookstore when you got here, but what made you actually come back?" Cora leaned back against the couch, her mind racing with the possibilities of his answer. He'd always been so lively and driven when they were younger. Did that mean she was officially old? No, no, it was just that his return seemed to have some deeper, hidden reason. She wasn't buying the whole "bookstore takeover" excuse.

There was a pause on the other end of the line, and Cora could practically hear him thinking—probably running through his mental list of ways to dodge the question. "You've always been curious, huh?" he said with a chuckle, clearly not even trying to hide the amusement. Yeah, because she definitely didn't have a million questions floating around in her head right now. But sure, let's go with "curious."

"I guess so," she admitted, her tone softening despite herself. "I just...I don't know. There's something about you being here, about how much you care about this place, that makes me wonder what really brought you back after being gone forever."

"Not like I wanted to be gone so long," Theo muttered, the bitterness in his voice low but unmistakable.

Cora felt the familiar tightness in her chest. She had to remind herself—he hadn't wanted to leave. He wasn't the one who'd dragged his family out of Valley Creek Hollow. He had just been a kid, powerless to stop any of it.

Silence crackled softly on the other end of the line, that uncertain kind that made her wonder if she'd pushed too far. But then Theo spoke again, quieter now, like he was choosing each word with care—something rare for him.

"When we left, my parents kept saying I had to move on. That there was nothing here for me anymore. I wasn't sure if I'd ever come back—or who'd even still be here if I did."

His voice hit a spot in her she hadn't touched in years. This wasn't just about the bookstore. It never had been. Cora swallowed hard, her hand instinctively brushing the jade shell at her neck, the one he gave her the day he left.

"The bookstore," he continued, "was everything to me. It wasn't just some building full of books. It was where we found our stories—where we *became* part of them. I didn't know it then, but it was my anchor. And when I left, it felt like I lost that."

She could see it all so clearly; thirteen-year-old Theo, red-eyed and shaking, fastening the necklace around her neck with trembling hands. *"Never forget me,"* he had said, the jade cool against her skin. *"This shell is for protection, for strength. That's what I want for you."*

And now here he was, sounding like that same boy again—only grown, and carrying the weight of too many quiet years.

"I didn't know what I was doing for a long time after," Theo admitted. "Tried to build a life, tried to figure out who I was. But no matter where I went, I kept thinking about that place. About us. About what it meant. And one day, I realized I wanted to give that same feeling to other kids—the way we had it. The bookstore...it was where everything started."

"So you came back," she murmured, her voice steadier than she felt. "To build something like that again."

Theo let out a breath. "Yeah. I guess I did."

And for a moment, that warmth between them bloomed again. Familiar, comforting.

But it didn't last.

Cora thought back to the stack of papers she found in the attic. The bookstore's financial records. Rent past due. Utility notices. Credit card debt she hadn't known about until she stumbled on them by accident.

She hadn't brought it up right away, hadn't wanted to corner him. But the words itched now, like a splinter in her chest.

"Theo," she said softly, her voice almost too gentle. "I saw the bills."

The silence on the other line made her heart quicken. She hurried to explain herself.

"I wasn't snooping," she added quickly. "They were just... there. And I couldn't ignore them."

She imagined his reaction now. Jaw clenched, shame creeping into his expression.

"I didn't want you to worry," he finally said, voice hoarse. "Didn't want to drag you into this. I didn't want to be the one who—" He exhaled sharply. "Who broke everything."

Her heart twisted. "You're not breaking anything, Theo. But you *can't* do this alone. You're drowning, and nobody even knows it."

He didn't speak for what felt like hours, but it was only a few minutes. She knew this conversation would be tough, but it had to happen. They had to do something if the bookstore was to stay afloat.

"What if we make the holiday event a fundraiser?" she offered gently, but with growing urgency. "Not just a cozy little gathering, but something bigger. We get the whole town involved. Turn it into a community push—add a crowdfunding campaign, do promo, even a silent auction or author readings. I can write about it in the paper, online, wherever people will see it."

Theo sighed. "I don't know... asking people for help like that—it's not easy."

"I know. But you said it yourself, this place is about more than just books. It's about belonging. And people *want* to help. They just need to know what's at stake."

He hesitated.

"I'll even help you write the campaign." She felt desperate now, but had to make him see. "Make it personal. Show them how much you care. Show them what this place means—not just to you, but to everyone."

Another pause, long and deafening. "You really think people will care?"

"I know they will. Because they already do. Just like I do. Valley Creek Hollow wouldn't be the same without you, Theo."

She couldn't handle the constant silence she faced, not when she didn't know how he looked or what he was thinking, so she continued. "You keep saying you didn't know if anyone would still be here when you came back, but...this town *needed* you to come back. *I* needed you to come back."

His breath hitched like he wanted to speak, but she didn't let him—not yet.

"You're the reason half of these kids even care about books," she went on, smiling softly. "You brought life back into the square just by opening those doors again. You remembered what made this place special, even when the rest of us kind of forgot. And I don't think you realize how rare that is. How rare *you* are."

Cora took a slow breath, letting her feelings dictate her words. "I don't know what it would've been like if you hadn't come back and I was the only one who had. But I do know things feel different now. Brighter. Like maybe there's actually room for something good again."

Theo let out a soft, unsteady laugh. "I didn't expect to find you here," he said, his voice rough around the edges. "Not like this. Not still wearing that damn necklace."

Cora's hand instinctively lifted to the shell. "You gave it to me the day you left. What was I supposed to do—*not* wear it? It's the only thing I didn't pack away when everything else fell apart."

Theo exhaled, and the silence that followed wasn't awkward this time. It was full—thick with unspoken things, with all the versions of them they used to be and might still become.

"I'm really glad you're here, Cordelia," he said finally, and the way he said her full name made her pulse stutter in

the way it always had—like it was stitched with something sacred.

Cora smiled, though it trembled at the corners. "Me too, Theo."

She didn't know what this was between them yet—not exactly. But in that moment, it felt like a beginning.

Chapter 11

"So," Cora said, clearing her throat as she slid into the seat across from Theo, a notepad balanced on her knee. The pages were already dog-eared from too many restless ideas. "About my fundraising suggestion."

Theo glanced up from his mug of lukewarm tea, one brow lifting. "Yeah? You planning to burn it down or save it?"

"Definitely the saving option."

His smile didn't quite reach his eyes. He leaned back, arms crossing—a motion she began noting when he wanted to distance himself. "Cordelia..."

"I know," she interrupted gently, eyes still on the notepad as her pen scratched something down—mostly to ignore the way his voice still stirred something inconvenient in her chest. She'd invited him over the next day so he'd feel more comfortable shifting their planning techniques, but it didn't seem to be working. "You don't want to make a big deal. You don't want people thinking the store's in trouble. But they care about this place, Theo. You *just* said it the other day—it's a foundation. It matters."

He hesitated, gaze drifting to the window. Somewhere out there, the town slept unaware. Or maybe not so unaware.

"Let them show up for you," Cora continued to encourage. She didn't know where this confidence came from, but she would use it. For Theo. "You've given so much of yourself to this town in a short span of time after Mr. Hargrove retired, and you didn't even have to!"

"It was more for selfish reasons..."

"Please. Because *anyone* would do late-night book deliveries, last-minute Yule gift wraps, and impromptu therapy at the checkout desk."

His fingers raked through his hair, and he let out a breath like it had been sitting in his chest for months. "It's complicated. I don't want it to look like I'm failing."

"You're not failing. You're being honest. There's a difference."

When he didn't answer, she flipped to a clean page, tapping her pen against it. "Okay, listen. Everyone's going to be out and about for Yuletide anyway, right? So why not add a little more to the workshops and cookie booths this year? We turn it into a community fundraiser. You already have the live readings and storytelling for the kids. We're just adding an aspect of donations."

His expression shifted—a mix of skepticism and the first flicker of reluctant curiosity. Cora pushed further. "I can help on the social media side, contact the paper, and yeah," she added with a glint in her eye, "I'll even interview you."

Theo groaned. "You're going to quote me out of context and make me sound like some tragic book boy, aren't you?"

"Obviously," she said, flashing a grin. "That's how you get donations."

Despite himself, he laughed, and there it was, the softening. The cracking open of something he'd been keeping sealed.

She leaned in. "And we could set up a crowdfunding campaign. Something simple, like GoFundMe. I'll help you write a personal letter—nothing fancy, just you being you. People respond to the truth, Theo. You don't have to put a bow on it."

He studied her for a long moment, trying to see through her. "How do you even know how to do all this?"

Cora hesitated, preferring to focus on Theo rather than revisit her past. "I picked a few things up while doing the advice column."

Theo blinked. "Back in Seattle?"

"*Witch, please,*" she mocked. "Tragic love letters. Passive-aggressive sibling disputes. One guy who was convinced his neighbor's cat was stalking him."

"Okay, but that's just writing. This is organizing, strategizing, marketing—"

"Lumi," Cora interrupted, her smile turning fond. "She started a handmade lingerie line for 'bigger baddies' as she calls it. I helped her launch it. Did her first logo, made her press kit, wrote all the product blurbs. During one of my visits back here we spent a weekend eating cookie dough straight from the tub while I taught her how to schedule Instagram posts and write SEO copy."

Theo leaned back into the couch, blinking at her in surprise. "You've got this whole secret résumé."

"It's not secret. I contain multitudes."

"You're full of surprises."

"And snacks," she added, pushing one of the cookies she and Lumi had baked toward him. "Which is how I win most people over."

He studied her for a long moment. He looked at her like she might be the miracle he hadn't dared to hope for. The flicker of belief started to take root as he took the cookie. "You really think people will care that much?"

Cora met his gaze, no hesitation in hers. "I *know* they will."

"Okay," he nodded, swallowing. "Let's do it."

Cora's smile bloomed—real and full and alive. She couldn't remember the last time she felt so dedicated to something. It filled one of the pieces inside of her that had been lost.

"Good. Because I already started drafting the post. And I may or may not have called a few businesses to donate raffle items."

Theo blinked. "How long have you been planning this?"

Her response was unapologetic. "Since I found the bills."

He narrowed his eyes at her, but the edge had melted into something softer. "You're a menace."

"Yeah," she admitted, shrugging. "But I'm your menace."

It slipped out before she could stop it, but her embarrassment was worth the grin that spread across Theo's face. She didn't hesitate, running to her room to collect all the post-it notes she'd accumulated and her laptop. When she returned to him, she shoved the notes into his hands and opened her laptop to a document titled *Operation: Save Sticks and Stones*.

Theo stared at the notes, suddenly ready to bolt. "Uhh, so we're doing this now?"

"Yes." Cora didn't even glance up. "I'm taking advantage of your willing state before you can change your mind."

"I still don't think anyone wants to hear me talk about feelings on camera."

"You literally own a bookstore. Your job is making people feel things."

"That's different," he muttered.

She finally looked at him, one eyebrow cocked, lips curving just slightly. "Why? Because this time *you're* the main character?"

He let out a pained groan and dropped his head onto the table. "Please don't say that again."

"Okay, fine," she said, nudging another cookie closer. "But you're doing it. Honest, passionate, mildly neurotic—that's your whole brand. Trust me."

He stared at the cookie, then took a slow bite. Baked goods seemed to be the only thing easing him up. "Only if you promise to edit out the part where I mess up and say something ridiculous."

"Deal," she said, lifting her phone and pressing record before he could back out.

The camera wobbled slightly as Theo shifted, then stared directly into the lens like it might bite him.

"Hey, um... Hi. I'm Theo, the owner of Sticks and Stones. And I guess I'm here to, well, to ask for a little help."

His breath hitched. He glanced off-screen, where Cora gave him a thumbs up.

"This store—it's been here for generations. It was my refuge when I was a kid. You all probably remember when Mr. Hargrove owned it. When I came back to Valley Creek Hollow, it was because I wanted that same refuge to still exist. For other kids. For anyone who needed it."

His voice softened, eyes dropping for a moment before lifting again. "But it's been hard. Independent bookstores don't have big safety nets, and I've been trying to keep it all going without saying anything. But someone..." he cast a sideways glance at Cora, who beamed, "reminded me that asking for help doesn't mean I've failed."

He took another breath. "So, if this place has ever meant something to you...if you've ever walked through these shelves and found a story that stayed with you...I'm asking you to help me keep that magic going."

He gave a small, crooked smile, the kind that made her heart ache a little. "Thank you. For caring. And for sticking with me."

Click.

Cora slowly lowered the phone, her throat tighter than she expected.

"That was perfect," she said softly.

Theo blinked. "Seriously?"

"Seriously. Let's save this bookstore."

Chapter 12

By the time Theo had eaten a second cookie and Cora had opened three new browser tabs, the two of them were seated cross-legged on the rug in her living room, surrounded by piles of sticky notes, half-drunk mugs of cocoa, and an alarming number of pens with no ink. The window fogged gently from the chill outside, while the warmth of planning—or maybe just proximity—kept the room from feeling too quiet.

Theo tapped his pencil against his knee. "Okay, so we've got the live readings. We add a costume contest—fairy tale themed. Extra points if someone shows up as a sentient candlestick."

Cora grinned. "Please. I'm just waiting for the inevitable 'hot lumberjack' interpretation of Paul Bunyan."

Theo chuckled, then reached over to adjust one of the notes on the coffee table. "And you're sure people will actually donate to this?"

"They will," Cora said again, with a confidence that surprised even her. "You're not just a bookstore. You're the cozy corner of this town's heart."

Theo paused, glancing over at her, the teasing fading just slightly from his face. "You really have a way with words."

She shrugged and gave a tight smile, eyes flicking down to her laptop screen. "Occupational hazard."

He was quiet for a beat, long enough that she looked up. He was watching her—not the sticky notes or the spreadsheet on her screen, but *her*, like he was trying to line up what he knew with what he still didn't.

"So," he said carefully, voice softer than before, "why Seattle?"

Cora blinked, caught off guard. Her fingers stilled on the keyboard. *He asks as if it's simple.* She reached for her cocoa to buy herself a second of calm. "That's specific."

"I'm just bringing back the conversation you avoided. Good time, right?"

She stared down at her hands, flexing them once before folding them in her lap. "It wasn't exactly strategic," she admitted. "I wanted out. Away. I loved this place, but after my dad died, everything here felt... too heavy. Too full of things I couldn't fix."

Theo didn't interrupt. He didn't even blink too hard. Just sat there watching behind his glasses.

"I needed to not be the girl from Valley Creek Hollow whose father used to coach little league and died too young. I needed to be somewhere I could breathe without running into someone who looked at me with grief."

She exhaled slowly.

"I could just be a girl with a laptop and a public transportation app who didn't burst into tears every time she passed the old pharmacy where her dad used to buy her gum."

A pause. Then another. She remembered those early days in Seattle. Standing in line for black coffee at a place that played French jazz too loud. Sitting on buses with strangers who didn't know her name. Waking up in a too-quiet apartment and pretending that was the kind of peace she wanted.

"And Seattle?" he asked gently.

"Far enough," she said, a faint, crooked smile pulling at her lips. "Big city. No one knew my name. I could disappear into it. Go to grad school and stay focused, write weird fiction, eat overpriced pastries alone on rainy days."

Theo tilted his head slightly. "Sounds poetic."

"It was. Then it wasn't."

He paused, then shifted closer. His scent calmed her, but only slightly. "That job in Seattle—the advice column. You don't talk about it much."

Cora hesitated. The pivot in topic wasn't abrupt; it was careful, deliberate. The kind of step you take when the floorboards creak.

"It was supposed to be a stopgap. Just something to pay rent while I figured out what kind of writer I wanted to be." Her fingers returned to the keyboard, not typing, just touching. "I was fresh out of grad school—low on options, high on debt. I applied for everything. Thought I'd end up teaching, or maybe ghostwriting memoirs for influencers who'd never read an actual book."

Theo's brows lifted. "That's a very specific example."

"It is," she muttered. "Don't ask. Anyway, the column took off. 'Witch, please.' People liked my voice. And my editor? She told me I had a gift for cutting through people's nonsense without making them feel like crap."

"That tracks."

She gave a short laugh. "Yeah, well. It paid the bills. Then it paid *really* well. Syndication. Podcast guest spots. People emailed from all over, thinking I had it all figured out. Answered letters from heartbroken people, confused people, furious people. Lonely people, mostly." She huffed a soft laugh. "Some weeks, I was more therapist than writer."

He smiled faintly. "Bet you were good at it."

"I was...something." She shrugged. "I could say the right thing. Or at least make it sound like I knew what I was doing. That's a kind of magic, right?"

Theo studied her, brows knitting just a little as his glasses dipped. "What made you leave?"

There it was. The question she'd half-hoped he wouldn't ask, and half-hoped he would.

She gave a careful smile, tucking a curl behind her ear. "Things got messy. Work got complicated. I wasn't writing the kind of advice I could stand behind anymore. I think I was trying to fix things in myself by fixing strangers."

Theo didn't answer right away. When he finally did, it was gentle. "That why you stopped?"

"Partly." Her gaze dropped again. "Nothing felt right anymore. I needed something quieter. More honest. So I thought, why not home?" She exhaled. "Turns out, the thing I spent years running from still had a little space for me."

Theo let that hang for a moment before reaching across the table to nudge her mug toward her. "Well, I'm glad you came back. Even if it took a detour through emotional chaos and overpriced coffee."

She gave a soft laugh. "You're not wrong."

"Is there more to the story?"

Her eyes flicked to his, then back to her screen. She felt the words rise—Avery's name, like a phantom in her throat—but she tucked them away for now. Not tonight.

"There is," she said, voice soft. "But not tonight."

He didn't push, as usual. Just nodded with an "Okay." After a long moment, Theo nudged her foot with his.

"So, when exactly were you planning to drop the 'advice columnist turned fairy tale fundraiser savior' part of your resume on your LinkedIn?"

She snorted. "Right after you add 'emotionally vulnerable bookstore owner' to yours."

He grinned, then gestured to the list between them. "All right, Miss Multitudes. What's next?"

"Raffle items," she said, already scrolling through her inbox. "Miriam from the flower shop is donating a centerpiece."

Theo raised a brow. "Please tell me it doesn't include the terrifying elf figurines she's been selling since we were five."

"I specifically asked her to leave those out."

"Shame. I think the murder in his elf eyes would've been a *lovely* addition to someone's home."

She laughed, this time fully, the sound pushing back a little of the weight in her chest.

"Lumi's also donating a custom robe from her winter collection. I may have offered free cookies in exchange for faster shipping."

"Bribery. Nice."

"I call it resourceful networking."

He looked genuinely impressed. "You've been busy."

"I told you," she said, smile softening. "I started the moment I saw those overdue invoices."

His expression shifted into something quieter. "Thank you. Really."

She shrugged, but it was the kind of shrug that held more than she'd ever say aloud. "You've given me something to care about, too. I think I needed that more than I realized."

They worked in tandem for another hour—scheduling posts, designing a flyer, jotting down ideas for kid-friendly activities. Theo kept glancing at her like she was an enigma he wanted to read cover to cover. And Cora—well, she let him.

Somewhere between raffle prizes and flyer font debates, the last guardrail between them slipped away—not with grand declarations or dramatic revelations, but with the steady click of keys and the sharing of silence that felt safe.

As the final draft of the event flyer slid out of the printer, Theo held it up, reading aloud: "**Yuletide Tales: A Community Fundraiser for Sticks & Stones. Stories, magic, and a little help from our friends.**"

He looked over at her, his smile quiet but certain.

"Let's save our story," he said.

And this time, Cora didn't hesitate.

"Let's do it."

Chapter 13

Cora truly appreciated the soft scent of old paper and polished wood as she stepped into Sticks and Stones. She found her usual spot in the back, sinking into the well-worn armchair and imbuing her magic into the sigil on the table for a sound proof bubble around her.

She'd come to write, or at least that was the plan. A romance story had been pestering her for days, growing louder and more insistent ever since she'd finished her short piece for Theo's fairy tale event. That story had come easily, the words smooth and ready. But this new one? It buzzed in her head like a fly trapped behind glass. Obnoxious. Persistent. Not the kind of story that waited politely.

Cora exhaled slowly and opened her laptop, fingers hovering over the keys. Between Theo's event prep and the fundraiser, she hadn't had much space to sit with her own words. She'd been too busy designing flyers, updating the shop's dusty social media accounts, and calling half the businesses in town to check in about raffle donations. She'd rewritten Theo's crowdfunding letter three times until it sounded like him—earnest, a little awkward, but heartfelt—and still made people want to pull out their wallets. Last night, she'd stayed up past midnight scheduling posts, making graphics, and quietly losing her mind trying to format the community calendar.

The list went on: setting up donation tiers, confirming authors for live readings, even wrangling a reluctant Theo into a decent photo for the campaign header. All of it had kept her grounded in something outside herself—something good. But now that things were moving, now that momentum had caught hold, the stillness pressed in again.

And with it, the story. This stubborn, lovesick idea with too much dialogue and a main character who was just as much of a hot mess as she was.

She rubbed at the ache forming between her eyebrows, glancing around the store mindlessly. Something had been in the air recently, part nostalgia, part magic, part guilt for all the holidays she'd skipped with her mom, who was currently making up for lost time with an endless stream of check-in text messages and lots of cooking. Her stare fell to a bookshelf, one where Theo had given her recommendations for her story, and she immediately looked away.

The thought of that last time had her cheeks flushing instantly, and she had to fan her face like a teenager caught sneaking out of a window. It wasn't like it wasn't still fresh in her mind. Of course it was. Her brain immediately flashed to the fantasy of her clutching the sheets as Theo crawled on top of her, leaving hot kisses against her skin. She could practically feel the heat of him against her neck, the intensity of his breath—God, the *heat* of his presence. And the way he'd—

Right. *Focus, Cora.* She barely had time to blink before a familiar voice interrupted her thoughts.

"Hey, you okay over there?" It was Tessa, perched at one of the nearby desks, squinting at a book that was probably far too dry to be that riveting. She shot Cora an amused look, clearly having noticed the flush creeping up her cheeks.

"Yeah, just...thinking," Cora muttered, hoping her tone sounded more casual than it felt.

Tessa raised an eyebrow, clearly not buying it. "Uh-huh. Well, if you're thinking about Theo, just let me know so I can leave the room."

Cora shot her a look, half embarrassed, half annoyed. "It's not like that—well, it kind of is, but it's *complicated*."

Tessa snorted and returned to her book, enjoying the drama she had stirred up. Meanwhile, Cora caught sight of Theo in the far corner, sorting through a pile of papers, oblivious to the electric tension in the air. His back was to her, but she could swear she felt him *somehow* sensing her distraction. That only made it worse. She couldn't even escape the thought of him for five minutes without her mind going on a full tangent.

Okay, maybe the writing thing wasn't going to happen today. Maybe she'd just sit here for a minute and let her brain catch up. She glanced up, hoping the calm would settle her nerves, but her eyes landed on a man in the nonfiction aisle giving her a curious once-over, like he could hear the mental spiral she was barely containing. His brow arched, amused. Perfect. Just what she needed—a mind reader in aisle three. She looked away quickly, cheeks flushing, and suddenly wished she could burrow into the floorboards like a startled mole.

With a sigh, she flipped open her notebook and clicked her laptop awake. Blank pages stared back at her like they knew things. Like they'd been waiting, smug and patient, for her to finally sit still long enough to confront them. This was supposed to be her writing time. Theo had unlocked the door early just for her, giving her that precious sliver of peace before the morning rush. And still, all she'd managed to do so far was lose a staring contest with a blinking cursor.

With a little flick of her wrist, her pen floated up, twirling absentmindedly in mid-air as she tried to channel some sort of divine inspiration—or at least the ability to string a coherent sentence together. Romance had always been her escape, but attempting to write it now felt more like an Olympic event than a creative pursuit, especially since her relationship had crumbled faster than a stale cookie. Since the breakup, she hadn't even come close to touching the genre—who wanted to write about love when the only thing her heart seemed capable of at the moment was avoiding anything that remotely resembled it?

She glanced out the window. Downtown was just starting to stir, shop signs flipping to open, and the scent of roasted coffee from the café next door drifting in under the doorframe. There was so much to do—more raffle items to confirm, another sponsor to email, a live stream to schedule—but her hands stayed still. For once, she wasn't in motion. Just...here.

She didn't even know if her words could breathe life into the characters that used to dance in her head so effortlessly, or if they'd just collapse on the page. Guess it was time to find out.

The back office door creaked open, and there Theo was. A book tucked under his arm, a steaming mug in hand, and his hair doing that perfectly tousled thing that suggested effortless charm. He wore a soft, time-worn sweater—charcoal gray and slightly stretched at the sleeves, like it had been pulled on a hundred sleepy mornings—and jeans that fit in a way that made Cora's gaze catch for a beat too long. His smile, easy and disarming, washed over her.

"I'm starting to think you're just using me for my bookstore," he teased, amusement practically dancing behind his glasses. The statement made Cora flush too easily, briefly thinking of other things she could've used him for that weren't as wholesome.

"Please," she said, letting a smirk pull at her lips. "You think *this* is the kind of place that tempts me? I'm clearly here for the overpriced coffee next door."

Theo chuckled and stepped farther into the room, close enough that his cologne—a mix of cedar and worn pages—brushed the air between them. It had become a habit lately, him drifting closer, like the space between them had always been optional. He probably didn't even realize he was doing it. Or maybe he did. Either way, it was starting to get under her skin in a way she didn't entirely mind.

Cora shifted in her seat, suddenly aware of the way her cardigan had slipped off one shoulder, the fleece-lined leggings bunched at the knees. The outfit screamed creative rut chic, as if her wardrobe itself had given up trying. Still, she tugged the cardigan into place and angled her laptop slightly, as if that would make her look more productive than she felt.

Theo set the book down on the nearest stack and handed her the mug. "Chamomile. Figured you needed something to calm your clearly tortured creative genius."

"Honestly?" Cora sighed, cradling the warm mug in both hands. "I'm trying to work on this epic romance that's been stuck in my head since I finished the fairy tale piece for your event. But so far," she nodded toward her screen, where the blinking cursor mocked her, "all I've managed is a blank page and a serious case of writer's block."

"That's how you know it's real," he called before moving back to the register. "If it doesn't torment you first, it's probably not worth writing."

Cora smirked and shook her head, eyes drifting back to the empty screen. But before she could spiral further, the soft thud of a book landing beside her pulled her attention up.

He placed his things down on the table she was occupying, making an oddly comforting sound. "Let me help," Theo offered, his eyes scanning the shelves lined with books. "Sometimes inspiration needs a little nudge."

With a finger snap, a few books stirred, then lifted into the air—floating down from the shelves with the gentle grace of autumn leaves. Cora couldn't help but raise an eyebrow—just a little bit impressed, but mostly entertained.

"Wow. You're just throwing around enchantments in front of customers now?"

"I'm multitasking," he corrected. "How about a little literary roulette? Read a few snippets, see what sparks something."

The books landed in a neat stack next to her laptop: a mythology collection, a thick volume on romance tropes, and something handwritten and worn at the edges—probably some obscure poetry chapbook only Theo would know about. She stared at the pile, then at him, and despite herself, her lips twitched with reluctant amusement.

"Fine. But only because the floating book thing is mildly impressive."

"Mildly?" Theo echoed, feigning being wounded. "I just summoned a curated love library from midair. Give me a sec."

Cora rolled her eyes but didn't argue. Truth was, she appreciated the effort more than she wanted to admit. Her motivation had been MIA for days.

He headed back to the register as the bell over the door chimed, greeting the new arrivals with his usual easy charm. Cora watched him for a moment—the way he switched so effortlessly between helping customers, re-stocking shelves, and somehow still making time to check in with her like it was the most natural thing in the world.

Among the customers trickling in, Cora noticed Mrs. Pemberly stepping through the door in her usual Sunday-best coat—too formal for a weekday, but perfectly in character. She hadn't seen the woman in years, but the old witch looked exactly the same with her clothes and long graying hair perfectly in tact. She looked around with a kind of polite curiosity, hands clasped over her bag as she waited patiently for Theo to finish ringing someone up.

"I just wanted to ask about the fundraiser," she said softly when he turned to greet her. "I saw the flyer at Marigold, and I know the Historical Society's already planning their own event, but there's plenty of support to go around." Her tone held the kind of warmth that didn't ask for attention but always carried assuredness.

Theo smiled. "We'd love that. We've got a donation jar up front and a raffle coming together. Cordelia's been organizing most of it."

Mrs. Pemberly turned her gaze to Cora with an approving little nod. "You always had a quiet talent, dear. It's good to see you here again. I'll see what I can do."

She gave Theo a brief smile and began to exit just as quietly as she'd come in before turning back to him.

"Mr. Hargrove took good care of this place for years. It's good to see the next generation continuing his love of knowledge and community."

And with that, she left, the bell above the door chiming gently behind her.

When things settled again, he returned with a receipt book in one hand and one of the romance anthologies in the other.

"Alright," he said, sliding into the chair beside her. "Let's do this properly. We read, we brainstorm, and if necessary, we dramatically overanalyze the concept of love until you're emotionally exhausted but creatively recharged."

Theo began to read aloud, his voice rich and soothing. Stories of heartbreak and devotion, mythic lovers and quiet yearning. The rhythm of his voice soothed her in their little sound bubble, allowing customers to browse quietly, the occasional rustle of jackets or creak of floorboards punctuating the softness of his words.

She didn't even realize she'd started scribbling notes until her pen was already moving. Scenes began unfolding in her mind—messy, tender, a little sharp around the edges. They didn't have structure yet, but they had feeling. They had breath.

"What do you think makes a love story truly captivating?" Theo asked, glancing up from the book in his hands. His voice was casual, but his eyes held something that lingered just a little too long. He leaned forward slightly, elbow resting near her notebook like he was asking more than just a hypothetical question.

Cora twirled her pen slowly, eyes narrowing on the swirling steam rising from her mug as she tried to will away the sudden awareness of how close he was—and how ridiculously good he smelled.

"I think," Cora began, "it's the moments between the grand gestures. It's the way two people look at each other when they think no one's watching, or the quiet comforts of sharing a cup of tea. Those little moments hold everything, at least for me."

She shrugged, trying to play it off, though her words felt more exposed than she liked. Those were the kinds of moments she craved—both on the page and, if she was honest, maybe a little off of it too. And right now, Theo was making it increasingly difficult to keep her heart in check.

Theo tilted his head thoughtfully. "So, the unscripted parts. The bits where people are just themselves."

"Yes, exactly!" Cora snapped her finger. "The quirks. The banter. The imperfections. Falling in love with someone's weirdness because it fits your own."

"Do you have a character in mind?" he asked, already drifting back toward the counter as a customer approached. He rang up a paperback with a few taps of the register, then returned without missing a beat.

"I have a rough idea," she confessed. "She's a witch—independent, stubborn, too busy holding everyone else together to let anyone in. She falls for another witch—quiet, patient, who sees through all her armor. It's slow-burn, smutty, messy."

Theo chuckled, shelving a newly donated box of titles with one hand while still half-listening. "Sounds like the kind of love that's earned in pieces."

Cora nodded. "Exactly. She hides her pain. He wears his. They clash, but they also... see each other. And eventually, they realize love isn't about pretending to be whole, but about letting someone meet you in the cracks."

Theo paused, one hand still resting on a shelf, the other dusting off a spine. His expression softened. "That's the good stuff. Vulnerability. Honesty. Letting someone stay even when they've seen the storm."

Cora's pen moved faster now, words spilling out like they'd been waiting for permission. Characters took shape, their world blooming in the margins of the notebook.

Theo returned once more with fresh tea and set it beside her without a word, offering her a quick wink before disappearing again behind the counter. The bell above the door chimed, a new wave of customers trickling in. As he helped someone find a poetry collection in the back, he tossed her a suggestion over his shoulder about giving her heroine a familiar with a snarky streak. She scribbled it down without hesitation.

Hours passed this way—Cora pacing, writing, muttering to herself, Theo drifting in and out of her orbit. He stocked books, organized the donation shelf, and answered questions for regulars, but never stopped checking in. A quiet nudge here, a comment there. It was the kind of support that didn't demand attention, just offered presence.

Eventually, Cora stopped mid-pace, notebook in hand, heart racing.

"I think I'm onto something, Theo," she said, turning toward him. "I actually see where this is going now."

He looked up from where he was restocking a display of local authors and smiled—that real, soul-deep kind of smile that could melt the edges off a snowstorm. "I knew you would. Sometimes all it takes is a change of scenery, a few good books, and someone to believe in the story with you."

Cora's breath caught at his choice of words.

Friend. That's what he'd said earlier. But it didn't land right—not with the way he was looking at her now. Like she was more than the story in her notebook. Like maybe she was something he wanted to read slowly, carefully, again and again.

She turned back to her pages before her heart could betray her face. Feelings weren't on the to-do list. She had words to write. A plot to untangle. And a maddeningly supportive bookstore owner to not fall for.

Totally doable.

Probably.

"Speaking of a change in scenery," Theo said, his voice light but unmistakably loaded. Cora winced, already bracing herself for the question she knew was coming. "You ready to tell me what made you finally come back?"

She exhaled through her nose, the weight of the past pressing down. "You know how I told you I was an advice columnist? Well... things went south after I ended my engagement." The word tumbled out before she could soften it. She hadn't meant to say it like that—not with so much finality, not with so much honesty. But with Theo, the filter always seemed to short-circuit.

His eyes widened, surprise catching his expression the same way hers had when they'd first reunited. "You... you were—"

"Engaged. Yeah." She nodded quickly, hoping to glide past the word and everything it carried, but it stuck in the air. "Funny thing? You and my ex were the only people who ever called me by my full name."

"Huh. I guess that makes me a rare breed."

She offered him a crooked smile. "You're rarer than you know."

As she spoke, Theo slipped behind the register, helping a customer check out with a quiet, "Thanks for stopping in." He returned to her table moments later, a little more serious now, but still with that steady presence that always made her feel just a bit more grounded.

Cora launched into the story—the real one this time. She told him about Avery Chen, the illustrator she met near the end of grad school. Their meet-cute in an art museum, how Avery's laugh had pulled her in like a tide, how fast it had all moved after that. Painting dates, long weekends with Avery's loud and loving family, plans for a wedding that always felt slightly too big, slightly too soon. "It felt like a fairy tale," she admitted. "But fairy tales have dragons. And some of them win."

As Theo stepped away to reshelve a few books, Cora kept going, the words pouring out with more ease than she expected. She talked about how the cracks in their relationship had started to show—Avery retreating into silence at the first sign of emotional tension, Cora trying to fill the space with logic and optimism. They'd pulled at each other instead of toward. And then, of course, the magic thing.

"But it became clear that me being a witch slowly became an issue," Cora continued, her voice quieter now. "At first, Avery thought it was fascinating. But then she started flinching. Not outright, but enough to notice. Enough to make me stop being myself around her."

Theo paused mid-shelf, eyes narrowing slightly. "Why stay with someone who couldn't accept you?"

"Exactly," Cora said, exasperated. "I kept telling myself it would get better. That she was just adjusting. But the truth is, I started hiding the parts of me that made her uncomfortable." She slumped back into the chair, her voice losing its edge. "I stopped doing magic around her. Did the whole 'mundane' thing. But it never felt like I could be all of me."

Theo moved back to the table without saying a word; just the warmth of his presence felt like reassurance. Cora reached for her drink, her fingers brushing against his.

"I ended it," she said after a beat. "But even though it was my decision, it wrecked me. I poured all that bitterness into my work without realizing it."

She told him about the advice column, about the moment everything fell apart—the letter from "Feeling Uncertain" and the chain reaction that followed. She'd given impulsive advice, more cathartic for her than helpful for the reader. It backfired... badly. The reader's response had been devastating, and her boss's disappointment sealed the deal.

"When Margo looked at me with pity," she murmured, "I knew it was over. That's the look that breaks you. Not anger, not even frustration. Pity."

Theo's hand found hers, a gentle squeeze bringing her back. "Cordelia, I hope you don't think you're a fraud. You were hurt. And honestly? Still healing. That's not failure—it's just life."

She gave him a tight smile, one part gratitude, one part disbelief. "Maybe. But I stopped helping people. I was just spewing pain disguised as advice."

He stayed quiet as she detailed her worst misstep—how she'd mocked a girl named Lisa in print, not realizing the cruelty of it until the backlash hit. And when she met with

Margo, when the decision was made for her to leave the column, it had all come crashing down. Seattle became too loud, too sharp. So she came home.

"Do you think coming back was the right choice?"

Cora looked out the window, watching the town move at its slow, comforting pace. "I think I needed to remember who I was without all the noise. Find the version of myself who used to write just for me. Not for a paycheck. Not for approval. But because the stories mattered."

Theo nodded slowly. "Sounds like you're finally writing from the place that matters."

She thought of her mom's words—the way she'd called out Cora's tendency to overfunction, to work through grief rather than feel it. "Mom's right. Black women are taught to push, to grind, to hold it all in. I thought if I worked hard enough, I could outrun the pain."

"But pain doesn't work like that. It waits."

Cora pursed her lips. "I've barely cried. I thought it meant I was handling things. Turns out, I've just been bottling it all up."

"Maybe now's the time to let it out. You're safe here."

Her throat tightened. *You're safe here.* When was the last time she felt safe? Not before this. Slowly, she started building toward that again.

Then came the question that caught her completely off guard.

"What was it about being a witch that was a problem?"

Cora scoffed, pulling her hand back to lean away from him. "That's the thing. I never got a straight answer. It just... became clear. Like my magic was something she tolerated, not embraced. Like I was a risk."

Theo's expression darkened slightly. "That's not love. That's fear masquerading as acceptance."

"Tell me about it. And the worst part? I made myself smaller for her. I dimmed things down. And for what?"

Theo didn't answer immediately. He just looked at her, eyes sad. "You lost a part of yourself."

"Two years. It felt like everything, until it didn't."

And just like that, the vulnerability was back, an ache behind her eyes. But with Theo sitting there, not pushing, not judging—just being—she didn't feel quite as exposed.

"You know," he said, reaching for her hand again. This time she let him intertwine their fingers, "it's never too late to start over in love either. Even if you had it all mapped out. Sometimes it's okay to get lost again."

Cora raised a brow. "That sounds exhausting."

"Yeah, well, they never told us adulting would be this emotional."

She leaned back, letting the warmth between them settle in. "I still don't know what I want to do for work. But I do know I'm done with trying to be everything for everyone."

"That's my girl," Theo murmured, pressing a light kiss across her freckles before pulling back. The move stole her breath.

She blinked, trying but slightly failing to regain herself. "Are you okay with still calling me Cordelia? Or do I need to start responding to Cora again for balance?"

His face crinkled in mock disgust. "Absolutely not. She doesn't get to take that from me."

Relieved, she grinned, right before throwing it back at him. "What about you? Any suitors in your orbit?"

He shrugged, focusing on their hands again. "A few flings. A relationship that ended too soon. I guess I'm still figuring out what love means for me, too."

Their eyes met. Something unspoken lingered there. And then, too quickly, Theo stood and started gathering his things. "Feel free to hang out if you need more inspo. I've gotta pretend I know how to run a business."

Cora watched him disappear behind the office door, unsure what bothered her more—the fact that she'd poured out her heart while he kept his mostly closed, or the possibility that she was falling for someone who might not be ready to fall with her.

She stared down at her notebook. The pages had stopped shaking. The words were flowing again.

But her heart? That was still a work in progress.

Chapter 14

The bookstore lights had dimmed, but Cora was still there. Her coat draped over the back of a chair as she and Theo tossed ideas back and forth for the reading and the fundraiser. Outside, snow began to cling to the windows unnoticed, a quiet curtain falling between them and the rest of the world. When Theo offered to walk her home again, he did it with a grin and a dry warning about icy sidewalks.

She made a show of pouting, deflecting the warmth his offer stirred in her chest.

They closed up the shop together, the wards humming softly as they locked the door behind them. The wards around the door responded to her mood with a soft shimmer when she passed, just a flicker like they recognized something shifting inside her. The street lamps bathed the square, flakes catching in the light. Cora's breath came in pale clouds, but the cold barely registered with Theo walking beside her. Their boots crunched in rhythm, the only sound save for a distant bell.

Still, her mind wandered.

They were both single. Both grieving. If Lumi were here, she'd tell her to stop overthinking and *just kiss him already*. The idea alone made her stomach knot. What did she even want? Theo was funny. Charming. Maybe a little too thoughtful. But this—whatever *this* was—felt like stepping into a story she didn't know how to finish. Grief left bruises, and Cora still hadn't figured out which ones were hers and which ones were Avery's.

Theo broke the silence, voice soft, breath fogging in the air between them. "I always thought holidays would feel more magical as an adult. But I think I was looking in the wrong place. It's not the celebration; it's the people."

His words hit a place in her chest she'd been trying to ignore. She stepped closer without thinking, their arms brushing. The cold wind slipped under her collar, but the heat from his body made her pulse skip.

"Sometimes it's the place too," she said quietly. "Back in Seattle...I don't know, I just couldn't find the same whimsy there as I do here."

Theo gave her a sideways glance. "Wait, wait—this sounds suspiciously like personal growth. Are you actually admitting something nice about Seattle?"

Cora cringed, but there was a smile tugging at her lips. "Don't get too excited. I didn't give it a fair chance. Honestly, I didn't want to. Everything just lost its color after dad died. I thought a new city, a new program, a new everything would help. But grief doesn't care about skylines or coffee shops."

Theo nudged her lightly with his shoulder. "Come on. I told you about my wholesome lawn mower story, as you so lovingly dubbed it. You owe me more than just a sad summary."

She groaned, but her smile widened. They turned down one of the narrower lanes that wound behind the square, where the sidewalk curved gently and old stone cottages leaned toward one another. Snow flurried down in gentle swirls, softening the edges of everything—fences, porches, rooftops glowing with the warmth of string lights.

"Okay, fine. But you asked for it."

Theo chuckled and tucked his hands into his coat pockets. "Hit me with it."

"It rained all the time. I know, big surprise. Seattle. But it wasn't the romantic, brooding kind of rain. It was the gray, persistent drizzle that gets into your bones. I rented this tiny apartment with zero insulation and paper-thin walls. You could hear everything. The couple next door used to fight at midnight and then, you know, make up around two."

Theo let out a soft laugh. "Sounds charming."

"I started grad school two months after the funeral," she went on, her tone quieter now. "I told myself it was what dad would've wanted. He believed in momentum. In not sitting still too long or letting emotions get the best of you.

But really, I think I just didn't want to feel anything. So I buried myself in research, and projects, and late-night papers. I told myself I was building a future, but I think I was just hiding."

As the words left her mouth, her chest tightened. She hadn't said that out loud before—not like this. The admission left her raw and exposed, like if she were to stand in this wind with no coat.

"I remember the first week so vividly. The air felt different—wet all the time, heavy with mist. I was constantly damp. And cold, but not in the crisp way it is here. I swear the chill seeped into my clothes, into my skin, until I didn't notice it anymore. That scared me."

She glanced at the soft golden lights glowing in windows around them—lights people had left on deliberately, maybe to welcome someone home or just to make the dark less lonely.

"I kept telling myself I was being brave. That I was starting fresh. But I wasn't. I was hiding. I was walking through the university with all these ridiculous expectations. I thought maybe if I just kept moving—classes, lectures, library shifts—I'd eventually forget how heavy everything felt. I tried to reinvent myself. New city, new degree, no one who looked at me like I might shatter. I went out to coffee with people I barely liked. Pretended I was fascinated by whatever theory we were reading in postmodern lit. I even joined this—gods, I can't believe I'm telling you this—I joined this urban hiking group."

Theo barked a laugh. "You? Hiking?"

"I know! I hated it. They all wore vests and talked about elevation gain. But it was something to do. Something to fill the weekends so I wouldn't sit in my apartment and wonder if I should've stayed."

Her smile faltered.

"It rained constantly. That kind of soft, endless rain that makes the city feel blurry. And I started feeling blurry too. I stopped using magic. Not on purpose, not at first. I was afraid of what would happen if I did use it. If I'd feel too much again."

Theo's brow furrowed. "You disconnected from it completely?"

"Yeah. For almost two years. I couldn't even light a candle without it feeling wrong. Like the energy in me had turned into something sour. I'd try, and it'd sputter out. Or worse, it would spark and remind me of what I'd lost."

Theo stopped. The snow fell in slow spirals around them. "I should've been here. You shouldn't have had to go through that alone."

"I had Mom and Lumi. Kind of. But I let this idea of grad school being a fresh start carry me farther than I meant to go."

"Sounds...lonely."

"Back then I didn't say much. I just ran. Every time I felt too much, I pushed it down and poured myself into something else. Something productive. Something that didn't ask me to feel anything."

She huffed a laugh and kicked at a patch of slush. "I made a few friends, sort of. I dated a bit. And I kept going back those first few years. Then I met Avery. And for a while, it felt like maybe I'd done the right thing. That everything I'd run from didn't matter as much because I had her. She became my momentum, and soon, visits home turned into phone calls."

The cold nipped at her nose, but she hardly noticed. She reached up to tuck a stray curl of hair back under her hat, her fingers chilled and stiff.

After a moment, he asked, "Was she into the holidays?"

Cora's breath caught. "Not really. Her family did dinner, but there weren't any traditions. No tree, no wreaths, no music. I missed Mom's Yule stuff, the cinnamon sticks simmering in the kitchen. But I didn't know how to come back. Not without feeling so ashamed."

Theo stayed quiet, gaze on the cobblestones. She noticed the way his fingers twitched at his side, like he wanted to reach for her but didn't know if he should.

"And now?"

She shook her head, looking away from him. "I'm trying."

"So, no Yule tree? That's a travesty."

Cora smiled, almost despite herself. "I had a sad little one in my apartment. A plastic twig with maybe two ornaments. One time I went to a department mixer with spiced wine and ironic sweaters. I snuck out early and stopped by a late-night grocery store for prepackaged cookies and went home alone. Not exactly magical."

"Sounds like something we need to fix."

He brushed her hand, just a graze, but it sent a jolt through her skin. Her magic stirred faintly, not enough to show, but enough to remind her it was still there. Always waiting.

"I had a rough holiday once, too," Theo started, voice floating in the wind. "The guy I was dating dumped me right before New Year's. My parents liked him. Took a while for them to get used to him, but liked what he could offer. Said he'd be a good influence. Thought he'd straighten me out."

Cora stopped walking. "Theo..."

He didn't look at her, just kept his gaze on the snow-covered path. "They thought he was the safe choice. Successful. Clean-cut. But I wasn't enough for him. Not serious enough, not stable enough. Not *something* enough."

Her chest ached with the weight of it, like it had settled deep into his bones. "I'm sorry. That's cruel."

"I'm still figuring out how to carry it," he admitted. "Trying not to let it harden me."

Cora thought of the years she spent running, of how easy it had been to bury grief under work and ambition. And how hard it was to claw her way back to something real and figure out who she was on the other side. But she had Lumi and her mom, the pillars of stability in her life. And Theo, Theo did a lot on his own.

Theo glanced at her, the tension in his shoulders easing. "You're shivering."

Before she could respond, he slipped an arm around her shoulders. The warmth of him was immediate. Her breath hitched as she leaned into his side, heart racing from something that had nothing to do with the cold. Magic hummed faintly in her veins, stirred by his touch. For once she didn't want to suppress how she felt, so she opened her palm and let a flicker of warmth escape, weaving it through the falling snow until the flakes danced.

Theo watched in quiet awe. "You've still got that spark."

Cora rolled her eyes, but her cheeks flushed. "If you or Lumi say that one more time..."

He grinned, tugging her closer. "You'll what?"

She didn't answer. Couldn't. He was close—closer than before. His hand brushed her cheek, feather light. A pulse of magic passed between them, gentle and familiar. She felt it in her chest, in her fingers, in the breath she didn't realize she was holding. The scent of him, woodsy and fresh, mingled with the crisp winter air, making her head spin. She could feel the heat of him through her layers, could feel his presence in every inch of her being.

Theo leaned in, slow, hesitant. She didn't move. She couldn't.

Then, a sudden gust swept through the square, cold and biting, scattering snowflakes and snapping the moment in half.

Theo stepped back with a groan. "Seriously?"

Cora chuckled awkwardly. "Maybe it's a sign."

Theo's hand, still warm from where it had brushed her skin, dropped to his side. He took a step back and nodded down the street with a small smile. "Come on. Let's get you home."

Cora nodded, forcing a smile that didn't quite reach her eyes. There was no denying the pull she felt toward him. But some things were just too fragile, too uncertain. For now, she would walk beside him in the snow.

Chapter 15

Cora bit her lip, eyes flicking nervously around the bookstore before returning to the glowing screen in front of her. Her fingers hovered over the keyboard like she was about to be caught in the act, trembling just slightly with anticipation. Ever since that impromptu brainstorming session with Theo last week, ideas had been flooding in at the worst moments—during coffee runs, family errands, even while fabric shopping with Lumi. What started as jotting notes in her phone had turned into typing entire paragraphs in public like a woman possessed. Subtle, she was not.

She wasn't doing anything wrong—technically—but still, there was something vaguely scandalous about what she was writing.

It had been years since she'd let herself write fiction, but her latest project had become the perfect excuse to dive back in. At home, she played it safe—character boards, plot outlines, folders neatly organized by theme. But here, in the cozy chaos of the bookstore, something else took over. Something reckless. It became the only place where her words seemed to catch fire. If she was being honest, it was also Theo's influence.

Dance Theo.

Her protagonist, a perfectionist with a bleeding heart and no sense of boundaries, was starting to feel too familiar. Cora pulled from years of advice column wisdom and late-night Googling to build a world that reflected her own—complete with meddling friends and emotional landmines. But that wasn't the scene she was writing now.

This scene was different. Hotter. Riskier. Just like the feelings Cora wasn't ready to confront.

Her fingers moved faster, skimming over the keyboard as her cheeks warmed. Her character was tangled up in a romance that scared her—and thrilled her. Unlike Cora, she embraced physical desire, even when her heart hesitated. Cora shifted in her seat, crossing one leg over the other and hyperaware of how it brushed against the table. Of how her cheeks warmed. The words spilled out, full of want and whispered promises. Her character wanted. Desired. Unlike Cora, who had mastered the art of hiding behind quips, layered sweaters, and the comforting logic of giving advice she barely followed. She wrote like no one was watching.

And then someone was. A low whistle broke her trance.

Cora froze. Her pulse jumped as she slowly turned and saw him—Theo, backlit by the bookstore's fading light, his coffee-colored hair tousled as typical. The glint off his glasses, slipping slightly down his nose, made him look like an anime character. Of course it had to be now.

"I thought you might need tea," he said, stepping around her chair, his presence alarmingly close. He set the mug beside her, eyes flicking to the screen. Then came that smirk. "But it looks like you've got enough steam."

Cora jerked her hands from the keyboard, instinctively trying to cover the screen with her arms. As if he hadn't already seen the line she'd just written about tangled sheets and aching skin. Her face flared crimson. "It's nothing," she croaked too quickly. "Just...experimenting."

"Experimenting?" Theo raised an eyebrow as he moved to lean against the table beside her, his hip brushing the side of her chair. "Looks more like a full-blown field study."

Her cheeks burned hotter than the tea. He was too close. Too comfortable. And she was too aware of the fact that his thigh was inches from her shoulder, that his voice had dropped into that teasing register he used when he knew he had the upper hand.

"It's just—" she tried again, but her brain was a scrambled mess of shame and something far more dangerous: want.

"Just what?" he asked, dipping closer, voice low. "Writing something to get you all hot and bothered?"

Oh. Her mouth parted, but no words came. She could talk about sex with Lumi without blinking. But Theo? His teasing hit different. His nearness buzzed against her skin, making her heart thunder.

She bit her lip hard to chase away the image now forming in her mind—of Theo pulling her to her feet, of the way his hands might grip her waist, the way he might kiss her like—

No.

She blinked hard.

He laughed softly under his breath. "You okay?"

She nodded too quickly. "Totally fine. Just writing."

"I could give you some tips," he said, brushing imaginary lint from her sleeve, fingers lingering a second too long. "Might help with, you know, realism."

She narrowed her eyes at him, trying to summon her usual bravado. "What, like how to write a convincing kiss?"

"I mean..." His eyes sparkled, daring her. "That depends. You basing any of this on real experience?"

She swallowed hard. "Maybe. But not my current reality."

Theo tilted his head, the playfulness fading just enough to let something real through. "And the fantasy? Is it about someone you know?"

Her stomach clenched. The question wasn't fair. It wasn't even really a question—it was a challenge. Her magic pulsed faintly beneath her skin, an itch at her fingertips.

"It's fiction, Theo. It doesn't matter."

He studied her. "Maybe. But *you* matter."

She looked away, fingers tightening around the tea he'd brought. It burned against her palms.

"I'm not ready," she said.

"I know," he replied softly. But the way he said it—it was like he saw all the cracks she tried to hide. Like he was still choosing to look at her even after seeing the broken pieces.

Silence stretched on. Then she sighed, the words clawing their way out. "I'm not ready because the last time I loved someone, it broke me."

She didn't mean to say it like that. She didn't mean to open that door. But now it was open.

Cora stared at the table. "Avery had been distant. I saw the signs, I just didn't want to. I kept convincing myself it was a rough patch." Her voice turned brittle. "So I planned this night. Candles, groceries, the whole domestic fantasy. Thought we'd fix things."

She shook her head, bitter. "Instead, I came home to her in bed with someone else. Laughing. Like I didn't exist."

Theo didn't move. His hand twitched slightly, but he didn't speak.

"I shattered everything," she whispered. "Literally. The books flew. The lights broke. I didn't even mean to. My magic just...exploded."

Theo's hand moved instinctively toward hers, but she flinched before he could touch her. His fingers clenched instinctively.

"I left the ring on the floor. Didn't even say goodbye." Her voice cracked on the memory. "It wasn't just betrayal. It was erasure. Like none of it had been real."

When she finally looked up, Theo's face had gone pale, jaw tense.

"I had no idea," he said. "I'm so sorry."

Cora gave a sharp, bitter smile. "Being a witch made me too weird. The pace made me too much. Apparently, she wanted 'normal.'" Her voice twisted. "She proposed, Theo. Then called *cheating* a 'mistake.' On Samhain."

Theo's expression darkened, his fury quiet but unmistakable. "That's not a mistake. That's cowardice."

Cora nodded, but it felt empty. "She said I was too intense. That I was always expecting something she couldn't give."

"And you believed her?" he asked, incredulous.

"I don't know what I believe," she admitted. "I just know I've been tired ever since. I thought she was my person. I thought—" Her voice faltered. "I thought we were going to get married."

Theo's eyes narrowed a bit as he took a deep breath, glancing at her. "And you didn't come home right away, did you? You stayed in Seattle for a whole month."

"I buried myself in work, tried to pretend it didn't matter. But I broke, Theo. And I've been trying to stitch myself back together ever since."

"I know it still hurts," he said gently. "But that doesn't mean you're broken beyond repair. You just...need the right adventure."

Cora moved her shaking hands to her lap, flinching at his use of words.

"I've had enough adventures," she snapped. "Avery was an adventure. I barely survived her."

Theo's expression softened, but the teasing was gone now. "Maybe the adventure wasn't the problem. Maybe it was who you trusted to go with."

Cora looked at him then—*really* looked. Theo, who had always shown up. At the boy who had grown into a man. Her stomach twisted with a feeling she wasn't ready to name.

"I don't know if I can risk it again," she whispered.

"Then don't think of it as a risk," he replied. "Think of it as a recalibration. A chance to redefine what love means. With someone who actually wants to stay." He reached for her hand again, and this time she let him take it. "And I, for one, am someone who wants to stay."

Chapter 16

"**H**e didn't!"

Cora winced, pressing her fingers to her temple. "Volume, Lumi."

"Sorry, sorry." Lumi tried again in a whisper. "He *didn't.*"

"He did, and I wish he hadn't."

After her emotionally messy heart-to-heart with Theo, Cora headed straight to Lumi's. Some people drowned their feelings in ice cream and reruns, Cora preferred hot chocolate, couture chaos, and her best friend's apartment, which currently looked like a fabric store had exploded. Emotional processing via lace and silk.

A Cora classic..

She'd managed to avoid the worst of the story—the cheating, the lies, the way she'd poured herself into someone who made her smaller. She didn't want to put that weight in Lumi's hands, too. Not yet.

Lumi, ever the opportunist, immediately roped her into modeling her latest designs. Cora didn't argue. Standing still while being pinned into expensive lace felt preferable to spiraling alone in her bedroom. Besides, Lumi made a mean hot chocolate and had already shoved one into Cora's hand while tossing a half-pinned corset at her before she could start sulking properly.

"Hold still," Lumi said, circling her with a strip of lace and a needle in hand. "Unless you've developed a love for being stabbed since you left."

"How'd you guess my latest kink?" Cora deadpanned.

Lumi snorted. "You're a terrible liar."

Cora smirked, her body still aching with everything she hadn't said to Theo—and the things she *had*. "You know I'm not actually model material, right?" *And not your target demographic.*

"Oh, please. You're a dream. And more importantly, you're here, which means you're mine."

Cora rolled her eyes. "Right. I return to my hometown and immediately get conscripted into a one-woman lingerie operation. How did you *ever* manage without me?"

Lumi hesitated, just for a breath. It was subtle, but Cora caught it—how the usual quick wit lagged by a second.

"I didn't," Lumi said, flicking her eyes back to the hemline she was adjusting. "Clearly the universe sent you back for the noble purpose of being my human hanger. I'm honored."

Cora chuckled. "Right, that's exactly why I left Seattle. To serve as an emotional support mannequin." But she let Lumi continue her work. The living room was a disaster of satin and lace, bolts of fabric cascading off every surface. And honestly? It suited her.

"I still can't believe you do this all from home."

"Imagine me with a storefront. In this economy?" Lumi waved a hand dismissively. "This is my empire now. Chaotic, fabulous, and entirely rent-controlled."

"Yes, very glamorous. Dodging piles of tulle to get to the bathroom."

Minutes passed in comfortable noise—snipping, muttering, the clink of pins on hardwood. Then came the wardrobe change. Cora slipped out of her garter and into a black satin nightgown that felt sinfully smooth against her skin. Lumi, clipboard in hand, studied her like a sculptor examining raw marble.

"Gorgeous," she declared, jotting something down. "But it needs lace."

"Has Jax seen any of this genius yet?"

"Nah, he's still in Paris. Off frolicking with his family while I keep the dream alive. So you're my full-time muse until further notice."

Cora tilted her head. "He's really missing out."

Lumi shrugged without looking up. "He's busy with baguettes and red wine. I'm busy running everything back here." A beat passed. "It's fine. Just...would be nice if he checked in more. I'll show him when he shows up for it."

That landed heavier than it should have, tugging at something in Cora. Lumi's voice, usually all bite and sparkle, had softened, veiled under sarcasm, like tissue paper over a bruise. Cora didn't push. Instead, she stepped back into the role Lumi needed—supportive, silent, wearing the clothes and pretending her heart wasn't tangled up over a certain bookseller. All giggles and deflection.

Cora struck half-serious mock-model stances while Lumi buzzed around her with fabric and fervor, capturing shots with the passion of someone who *needed* the distraction. Cora played along, grateful for something to focus on that wasn't Theo's voice echoing in her mind.

"Oh, yes, this is it," Lumi gushed, snapping a photo of Cora in a particularly delicate lace slip. "Who needs Paris when I have you right here?"

"I feel like I'm starring in a boudoir ad for confused witches," Cora commented, adjusting a strap. "Very mysterious. Very 'haunt your ex.'"

Lumi grinned, wicked. "Speaking of haunting. Imagine Theo seeing you in this."

Cora froze. "What? Lumi—no. Absolutely not."

"Oh, come on. Tell me you don't want him to."

"I've never worn this kind of thing for anyone before," Cora muttered, crossing her arms. "And even if I did, Theo and I are just—"

"Friends?" Lumi finished, unconvinced. "Sure. Friends who undress each other with their eyes and share emotionally intimate snow walks."

Cora blushed so hard she nearly combusted in red lace. She turned to the mirror, barely recognizing herself. The bodysuit clung like a second skin, delicate and bold all at once. It made her feel exposed—but not in a bad way. More like she was standing in front of a version of herself she didn't quite know yet. Powerful. Vulnerable. Present.

She bit her lip. "I don't even know what I want right now."

Lumi didn't answer right away. Her teasing smile had dimmed a little. "You don't have to know. But it's okay to want things again, Cora."

Cora nodded, her throat tight.

Lumi turned away, fiddling with fabric. Her shoulders were a little tenser now. And Cora realized the teasing wasn't just teasing; it was Lumi's way of keeping things surface-level. Of avoiding her own mess. "Well. Just saying. It'd be a crime if someone didn't get to see you like this."

"You mean like you?" The words slipped out before Cora could stop them—half a joke, half... not.

Lumi stilled. Her mouth twitched into something unreadable. "Please. You'd never survive my dating habits."

Cora looked away, adjusting the hem of the bodysuit to hide her rising blush. "Right. Wouldn't want to complicate things."

Lumi went back to draping fabric like nothing had happened. But her hands moved slower now. Less show. More care. Cora watched her in the mirror. How her focus sharpened when she worked. How she bit her bottom lip when she pinned something just right. How she'd always, always been the first to show up, even when Cora hadn't known she needed her.

"I missed this," Cora said, almost to herself.

Lumi met her gaze in the mirror. "Yeah. Me too."

"You okay?"

Lumi glanced back over her shoulder, the smirk returning like a mask slipping back into place. "Of course. Why wouldn't I be? I have you here, half-dressed, and utterly at my mercy."

But the uncertainty lingered, the unspoken things between them stacking up like pins in a cushion. And for a moment, surrounded by luxury fabric and banter, it hit her how easy it was to avoid healing when everything around you looked beautiful.

Still, she smiled. "Whatever you say, Lumi."

Chapter 17

S he hadn't meant to end up at the Pine Cone Cream-
ery.

Cora'd spent all afternoon buried in fundraiser logistics,
mainly emails and donor spreadsheets, until the screen
started to blur and the words stopped making sense. She
toggled between productivity and distraction, the rhythm
of the work helping for a while. But the house was too

quiet, her thoughts too loud, and the ache she still hadn't figured out how to name became ever more present. So she grabbed her coat without thinking much of where she was going, only that she needed air, and let her feet steer her.

Her body knew where it was going before her mind caught up.

The old ice cream parlor still had the hand-painted teal awning, still had the same smudged glass case full of rainbow sprinkles and gummy bears, and still smelled faintly of waffle cones and nostalgia. The bell on the door jingled when she stepped inside, with low folk music playing from the speaker.

She stood at the counter, scanning the menu as if she didn't always get the same thing—French vanilla ice cream with brownie bites in a waffle bowl. She and Theo used to come here after school, back when ice cream was the go-to fix for anything, including quizzes they didn't study for. A flash of memory hit her as she stepped inside—Theo, ten, daring her to try dill pickle ice cream, and her laughing so hard she nearly snorted caramel swirl.

Now? Now things didn't melt away so easily.

She took her bowl and slid into a booth by the window—the one they always used to cram into, knees bumping, sticky fingers trailing napkins behind. She hadn't expected to feel *this* much just by walking in. It was like floating somewhere between lives, the ignorance of her youth and the woes of her adult years.

Just weeks ago she'd taken off her ring, turned the page, and stepped into a version of herself she didn't even know yet. She'd told Theo, but the words still tasted like loss.

The bell jingled again. She looked up and there he was, summoned by her thoughts.

Theo.

He paused in the doorway like he wasn't sure he was seeing her right, then smiled that same crooked smile that had always undone her a little. "Seriously?" he said, stepping inside. "We've been apart for two hours."

She blinked, then laughed, a sound that felt surprisingly real in her chest. "It's either fate or you're following me."

He lifted his hands in mock innocence. "Guilty. I bribed the staff to text me when you walked in."

She snorted and waved him over. "Get your order and sit. If I knew I was going to run into you, I would've ordered the giant sundae and made you help finish it."

Theo wandered over to the counter and ordered—mint chocolate chip in a cup, classic—and then slid into the booth across from her. For a second, neither of them said anything. And just like that, it was easy again.

Or almost.

"I thought I was the only one who stress ate ice cream," Theo said, spooning into his.

"I'm not stressed," Cora lied.

His eyebrows lifted. "You color-coded our fundraising schedule."

Cora shrugged, licking her cone. "It's efficient."

"You also named the spreadsheets."

She cracked a small smile. "Again, efficient. I'll admit, that's what I was working on when I gave up," Cora dug out a brownie. "You?"

"Trying to write thank you notes without sounding like a robot," Theo explained. "I think I failed."

"You have the handwriting of someone who's been held hostage."

He groaned. "You're not wrong."

The joke faded and left a quiet between them, more honest than before. Cora looked down at her ice cream. "Mom hadn't come back from her shop yet. I guess I just needed to get out of my head. You ever feel like the quieter it gets, the louder your thoughts are?"

Theo's spoon paused midair. "Lately? All the time."

They both went quiet again. The windows glowed with the last of the evening light, and the soft sounds of families and laughter drifted around them. Cora took another slow bite, the cold biting her teeth.

"You've been really... great," she said eventually. "About all of this. The bookstore, the fundraiser. Letting me help."

"You're the one keeping everything from falling apart."

"I think I needed something to hold together," she admitted, quieter now.

Theo looked at her then. Not just glanced—*looked*. "You okay?"

She hesitated. The words almost came out.

That she wasn't. That she left an entire life behind in Seattle. That she'd spent the last few weeks pretending to be okay because it was easier than explaining the unraveling of her future. That some mornings she still reached for her phone to text someone more from habit than longing.

But she just gave him a small smile. "I will be." She hoped she would be.

He didn't press. Just nodded like he understood, as he usually did. After a moment, he leaned back in the booth. "You know, you haven't changed as much as you think."

She raised an eyebrow. "Oh yeah?"

"You still eat your ice cream like you're rationing it. Bite, pause, overthink, repeat."

Cora laughed, caught off guard. "It's called savoring."

He smiled. "Sure. And you still hate mint chocolate chip, but you're too polite to say it."

She gestured toward his cup with a look of disdain. "It tastes like toothpaste."

"Wrong. It tastes like excellence."

They grinned at each other, something lighter rising between them.

Then Theo's expression softened. "But really, Cordelia. You've changed, too. There's something... I don't know... quieter about you. Not in a bad way. Just...different."

She looked down. "A lot can happen in the time we've been apart."

Then Cora met his gaze, her chest tightening in a way that surprised her. "You've changed."

Theo's brow lifted. "Yeah?"

"You're more grounded," she commented. "Still a total mess when it comes to calendars, obviously. But there's something steady about you now."

His smile faltered just enough to make it real. "That means a lot. Especially coming from the queen of color-coded schedules."

Cora smiled. "You always had the heart for this bookstore. But now you've got the follow-through."

He looked at her, really looked. "And you. You're still the same Cordelia who takes on too much, who makes things happen. But you laugh more now. I noticed that. You let yourself slow down sometimes."

Cora blinked. She hadn't really laughed most of the year. But here Theo was saying she was laughing *more*. She wondered if coming back home changed something, or if it was Theo.

Cora looked at him now and noticed the details she hadn't clocked before. He'd changed his hair, sure, and there were faint creases near his eyes she didn't remember from middle school. But his expression—the mix of curiosity and quiet mischief—hadn't changed at all.

"You still do that thing," she commented.

"What thing?"

"That little tilt of your head when you're trying to figure someone out."

Theo laughed softly. "I do not."

"You totally do."

He scooped another bite of ice cream, pretending to be offended. "Next you're going to accuse me of still getting brain freeze every time."

"You *absolutely* do that."

They both laughed. But under the humor, Cora felt something loosen in her chest. Not all the way. Not yet. But enough.

It had been easy to fall into this rhythm again—working with Theo on the fundraiser, texting during the week, planning late into the evening on video calls. But being *here*, face to face, just talking like this, made it more real.

Made her miss him in a way that surprised her.

He looked down at his empty cup, then back at her. "You've been showing up. For the fundraiser. For me. It's meant a lot."

"It's meant something to me too," she said. And then added, softer, "More than I expected."

She didn't mean just the project. She meant *him*. The time. The space he gave her without asking too many questions. The way being around him made the parts of her that still hurt, hurt a little less.

Theo smiled. "I like being around you."

Her gaze warmed. There it was, that flutter in her chest again. Not the one that would come when she tried holding herself together in Seattle. This was quieter. Sweeter. Made it easy to breathe.

"I like being around you too," she admitted quietly.

They finished their ice cream slowly, talking about nothing and everything the way they used to. She teased him for still eating around the chocolate chips, and he called her out for never finishing a cone all the way down.

As the sky outside turned lavender, Theo glanced toward the door.

"I should probably walk you home," he said, then added with a half-smile, "If you want company."

Cora hesitated, but just for a moment. Then she nodded. "Yeah. I'd like that."

They stood. She tossed her napkin and bowl, and he held the door open for her like he always used to. Their arms brushed as they stepped outside, and she didn't pull away.

She was grateful he didn't pry more into her problems. That she could give a little until she was ready to give more. He didn't ask. He didn't need to.

And that—*that*—was part of what made it so easy to be near him.

Chapter 18

Deciding to keep the habit of visiting her old stomping grounds, Cora slipped into her old corner at Marigold Café like no time had passed at all. The café still smelled like orange peel and fresh bread, wrapped in the cozy haze of mismatched furniture and half-wilted plants that looked better in the golden light than they probably deserved to.

It was a place that never asked questions—except for the owner, who launched herself at Cora the second she walked in, arms wide and words louder.

After a barrage of questions and unsolicited life advice, Cora was handed lavender croissants and orange peel tea, no charge, no escape. She gave the bare-minimum run-down—travel, burnout, a brief detour through emotional chaos. Mostly true. Mostly vague. Just enough to earn a moment of peace.

Finally free, she settled into her chair and let the café's rhythm steady her pulse—the clink of ceramic, the low hum of chatter, the occasional hiss from the espresso machine that sounded vaguely judgmental. Around her, life unfolded like a story mid-sentence—students pretending to study, a couple tangled in whispered laughter, an older woman knitting like she knew the secrets of the universe and wasn't sharing.

Cora also peeped a few magic folk milling about. A barista casually coaxed flame to the bottom of a milk pitcher. A reader flipped through her book without touching it. Another patron murmured to the flickering light hovering above his cup. Looks like he needed something more than a pick-me-up.

She opened her laptop, not to draft a column, not to get back to some version of the person she used to be. That door was closed. But the habit remained, fingers hovering above the keys, like muscle memory alone could summon purpose. The cursor blinked against a blank page, waiting for a thought that never came.

She didn't even try to type.

Her fingers curled into her palms, then relaxed. Stilled. Nothing.

A sigh slipped past her lips, barely louder than the café's ambient hum. She wasn't here to chase old routines or resurrect a voice that didn't fit anymore. The pull to prove she was okay—still capable, still useful—had faded to static.

With a soft flick of her wrist, she stirred her tea without touching the spoon. The quiet magic felt more honest than anything she might've written. The café door swung open again.

I'm being tested. The universe must think this is funny.

In walked Theo. Confident, relaxed, that impossible mix of charming and completely unaware of it. Sunlight hit his hair just so, golden glints catching. Her heart flipped. Again. She was used to this. Used to Theo being too close, too kind, too something. It was like being the unwilling subject of a very specific experiment in personal space and emotional volatility.

But this time, he wasn't walking toward her.

He leaned down beside someone else—a small figure in an oversized sweater, green glasses sliding down their nose, laughter already shared before they even reached the counter. Jordan. Even their name sounded effortless.

Cora's hand clenched around her cup, but it was the force of her magic that created a hairline crack near the handle. She told herself it didn't matter. She told herself she didn't care.

She lied.

They looked good together. Comfortable. Intimate in that casual way that comes from *being chosen*, not just tolerated. Jordan laughed like they and Theo had an inside joke carved over weeks, not hours. Theo's smile hit harder than expected. It had always been her safe place. Until now.

Something inside her curled, sharp and humiliated.

Cora ducked her head, cheeks burning, pretending her tea was suddenly the most fascinating thing in the room. She wasn't okay. And she hated that.

Theo's laughter carried across the room, warm and familiar. It should've felt like home. Instead, it knocked the air from her lungs. What *was* she even feeling? Jealousy? No. She didn't get jealous. Not really. Not even with Avery. But this wasn't about ownership. It was about presence. About absence. About not realizing she'd counted on a place at the table until someone else had taken the seat.

Then Jordan glanced up, Theo leaned in, and that was enough to make Cora stand. Not because she was brave. Because she was done sitting still. She crossed the room, curls shifting behind her headband, sweater sleeves pulled just over her wrists. When Theo spotted her, his smile lit up. And suddenly, it wasn't so hard to breathe.

"Hey, mind if I join you?" she asked, voice level despite the pounding in her chest.

Theo beamed. "Corde—erm, Cora!" He stood, practically glowing, and pulled out a chair for her. Jordan looked at her with that too-knowing smile, like they already knew who she was.

She wouldn't be surprised if they did.

Introductions happened in a blur. She caught the name Jordan. Then something about book clubs. Something about her mom. Something about Theo "not shutting up about her."

Cora was barely listening. She was *watching*. Watching the way Theo shifted his chair closer. The way his arm rested behind hers. The way he always, *always*, made room for her, no matter who else was at the table.

And just like that, her panic started to loosen its grip.

When Jordan excused themself with a theatrical sigh about needing a break from "Theo being Theo," the air changed.

Theo turned to her, all focus, all warmth. "You okay?"

No, she wasn't. Not even close. But she smiled anyway, tight and brittle. "Just lost in thought."

He didn't buy it.

"You looked more than thoughtful earlier." He didn't move. Just studied her, head slightly tilted, as if trying to decode the cracks in her voice. "You looked...jealous."

There it was. The word hung between them, deeply, deeply uncomfortable but accurate.

Cora flinched. She didn't mean to, but the word hit a nerve she didn't realize was exposed. Her eyes dropped to the table, where her fingers clutched the mug with too much force, white-knuckled and trembling. *Dammit*.

"I didn't know I could be jealous," she said finally. "Not like that. Not over something that wasn't mine to begin with."

Theo didn't interrupt. He waited, like always—patient, steady. A lighthouse she was trying very hard not to crash into.

"I just saw you two and...it caught me off guard." Her voice cracked like a poorly sealed envelope. "I felt left out. Not in a petty way, just like I wasn't supposed to be on the outside looking in."

Theo leaned forward. "You don't have to pretend. Not with me."

She hated that he said it so gently, like she was something breakable. Because he wasn't wrong. Her throat tightened, and she stared into her tea like it might give her the answers her heart was dodging.

"I'm scared," she whispered.

"Of what?"

"Of this. Of what it means. Of what happens if I say yes to whatever this is becoming and ruin the one thing that's never let me down."

Still, he said nothing. Let her speak the fear aloud, let it breathe instead of swatting it away. That was Theo, always making space, even when it hurt.

"I've already been gutted once," she murmured. "And it took everything to rebuild after that. I don't know if I can survive another collapse."

Theo's eyes didn't flinch. "I told you," he said, quiet, deliberate. "I've only ever loved one person."

Cora looked up, startled by the way he said it. Like it was inevitable. Like it had always been the truth.

"And it's not Jordan. Or anyone else that's come through the bookstore. Well, except this one witch who's been helping me out with my event."

Something deep in her chest pulled taut, the last thread of a secret she'd been pretending she didn't know. Her pulse roared in her ears. She could feel his honesty radiating across the table, quiet and absolute, the kind of confession that didn't beg for reciprocation—it just *was*.

She wanted to believe him. Wanted to fall forward into that warmth and let it melt away the years of doubt, the ache Avery left behind, the fear that she was too much or not enough. But even in the presence of that truth, another truth tangled her up; she wasn't ready. Not yet.

Her voice was hoarse with restraint. "I want to be brave enough for this. I do. But I'm not there. Not after everything. Not yet."

Theo didn't flinch. Didn't sigh, or frown, or shrink. He just nodded. A slow, careful nod that carried something weightier than disappointment. Understanding.

"I get it," he said. And it didn't feel like a dismissal. It felt like a promise. "I'm not going anywhere, Cordelia. But I need you to promise something too."

Her gaze lifted cautiously.

He leaned back slightly, still watching her. "Don't shut me out. Even if you don't have the answers yet. Even if it's messy."

Cora exhaled, trembling, like she'd been holding her breath for weeks instead of minutes. "I won't. I don't want to."

That was as much of a beginning as she could give him.

And Theo? He accepted it like it was everything.

Chapter 19

Cora's thoughts drifted as she walked, the past few weeks looping in her head like a reel stuck on play. Theo reappearing like he'd never left, charming as ever. That almost-confession of his—sweet, sure, but also completely disarming. It should've made her heart race in a good way. Instead, she kept circling the same question: was this something real, or just nostalgia in a shiny new coat?

Next to her, Lumi's boots clicked softly on the icy sidewalk, their steady rhythm a weird contrast to the city noise around them—cars, chatter, distant music. The kind of moment that should've felt peaceful. But Cora's stomach was all knots.

"Hey, can I ask you something?"

Lumi looked over, curious. "Shoot."

Cora fiddled with the zipper on her coat. "Do you think Theo actually...*feels* something? Or is it just the thrill of running into each other again?"

"You mean, is this about you or just about the timing?"

Relief flared through Cora. "Exactly. Thank you for translating my brain into English."

"That's what I'm here for." Lumi winked. "But honestly? Sometimes seeing someone again reminds you of what you felt before. But it can also make you realize how much it's changed."

Cora let out a breath, watching it curl into the winter air. "He's always been smooth, you know? Like, *effortlessly* good at being the version of himself everyone wants to see. I keep wondering how much of that is real."

"I mean, most people have a public setting and a private one. The question is, which version does he show you when it's just you?"

That landed heavier than Cora expected. Because the truth was... she wasn't sure.

Lumi bumped her shoulder playfully. "What you need is context. People act differently around others. We see how he handles a little pressure, like a badly timed mini golf putt."

"You just want an excuse to make fun of my form."

"Obviously," Lumi said, deadpan. "And to see if he looks at you like you hung the stars."

Cora laughed, the kind that came from deep in her chest. "Okay, fine. Let's test him. There's a winter-themed mini golf spot on Chestnut. You in?"

"Always. Let's see if this guy passes the vibe check."

Holiday chaos hummed through Center City—blinking snowflake lights, harried shoppers, the distant clang of bells. Wrapped in her green coat and scarf, Cora let herself feel *almost* festive.

"Can you believe we're actually doing this?" she said, grinning.

Lumi and Theo were both bundled up and already bantering like siblings. Theo's laugh was too warm for the cold air, and of course, he looked unfairly good in that jacket. Cora told herself she wasn't swooning. Not really. She was just *noticing*.

"Let's hope my skills in mini golf live up to my skills in binge-watching holiday movies," Lumi teased, adjusting her beanie.

The course was like a Christmas fever dream—sliding penguins, glowing elf statues, candy cane arches. Kids shrieked. Couples posed. A cocoa stand promised both sugar and spiked options.

"Ladies first," Theo said, mock-formal, gesturing to the first hole.

Cora rolled her eyes, but her cheeks flushed anyway. She took the club and tapped the ball through a windmill with suspicious ease. Lumi whooped.

They played on, the course winding through the fake snow-dusted maze. Cora tried to focus on her swing, but

Theo's celebratory dances each time he made a shot made it impossible not to laugh. She watched him more than she should've—how his grin made everything brighter, how easily people gravitated toward him. Was this who he really was? Or just the version he wanted them to see?

Lumi elbowed her halfway through the course. "You're trying *so hard* not to look smitten. How's that going?"

Cora groaned. "I don't know what you're talking about."

"Mmhmm."

They hit a new section, one designed for selfies and cocoa breaks. Stalls sold overpriced ornaments and marsh-mallow-stuffed mugs. Theo was already at the cocoa counter, charming the vendor like he was born to do it. Cora watched him, fingers curling tighter around her cup. There was something about him tonight—his energy, his attention—that made her feel exposed. Like he saw her, really saw her, and wasn't looking away.

"So?" Lumi asked, sipping her drink. "Still pretending you're not in trouble?"

Cora just sighed. "Why are you like this?"

"Because I'm right."

They finished the course, laughter echoing under the glow of string lights. At some point, Cora stopped caring whether this was about nostalgia or timing or whatever excuse she'd been clinging to. She was having fun. Real, uncomplicated fun. It made her ache in a way that wasn't entirely terrible, but it was confusing enough to make her question everything she'd just convinced herself of two minutes ago.

She tried to brush it off, because surely the lingering glances, the easy laughter, the way they were so... *comfortable* together, couldn't mean anything, right? *Just friends* doing *friend things.* But every time he caught her eye, she was hit with a truckload of warmth and sincerity, making her feel giddy.

"Careful, don't want you swooning all over the place," Lumi whispered. Cora stuck her tongue out in response.

Theo lined up his shot at the final hole with exaggerated drama. "This one's going in with style."

Cora smiled, until a flash of something old hit her. A memory. Avery. That same confident grin, the way she could turn charm into distraction. Her stomach clenched in doubt.

Theo nailed the shot, arms raised in triumph. Cora clapped and forced a smile, hoping he didn't see the way her hands trembled around the club.

"You're on fire today!" Lumi grinned, giving Theo a playful nudge.

Theo, clearly enjoying the attention, turned to Cora with that smile of his, the one that could probably make a rock melt. "What about you, Cordelia? You've got skills too! I'd say we're quite the team!"

Cora chose to ignore the obnoxious kissy faces Lumi made behind Theo's back. Instead, she focused on Theo, his look of admiration making her feel like she was the only person in the room. Great, now she was getting soft.

"Hey," Theo started as they wandered from their finished course, "how about we grab some peppermint hot chocolate before we call it a night?"

Lumi yawned suspiciously loud. "I'm actually pretty beat. You two enjoy your little hot chocolate date."

Cora blinked. "Wait—what?"

"Bye!" Lumi chirped, already walking off with a wave that practically screamed *wingwoman mission complete*.

Theo, blissfully unaware of the drama unfolding, just waved casually, his mind clearly on the peppermint hot chocolate he was about to get. Cora, on the other hand, watched as Lumi's wave turned into an over-the-top, exaggerated flourish. This was totally a set-up.

Theo turned to her. "Still down for a peppermint journey?"

Cora hesitated, still puzzling over Lumi's bizarrely dramatic exit, but then shrugged it off. She'd deal with that later. "Yeah, I'm down."

They headed to the café just around the corner, the scent of cinnamon and chocolate practically dragging them inside. But just as they reached the door, Theo's phone buzzed. He pulled it out, his smile suddenly dipping as he glanced at the screen.

"Sorry, I gotta take this," he muttered, his tone shifting slightly, before quickly stepping away.

"Everything okay?"

"Yeah, yeah, just a sec." Theo's voice was suddenly sharp, his usual relaxed tone replaced by something more clipped. Cora watched him, her brows knitting together as his carefree expression shifted into being unreadable. His posture stiffened, the easygoing charm he wore slipping away, and she felt a tight knot of worry form in her chest.

She stayed by the entrance, cold creeping into her gloves as she watched him pace a few steps away. His back was to her, but his voice, though muffled, carried just enough. Low. Clipped. Not the easy drawl she was used to. Whatever he was saying, it wasn't casual.

"Yeah, I said I'm out. No, I'm not—" A pause. "Look, I don't care if he thinks—"

Theo glanced over his shoulder mid-sentence and saw her watching. His face shuttered instantly. That mask of his, so practiced, fell back into place. The rest of the call was inaudible.

When he returned, his phone was already in his pocket, hands tucked into his jacket like he needed to keep them from doing something reckless. "Sorry," he said, voice lighter now, too light. "Just...family stuff."

Cora tilted her head, catching the stiff edge still clinging to his expression. "Everything okay?"

He gave her a smile that didn't quite fit. "Yeah. Just my dad being... my dad."

There it was. A name without a name. She remembered Theo's dad, vaguely. Stern. Formal. Always seemed like he was sizing people up. Even back then, Theo had brushed it off like it was nothing—like it was normal. But now, that tension in his shoulders, the tightness in his jaw—it didn't look like nothing.

Cora didn't push. But she tucked the detail away. Filed it under *noted, probably important later.*

Theo nudged the door open with a crooked grin. "C'mon. Peppermint cocoa's calling."

She watched him closely. "Theo, if you need to talk about it, you know you can, right?"

Theo let out a breath, motioning to the door. "I'm good. Really."

She stepped in beside him, the scent of sugar and steam hitting them. But the tension from outside didn't fully melt. It clung to Theo in the way he avoided eye contact with the barista, in how he fidgeted with the sleeves of his coat as they waited. And Cora, despite the warmth of the café and the promise of something soft between them, couldn't shake the feeling that Theo was carrying more than he let on—and had been for a long time.

"Two peppermint hot chocolates?" she asked the barista, glancing back at him for confirmation. He nodded, eyes elsewhere.

As she pulled out her card to pay, Theo finally stirred behind her. "No, let me. I owe you for carrying the team at mini golf."

She almost argued, but his tone had that threadbare cheer again. Instead, she stepped aside and let him pay, watching as his fingers tapped out a rhythm on the counter. Not impatient—nervous. Once they'd settled into a corner table, mugs warm between their palms, Cora let the silence stretch. Just a little. Enough to see if he'd fill it on his own.

He didn't.

She sipped the cocoa, peppermint sharp and rich. "So... your dad?" she asked gently, wrapping both hands around her mug. "I don't remember much about him. You guys close?"

Theo gave a short laugh, though it didn't sound particularly amused. "Define 'close.'"

Cora raised an eyebrow. "Okay. Define *not* close."

He exhaled through his nose, then leaned back, eyes scanning the café, suddenly hyperaware of everyone around them. "It's complicated," he said finally. "We don't see eye to eye on a lot of things."

That didn't surprise her. She remembered the sharp way his dad had spoken, how he always seemed to lead with expectation rather than warmth. Even in their youth, Theo had always been adjusting, modulating himself depending on who was in the room.

"Because of..." she hesitated. "Work? Life?"

"Everything." Theo gave a faint smile. "He's always had a specific idea of who I should be. What I should do. Who I should love." He looked away, fingers tightening around his mug. "And I've never quite fit the mold."

She thought about the one time she'd been to his house years ago. His mom had made peach cobbler and kept insisting she eat more. She'd been warmth personified—soft, funny, always checking in. His dad, by contrast, had barely said a word the entire evening. But the silence hadn't been passive. It had been calculated. Like he was always measuring something. Maybe everything.

"You ever talk to your mom about it?"

Theo's smile twisted. "She tries. She always tries. But in some ways they're similar in their expectations. And you can tell she's tired of fighting battles that aren't hers to fix."

She studied him, this version of Theo that wasn't all jokes, and mischief, and warmth. This version that carried shadows under his charm. It hit her then how little he actually talked about his life back home. Even when they'd reconnected, he'd mentioned St. Louis, sure, but not much else.

"How long's it been this tense?" she asked, voice softer now.

Theo didn't answer right away. Just stared into his cocoa like it might reveal something.

"Since college," he said finally. "And a good amount before that. He always saw my choices as rebellion. Even when I wasn't trying to rebel. I just wanted to be me. And I guess that wasn't what he had in mind."

Cora nodded, understanding curling in her chest. She didn't know everything, but she knew what it felt like to constantly recalibrate yourself just to keep peace in a room. She'd done it with Avery plenty of times.

Theo looked up again, and for a second, he wasn't guarded. Just tired. "Anyway. Not exactly peppermint cocoa conversation, huh?"

"It's real," she noted. "And I'm not going anywhere, so... You don't have to pretend."

That earned her a flicker of a real smile. Small, but genuine. Outside, the snow kept falling, slow and sure. And inside, Theo's armor stayed down. Just a little longer.

Chapter 20

"So," Lumi said, drawing the word out like a tease. "What happened after I left you two lovebirds?"

Cora groaned, a hand flopping over her face. "Please, for the love of all things sacred, never call us that again."

She tried to sound annoyed, but a traitorous smile tugged at the corner of her mouth. Cora lounged across her bed, legs tangled in her comforter as she balanced her laptop on her knees. Lumi's face filled the screen, framed by warm studio lighting and the creative chaos behind her—half-finished sketches, tangled string lights, an old espresso machine humming in the background.

"It was chill," she added, trying to be casual. "We walked around, got hot chocolate, talked about his event. Nothing scandalous."

She left out the part where melted marshmallow had stuck to her lip, and Theo—without hesitating—had reached up to wipe it off with his thumb. Left out how her breath had caught in her chest as he licked it away, like it was nothing, like it hadn't set her thoughts on fire. She'd spent the rest of the night trying to pretend her pulse wasn't sprinting in his direction.

Some things didn't need to be said out loud.

Lumi tilted her head, one brow arching. "You *say* that, but ever since Theo came back, you've been...how do I put this?"

"Self-conscious?" Cora offered. "Idiotic?"

"Happy."

That one landed like a soft punch to the ribs. Cora blinked at the screen. She hadn't expected that. She hadn't realized how much she'd missed feeling seen until Lumi said it out loud. But Lumi wasn't done.

"You're lighter. You laugh again. I'm finally seeing the real you. The you from before Avery."

Cora's brows drew together, sitting up a little straighter to rest her back against the headboard. "I was happy with Avery. It was just the last year that got complicated."

Lumi gave a slow, skeptical nod, the kind that said she was treading lightly—just enough to be kind, but not so much that she'd let Cora lie to herself. *Uh oh.*

"Complicated, sure. But let's not rewrite history. When you first got together with her, you were glowing. You couldn't stop talking about the tiniest things—her weird coffee orders, her dumb jokes, the way she did this thing with her eyebrows when she was lying. You'd call me just to tell me she wore mismatched socks on purpose."

Cora huffed a quiet laugh. "Gods, yeah. I'd forgotten about that."

"But then something changed," Lumi noted, pursing her lips. "You started...disappearing. During our calls, you looked so drained. Not just tired, like *tired-in-your-soul* tired. You weren't you anymore. You'd go quiet for long stretches, and when I asked what was wrong, you'd brush it off."

Cora didn't answer right away, instead toying with the edge of her comforter. "I thought it was just stress. The advice column was taking off. I was adjusting. Juggling things."

"Sure. But it wasn't just that. You stopped talking freely. You second-guessed yourself constantly. Like you were afraid to say the wrong thing. Like you were trying to be perfect for her all the time."

Cora swallowed. "I thought if I just kept showing up, kept loving her enough, it would click."

"But it didn't, did it?" Lumi asked softly. "You started shrinking. You stopped laughing at the stupid stuff. You stopped being curious. You were performing. Editing yourself."

"I didn't realize I was doing that."

"You were surviving," Lumi said, "and you're allowed to name that. But now? With Theo? It's different. You're not holding back anymore. You don't censor yourself. You even have that I-don't-give-a-damn sparkle in your eye again. I haven't seen that in *years*."

"I guess with Theo, I don't feel like I have to audition just to be in the room."

"Exactly. He sees *you*. Not some filtered version of you."

Cora dropped her head back. "It's weird. I didn't realize how much of myself I'd shoved down until now."

"Because you were in survival mode. And now you're not. Now you're finally remembering what it feels like to breathe. Be honest, how did Avery actually make you feel?"

There was a long pause, Cora's mind immediately going to 'inadequate.' But that couldn't be right. She remembered thinking she was cool, and adventurous, and unique. But maybe what she thought of Avery and how Avery made her feel were actually two different things.

"She made me feel... othered," she admitted solemnly. "Not in a 'you're so special' way. More like...we were on different planets. And I was the only one trying to build a bridge."

Lumi exhaled slowly. "You shouldn't have had to. Relationships shouldn't feel like you're clapping with one hand."

"At the time, I thought it was normal. That if I just worked harder, loved better, I could make it last."

"But now you know," Lumi said gently. "You were trying to hold it all together on your own. And it broke you a little."

Cora looked down at her lap. "With Theo... it doesn't feel like that. I don't feel like I have to prove anything. I just... get to be."

"That's what it's supposed to feel like," Lumi said. "That's what *you* deserve."

"It really is." Then she tilted her head. "Can I ask something without you deflecting?"

Lumi squinted suspiciously. "Doubt it. But go on."

Cora leaned closer to the screen. "Is it just me, or does some of what you're saying about *me* apply to *you* and Jax?"

Lumi blinked. Then stiffened. "We're not like you and Avery, Cora."

"I didn't say you were," Cora replied calmly. "But you've mentioned him less. You've said he doesn't check in much. You brush it off, but it doesn't really sound okay."

"He's busy. I'm not needy."

"No, but maybe you are *lonely*."

Lumi didn't answer right away. Her gaze dropped to her mug.

"It's just a phase," she replied with a clipped tone. "He's with his family. I've got my own stuff going on. We don't need to be in each other's pockets."

"Maybe. But it feels like you're doing all the heavy lifting and trying really hard to act like it's not wearing you down."

Cora watched her best friend—strong, capable, independent Lumi—pretend like her heart wasn't cracking a little every time Jax forgot to text back. It wasn't dramatic. But it was quiet, and it was real. "I'm managing."

Cora didn't push. She knew that tone. She'd used it herself, too many times. After a long beat, she shifted the conversation. "Something weird happened after you left us."

Lumi perked up. "What happened?"

"He went to take a call from his parents. When he came back, the vibe was just... gone. Like a switch flipped."

"Gone how?"

"He smiled, but it didn't reach his eyes. Said everything was fine, but it felt *very* not fine."

"Did you ask?"

Cora paused, knowing it was Theo's business and that she shouldn't say too much. "He initially brushed it off, but then we had a little heart to heart about some family troubles. It still felt like he was hiding something though."

Lumi raised an eyebrow. "And now you're spiraling."

"I'm not *spiraling*," Cora defended, tone completely unconvincing.

"You're more worried than a regular-degular friend would be."

Cora buried her face in a pillow with a groan. "I am not ready to unpack that. That is *not* why I came home."

"Nope," Lumi said with a grin. "But the universe did not get that memo."

Cora peered out from behind the pillow. "Wait—if you noticed all that stuff with Avery, why didn't you call me out harder?"

"I did. Repeatedly. But you were too busy building a new life without room for the people who mattered."

That stung more than she expected. Cora's frown deepened.

"I didn't mean to shut everyone out."

"I know. But you did." Lumi softened a bit. "Why did you leave, Cora? Not just when you met Avery—when you went to grad school. There were programs here."

"I had to," Cora said quietly. "Nothing felt right anymore."

After her dad died, after her magic went sideways the first time, after everything that used to feel like home cracked beneath her feet, leaving had seemed like the only option. Staying felt like standing in a graveyard of who she used to be.

Lumi looked away, her expression unreadable. "Maybe that's because you've never known what home really feels like. Not without all the things you've been running from."

And just like that, Cora felt the sting behind her eyes.

Her journey wasn't just about Theo. Or Avery. Or even love.

It was about *everything* she'd been avoiding.

Chapter 21

The scent of rosemary and lavender lingered in the air, soft and grounding, as Cora adjusted the flickering candles on the mantle. Each flame cast dancing shadows along the walls, the kind that always reminded her of childhood winters—of warmth, wonder, and the rituals her mother never let slip, no matter how fractured the years had been. She straightened the Yule candle—gold and intricately carved, its wax etched with ancient symbols for light and return—then stepped back, brushing wax flecks from her fingertips.

Outside, the wind curled against the eaves, a quiet reminder that this was the longest night of the year. The Winter Solstice had always been her favorite, a celebration of stillness and slow-burning hope. As a girl, she'd loved the way her mother made the night feel enchanted, even if the world beyond their doorstep felt anything but.

Tonight, that old magic felt closer than it had in years.

Cora glanced around the room. The table in the dining room was set with polished china and scattered sprigs of holly, the air still heavy with the scent of the rich stew that had simmered all afternoon. Evergreen branches stretched across the center like a quiet blessing. She ran her fingers along the table's edge, remembering winters long before heartbreak had ever entered her vocabulary. There had always been rituals—candles, herbs, songs without lyrics. Her mother's quiet brand of magic.

It was the first Solstice she'd spent here in two years.

Last year she'd been in Seattle—drinking mulled wine out of mismatched mugs, trying to stitch together new traditions with Avery that never quite held. They had smiled through it, both pretending not to notice how things were slowly unraveling—missed calls, curt answers, unspoken resentments. A kind of soft decay that no candlelight could disguise.

Cora had spent so long avoiding her grief for Avery—months of burying it under distractions, pretending her heart hadn't been slowly unstitched. And then there was Theo. The thought of him made something flutter low in her chest. She wasn't sure when it shifted—when the easy laughter turned into warmth in her palms, when the way he looked at her stopped feeling like familiarity and started to feel like possibility. He hadn't tried to fix her. He just listened. Like he knew the difference between silence and stillness, and respected both.

Her mother's voice drifted from behind. "You're going to want to save a spot for these."

Cora turned to see her entering with the bundles—dried herbs and tiny flowers tied in twine, floating neatly in a row behind her, charmed into calm obedience. Nicole's dress was deep velvet, the color of midnight, and shimmered faintly when she passed by the firelight. Her presence was always a little otherworldly, like she'd stepped from one veil into another and carried traces of it with her. Cora caught herself glancing down at her sweater—earth-toned, cozy, practical—and felt oddly rooted in it. Not glamorous. Not curated, but more present than she'd been in a while.

"These are for the fire later," she said, placing them down. "Protection, renewal, clarity. The usual."

Cora smiled, brushing a hand across one of the bundles. "You always know what's needed."

"It's not knowing, it's listening." Her mother's gaze softened. "You've gotten better at that."

Maybe. It hadn't felt like it, until recently. But being home in Valley Creek Hollow had brought a stillness back into her life—one she'd forgotten how much she needed. And maybe Theo had something to do with that too.

They moved in tandem, adding the bundles to the table. No big declarations, that was for all the other Yuletide happenings. Just the familiar rhythm of shared preparation. And under that silence, something inside Cora began to loosen.

Later, they sat down for dinner—their movements soft, the conversation easy. It wasn't about catching up. It was about simply being. And for Cora, who had spent months sprinting away from feelings she didn't want to name, that stillness was a gift.

When the plates were cleared, they stood at the hearth. Nicole retrieved the gold Yule candle, placing it gently in the center of the living room table.

"It's time," Nicole said, lifting the Yule candle gently. "The return of the light. A turning of the wheel."

Cora nodded. "And a reminder that even endings are beginnings."

She lit the wick. Flame caught and rose, warm and alive.

"Now," Nicole continued, "honor the year behind you. Think of what you've learned. What you're letting go. What you're ready to welcome."

Cora closed her eyes.

She thought of Avery—not just the loss of her, but the loss of the person she'd been with her. That girl who bent herself to fit into someone else's story. There had been love there, real and messy and bright, but there had also been fear. Of being too much. Or not enough.

And then Theo's image emerged—not a memory, but a feeling. The heat in her cheeks when he brushed her shoulder in the bookstore. The way his eyes stayed on her a second too long when she was talking about her writing. The moment he slipped that dog-eared poetry book into her coat pocket with a post-it: *"This reminded me of you."*

He didn't pull. He didn't chase. He waited. And that patience? It stirred something that felt dangerously close to hope.

"I'm ready," she whispered, opening her eyes. Her voice didn't shake. "Ready for more."

Her mother's hand found hers. "And are you ready to let yourself be loved?"

The flicker of flame reflected in Cora's eyes as she spoke. "I think I'm learning that love doesn't have to mean losing myself."

Nicole's expression softened. "Let the winter hold your fears for a little while. Spring will handle the rest." She turned, picking up the herb bundles. "Come on. Let's burn what no longer serves us."

Cora opened the window just a crack—the old tradition of letting the stale energy out, welcoming in the new—before joining Nicole. Together, they knelt by the hearth and fed the bundles to the fire. The herbs cracked and curled, smoke drifting upward. Rosemary for clarity. Lavender for peace. Cedar for protection. The scent wrapped around her like a whispered promise.

Nicole leaned back, gaze still fixed on the hearth. "The solstice reminds us," she murmured, "that darkness isn't the end. It's just the middle. The turning point."

Cora nodded. "Even when we can't see it yet."

Nicole leaned in, kissed her forehead, and whispered, "Happy Solstice, my heart."

Cora lingered in the warmth for a moment longer before returning upstairs. After her mother's last ceremonial flourish—shadow-casting via flashlight—Cora returned to her room, cheeks warm and hair smelling faintly of woodsmoke. She curled onto her rug, the wind singing outside, and reached for her tarot deck. It had been too long since she'd done a proper reading, too long since she'd trusted her own intuition.

She lit a small lavender candle and shuffled. "What must I release this Yule?" she asked aloud, drawing the first card.

The Five of Cups. *Of course.* A cloaked figure stared at three fallen cups, two still standing behind them, nearly forgotten. Grief. Regret. The not-so-gentle reminder to stop mourning what couldn't be undone.

She placed it down, exhaling. "Alright," she said. "Message received."

Avery's name didn't cross her lips, but her presence ghosted the edges of Cora's thoughts. She would always be part of the story—but not the ending. Not anymore.

"What have I learned this year?" Next card. Ace of Pentacles. Growth. Renewal. Beginnings that sprouted from uncertain soil. A smile tugged at Cora's mouth. This year had cracked her open. And in all that brokenness, new things had quietly started to bloom—writing again, reconnecting with her mother, Theo walking into her life like a chapter she hadn't realized she'd left unfinished.

"How do I bring balance into the new year?" Final card. Temperance. She tilted her head. *Of course it would be this.* A call to balance, to integration, to patience. She ran a finger along the card's edge. A way forward that didn't require extremes, didn't demand all or nothing. Maybe she didn't have to choose between solitude and connection. She didn't have to choose between herself and love. Theo didn't throw her off balance; he reminded her what equilibrium felt like.

She laid the cards in a line and studied them, their message quiet but firm. Release the past. Honor what you've learned. Trust your ability to hold more than one truth at a time.

She gathered the cards slowly and leaned back, watching the candle flicker. The universe had a flair for dramatic timing, sure. But tonight, she wasn't rolling her eyes at it. Tonight, she was listening. She wasn't just hoping for the light to return.

She was ready to meet it halfway.

Chapter 22

Theo seemed more off than usual.

Cora told herself it was just party prep jitters. Who *wouldn't* be frazzled before hosting a bookstore-wide Yuletide bash with enchanted decorations that refused to stay in place, a hundred little things threatening to go wrong, and the hope that they had the finances to last another year?

But then she caught him fumbling with an ornament, his usually steady hands uncharacteristically shaky, and his eyes kept darting to the door, like he was waiting for someone—or something—to come walking through. Or bracing. He'd been like this a couple of weeks ago when they first started planning, carrying some invisible weight she couldn't name. He was physically there, but mentally somewhere else.

They were adjusting a crooked banner of holly over the window when Theo broke the silence, his voice low. "How's the fundraiser coming along? I saw the numbers this morning, but I wasn't sure if you'd gotten any more last-minute donations."

Cora blinked, surprised by the shift in focus. "It's better than I expected, honestly. Not a miracle, but we might actually break even if the auction goes well."

Theo nodded, but didn't look relieved. He was chewing the inside of his cheek, his eyes scanning the room like he couldn't get comfortable in his own skin.

"I've been running the numbers too," he said after a pause. "Even with the extra push from this event, I'm not sure the shop's going to make it another year."

The words hit heavier than the banner tacks they were hammering in. Cora set down her end of the garland, glancing at him. "It's that bad? I know I saw the bills, but still..."

Theo shrugged, but it wasn't casual; it was the kind of shrug people did when the truth was too big to say outright. "Rent's going up again. Utilities are brutal. And traffic's been slow unless there's an event. We had a good fall season, but..." He let the rest trail off, the silence filling with all the things he didn't say. "There were moments I thought I was catching up to Mr. Hargrove's debt, just to have another thing to take care of."

"I wish I'd known sooner," Cora said gently.

"I didn't want to worry you. You just got back. You've got enough on your plate."

She wanted to argue, but the tired set of his shoulders stopped her. He was always the one trying to keep everything together, make the crisis feel manageable. But now he looked like someone unraveling in slow motion.

And that's when it clicked. The nervous energy, the distracted glances, the long hours at the shop, even the strange phone call she'd overheard the other day. This wasn't just holiday stress. Something was off, and now she was sure; Theo was holding something back.

So when the garland was finally up, Cora took a breath and decided to shift the conversation, just enough to draw him out of his head.

"Is your family coming here for Yuletide things?" she asked, keeping her tone light, casual.

Theo blinked. "What? Oh." He ran a hand through his hair. "Nah. They're still out west. Said it was too much of a hassle."

"But this is big," she said before she could stop herself. "Can't they come support you?"

"They figured I'd go there like I did last time. When I told them I had responsibilities here..." He shrugged, but it didn't read as indifferent. His voice dropped. "They didn't change their plans."

His eyes never met hers. The words hit her with a delayed sting. Cora remembered that strange phone call a few days ago where he'd stepped outside and come back looking like he'd seen a ghost. She knew they weren't very supportive, but didn't expect this.

She placed a hand on his arm. "You should come by our Yule party," she said gently. "Or just come over before. My mom would love to see you."

He gave her a crooked smile that didn't quite reach his eyes. "I don't wanna crash your family's holiday."

"Theo. You *are* part of my family. You've always been."

His gaze finally met hers, and there, for just a breath, the mask slipped. The charm, the calm, the easygoing bookstore owner thing. Underneath, something bruised lingered.

"So, it's not...pity?" he asked, almost like he was joking. Almost.

She snorted. "You dork. No. It's not pity. I just—I don't want you alone. And honestly?" Her fingers tightened slightly around his. "It would be selfish of me not to invite you. I missed this. I missed *you*."

His shoulders eased, a barely visible thaw. "Okay," he whispered. "But only if your mom makes her rosemary rolls."

Cora grinned. "She already has three batches pre-spelled. You're in luck."

But even as she pulled him into a hug, she felt it—like touching a charm that used to glow but now hummed with something different. Grief. Distance. A spell cast in reverse.

"They don't support you," she whispered, not quite a question.

Theo went still.

He pulled back, fiddled with his glasses. "They never really have," he said finally. "They thought the bookstore thing was temporary. They still call it a phase. Like I'm going to wake up and decide I want to go to grad school."

Cora didn't say anything right away. She was too busy remembering. How often he'd been at her house growing up. How her mom made him lunch without asking. How her dad let him crash family dinners and didn't bat an eye. At the time, she thought he just liked the chaos. But maybe he just liked being seen.

Her voice wavered. "You didn't just leave me when you moved away. You left *them*, too. The people who gave a damn."

Theo didn't respond, but he didn't have to. His silence said everything.

"Hey," she said after a beat, her voice steadier now. "You're not alone anymore, okay? You have me. You have *us*. You always have."

Theo gave her a small, almost imperceptible smile. "Thanks, Cordelia. I really mean it."

Later, when Theo rang the bell at her mom's house, Cora had to remind herself not to sprint. He looked...safe. Comfortable. Like her favorite book spine after years of wear. And maybe that was why it was so terrifying.

She wore red—not for the party, not really. The dress clung at the waist and flowed everywhere else, and when his eyes lingered just a little too long, her stomach did a strange, fluttery somersault. Magic always got a little weird around Theo. Like the universe was paying too much attention.

"This place hasn't changed at all," he said, stepping into the warmth and the scent of cinnamon and candle smoke. "I think even that garland is the same."

She laughed. "She's a nostalgic witch, what can I say?"

Then, Theo pulled something from his pocket. A small, neatly wrapped package. "I got you something."

Her breath caught. "Why?"

He shrugged, trying for casual. "Just...thought of you."

She peeled the paper. A delicate gold bracelet. On it, a lumpy, stone-like pendant—glinting faintly under the fairy lights.

"I don't get it," she said softly.

"You used to collect rocks. Remember? Any time we were out walking. You said some of them had stories in them."

Cora blinked. Something sharp and warm pressed at her chest. "I can't believe you remembered that."

"I remember a lot," he said.

And maybe that was the problem. Because she did, too. Every moment. Every spell. Every almost.

"Thank you," she managed, her voice a little thicker than she'd intended. She clasped it onto her wrist and gave it a little jiggle. "I really love it."

Theo's smile widened, a little relieved, a little shy. Cora broke the silence with a small cough. "Ready to face the madness?" she asked, motioning toward the living room.

Theo glanced over at the sounds of chatter coming from beyond the hallway. "I'm here for it."

By the time Aunt Vern was declaring their future engagement and offering to officiate the wedding herself, Cora
was ready to melt into the carpet. But Theo took her hand
like it was nothing—like it was *normal*—and squeezed it.

"You're part of the family," she'd said.

He didn't seem to want to let go.

Later, when they escaped to the outdoor tent, the sky
overhead twinkled with stars.

"Thanks for having me," Theo said, his voice low, honest. "I needed this."

She could've said *me too*. She didn't. Her mind was spinning too fast, full of tangled feelings, memories, tension,
and longing. It all pulsed beneath her skin like static.

Theo looked at her with a mixture of curiosity and
something else—something she couldn't quite name. He
leaned in just a little closer, and for a moment, the noise
of the party seemed to disappear entirely. The tent, usually spacious and warm, suddenly felt too small. Her skin
wasn't burning from the heater anymore; it was his near-

ness that made her pulse quicken. The space between them shrank until it felt like the two of them were the only ones left in the world, suspended in this strange, familiar moment.

"I didn't think it bothered you," he said, his voice barely above a whisper. "Not when I first came here tonight. You seemed... comfortable."

Cora was hit with a rush of memories, back to Sticks and Stones, the way Theo had leaned in just as close that day. Everything about him felt like it belonged—his warmth, his presence, it all felt like home. She felt her breath catch in her throat as they both leaned in, hearts thundering in sync. Just as their lips were about to meet, a loud shout broke through, her cousin's voice cutting the air from inside the house, yelling about some ridiculous game.

With a jolt, they pulled apart, the sound of laughter from the party slicing through the moment like a sharp knife. Cora felt a wave of disappointment rush over her, but even stronger was the exhilaration that lingered. Their connection was undeniable, but she wasn't quite ready to face it—especially not now, not with the mess of emotions swirling between them.

"Looks like we should get back," Theo said, his tone laced with a hint of reluctance as he shoved his hands back into his pockets. But as they turned to head inside, Cora took a deep breath, her heart still pounding. A quick glance at Theo made her realize this was just the beginning. No matter what her family thought, their friendship was evolving into something breathtaking, something undeniably real.

Inside, the celebration was in full swing—family members dancing, music blaring, and laughter echoing—but all Cora could focus on was the almost-kiss outside and the chemistry crackling between her and Theo.

The rest of the evening flew by in a blur of festive chaos and half-caught moments. As guests came and went, she and Theo slipped back into their easy rhythm of friendship—trading playful jabs, sharing stories, and laughing. But now, something was different. Her heart felt fuller, her laughter lighter, and beneath it all, that stupid, nagging yearning refused to go away.

But instead of feeling thankful, she just felt anguish.

Back in the kitchen, Cora gripped the counter like it might anchor her to something solid. The cool surface pressed into her palms, grounding her, but it wasn't enough to still the quiet, rising panic in her chest. From the outside, it probably looked like she was catching her breath, maybe even basking in the glow of a successful night. But inside, her thoughts spun into a storm.

Not again, her heart warned. *Not this close. Not when everything feels good.*

She pressed her eyes shut, jaw tight. The solstice had been only days ago. She'd whispered that she was ready; ready to let go of the walls she'd built so carefully around her. To choose warmth over armor. Connection over control.

She'd meant it. Every word.

But now, standing in the very heart of the life she swore she wanted—this home, this night, this man—her instincts screamed retreat. The closer she got to Theo, the more the ache of wanting twisted into fear. Because what if needing him meant breaking herself open in a way she couldn't survive? What if this wasn't enough to keep him? What if she wasn't?

A familiar heat rose behind her eyes, sharp and frustrating. She didn't want to cry. She wanted to be better than this.

And then, of course, he found her.

Theo appeared in the doorway like he belonged there—and he did. Not just in the building, but here. In her orbit. In this quiet space she kept trying to guard even as she longed for someone to walk into it.

"I was looking for you," he said, gentle as always, voice low enough that it brushed up against her like a hand on her shoulder.

Cora blinked hard, forcing her expression into something neutral. "I just needed a moment."

He didn't answer right away, and when she turned slightly to glance at him, he was watching her with that steady, quiet gaze that always seemed to see too much.

"You're not fine," he said.

She hated how the words cracked something open in her. She wanted to lie. To deflect. To reach for an easy, flippant reply. But he knew her too well.

"No," she admitted, voice flat. "I'm not."

He stepped into the room without rushing her, leaning against the opposite counter. Waiting, like always.

Her hands flexed against the stone. Magic shimmered faintly at her fingertips, restless and sparking—an echo of the storm in her chest. It responded to emotion whether she wanted it to or not.

"I'm scared," she said at last, the words scraped raw from her throat. "Scared of messing this up. Of needing you too much."

It was the truth, bare and biting. There was no undoing it now. Theo didn't flinch. He didn't look surprised. If anything, his expression softened, like he'd known and had just been waiting for her to say it out loud.

"You don't have to jump," he said quietly. "Just lean a little closer. We could go on dates, still tease each other, keep the banter, but maybe...closer. A little more intimate." His expression softened, and he reached out, his hand brushing against her arm. "Cordelia, nothing has to change if you're not ready for it. But if it does, I'm here."

The words struck something deep, an ache that told her for years that closeness wasn't safe. That love meant leaving. That opening up only led to being emptied out.

But he wasn't asking for everything. Just a little closer.

The weight of her breath eased slightly. Not gone, but less crushing.

"I made a promise at Solstice," she said, her voice barely audible. "That I'd stop closing every door the second things get too bright. That I'd open up. Let go."

She looked down at her trembling hands, at the way her magic curled and licked along her skin like fire refusing to be hidden. "I didn't think it'd still be this hard."

"It's okay that it is," Theo comforted. "But you're not alone in it. Not anymore."

Cora met his eyes. For a moment, neither of them moved.

"After the holidays," she whispered. "We'll talk. Really talk."

Theo didn't answer right away, but he didn't pull away, either. He stood there, close—so close to what they could have. His eyes softened, and for a long moment, it felt like everything else in the world had faded into the background. It was just them, standing there, present and patient, waiting.

"Okay."

Chapter 23

C ora wasn't sure how she was supposed to face Theo after last night. There their feelings were, sprawled out like a buffet she wasn't brave enough to touch. Now, every glance backward threatened to pull her into that flicker of warmth by the heater, of knees nudging and silence stretching and the undeniable sense that they were both waiting for something she wasn't ready to name.

"A mistake. Definitely a mistake," she muttered, tugging her coat tighter against the morning chill as she approached *Sticks and Stones*. But her heart wasn't buying it. Not when it kept latching onto the way his voice softened around her name.

The bookstore should've been a haven—a place of dusty magic and comfort. But as she shoved at the front door, expecting the familiar creak and musty paper scent, she was met with resistance. The door didn't budge. Inside, the lights were dim, the air unnervingly still. The 'closed' sign hung lazily in the window like an afterthought. And behind the counter, Theo sat with his fingers drumming a nervous rhythm against a stack of books, his eyes locked on the clock. Something was wrong.

Cora knocked. "Hey! You gonna let me in, or should I start reciting fairy tales on the sidewalk?"

Theo startled like someone caught mid-thought and moved to unlock the door, his motions quick and jittery. He barely met her eyes as she stepped inside, and she immediately noticed the air cool with the usual tinge of magic hummed sharp and anxious.

"You okay?" she asked, scanning the cluttered counter. Flyers were strewn everywhere and Theo looked like he hadn't slept, eyes bloodshot and hair down in disarray.

He shoved the nearest flyer toward her. "The date's wrong. On all of them. Hundreds of these are floating around town, and I didn't even notice until this morning."

Cora snatched it up, her stomach flipping as she scanned the bold, unmistakably incorrect date. "Oh. Wow. Yeah, that's...not great." Her fingers tightened around the paper, mind already racing through options.

She chewed her lip, then glanced at Theo. "What if we didn't need to reprint them? What if we just changed them?"

Theo blinked. "What, like, go house to house with a Sharpie?"

"No, I mean magically," she corrected, mentally flipping through the pages of her mother's grimoire she studied in her youth. "There's a charm—kind of like an object tether spell. If I anchor it to the printed flyers, we might be able to push a date-correction ripple across all of them. Like a chain update."

Theo stared at her, mouth slightly open. "That's advanced. And messy. And exactly the kind of thing you always say we shouldn't attempt without backup."

"Which is why I'm asking for help," she said, leveling him with a look. "You're the detail guy. You're precise. I can anchor the spell, but I'll need you to keep it from melting any ink or, you know, setting anything on fire."

She spoke with a surprising amount of confidence. It was a tricky spell, even more so with Cora's magic not exactly being consistently cooperative lately. But something had to be done.

His brow furrowed in thought, but a familiar glint sparked in his eyes. "If we channel it through the original design file, we could use that as the central link. A sort of... magical reference point."

"Exactly. We don't need to chase the flyers down if we can make them fix themselves."

Theo exhaled slowly, the edges of his tension starting to lift. "Alright. Let's try not to cause a paper apocalypse."

Cora smiled. "Deal. Let's fix your disaster the magical way."

Theo leaned back, rubbing his temples. "It's not just the flyers, though. I forgot markers for the coloring station, and the cocoa situation? Dire. I mean, we've got enough to serve exactly one very lucky child."

His voice cracked slightly at the end, and Cora had to fight the smile tugging at her lips. "Then we fix that, too. I'll call around, see who can get us supplies. My mom and I can make more cocoa tonight—magic-grade, not the powdered stuff. You just breathe. We've got this."

His shoulders slumped with a mix of relief and exhaustion. "You make it sound easy."

"It's not," she said, stepping closer, "but that's the point. We don't need easy. We just need each other."

Easier said than done, Cora realized, when the next morning began with cider.

Lumi barreled into the bookstore kitchen, cradling a large jug like it was a bomb. "Don't panic," she said, which of course made Cora panic immediately. "But the cider may have...fermented."

"What?" Cora blinked at the jug. "How?"

"My grandmother's recipe. When you sent an update I really wanted to help out and cheer up Theo. But apparently it works a little *too* well. It smells like a frat party in autumn."

Theo wandered in at that moment, fairy lights tangled around his shoulders. He sniffed the air and recoiled. "Why does it smell like bad decisions in here?"

"Long story," said Lumi and Cora in unison.

And then there was the stage.

They had borrowed it from the community center. Small enough to not take up too much space, but large enough to really put the readers in the spotlight. It was supposed to be sturdy. Instead, it collapsed mid-setup as Theo was testing the mic. One moment he was checking for feedback, the next he was sprawled on the floor, blinking at the ceiling while the mic screeched like a banshee.

"Oh my god, are you okay?" Cora asked, kneeling beside him, biting her lip to keep from laughing.

"I'm fine," Theo groaned. "But the mic just exposed all my insecurities in surround sound."

"How about we scrap this and pray people can project their voices."

Lumi stuck her head in. "The cider's now being served cold and in shot glasses. We're calling it *Cozy Courage.*"

He slumped into the nearest chair beside Cora, who handed him a gingerbread cookie shaped like a disturbingly muscular Santa.

"Everything is falling apart," he mumbled.

Cora patted his shoulder. "How about we switch gears for a bit and work on that spell?"

Theo obliged, and they spent the next hour hunched over Theo's laptop and a half-burned bundle of sage, working the tether spell line by line. It wasn't glamorous, more muttered incantations and carefully controlled panic, but slowly, impossibly, the date on the flyers shimmered, then shifted. Everywhere they'd been printed, the typo corrected itself with a quiet pulse of magic. Cora felt it echo in her ribs like the thrum of a finished spell. They high-fived—clumsily and maybe a little too hard.

While Theo went back to all the other emergencies that needed his specific kind of focused meltdown, Cora focused on her own mission of sugar, milk, and enough hot cocoa to satisfy a small, magical army.

By the time she got home, her jacket smelled like paper, dust. and lavender incense, and she was already rolling up her sleeves as she stepped into the kitchen. Without a word, she headed for the biggest pot they owned and began measuring out ingredients with the kind of intensity usually reserved for potion-making.

LILY A. LARKSPUR

Her mom breezed in a moment later with her usual air of grace, surveying the scene with amused eyes. "You're examining everything like the fate of the kingdom depends on it," Nicole said, slipping off her coat and summoning a spoon from the drawer with a flick of her wrist.

"The fate of Theo's event depends on it."

Nicole raised a brow. "I'd like to hope this doesn't all hinge upon your ability to make holiday drinks."

"There's a part of me that wants to make it like a mundane would," Cora huffed in response as she poured milk into the pot. "Don't want my magic creating another catastrophe to the list of things Theo is having a breakdown about."

Nicole chuckled and waved her hand. The ingredients lifted, swirled, and folded themselves into the pot in a graceful arc of magic. "But you're not mundane. And it's okay to make it a little extra special. Even if it's just cocoa."

She turned, reaching into her bag and producing a small bouquet of cheerful flowers. "Here. For good luck."

Cora stared. "Mom..."

Nicole held them out anyway. "I've watched you build something out of nothing, and I know your father would've been just as proud as I am."

Cora's throat tightened as she accepted the flowers, blinking quickly. "You're really laying it on thick today."

"That's my job. I know this event will be a success, and you'll handle it just like you always do; with personality." Nicole kissed her cheek and added, "Now go rest up. I'll make sure this batch of cocoa wins hearts."

Cora watched her mom command the kitchen with her usual graceful authority and couldn't help but feel steadier, more rooted. She wasn't alone in this.

She wasn't alone at all anymore.

Chapter 24

T he bookstore had never looked quite like this.

Strings of fairy lights glowed like bottled stardust, suspended from the rafters in gentle arcs. Glimmering charms floated near the ceiling; spinning snowflakes and soft candlelight orbs enchanted to hover midair and pulse in time with the festive music. Tinsel hugged the bookshelves while enchanted snow globes flickered on every table, casting tiny scenes in wintry motion. It was magic—literal and atmospheric—and it was all for the Fairytale Reading Night and fundraiser that Cora and Theo had spent weeks planning.

Tables lined the shelves, stacked with carefully curated silent auction items—enchanted first editions, rare herbariums, hand-poured potions, a wand carved by a now-retired artisan whose waiting list used to span years. Each one shimmered with quiet enchantment under glass domes or nestled in velvet-lined boxes.

But despite the glittering presentation, the heart of it was still the story nook—pillows and blankets piled high under twinkling lights—where children lounged with hot cocoa and crayon-scribbled stories. The scent of cinnamon and old paper mixed with gingerbread and melted wax. It was chaotic. It was warm. And it was working.

Cora weaved between the story circle and the auction tables, clipboard in hand, the hem of her red velvet dress catching the light as she moved. Her cheeks were already flushed, half from cider and half from adrenaline, pausing to chat with her mother and Lumi, both there for moral support and for her big "debut." Nicole, sipping on her cup of tea, looked around with pride, her smile shining brighter than any of the holiday lights. Lumi, who had apparently read at least half of the books in the place, gave her a nudge.

"You ready for this?" Lumi asked, a smirk playing at the corner of her mouth.

Cora shot her a look that was a mix of sarcasm and gratitude. "If by ready you mean terrified, then yeah, I'm ready. But you should totally write a little something yourself. You've got the imagination for it." She threw a quick glance at her mother, who was still looking blissfully unbothered by the event. "Mom, what about you? You've got a whole universe of stories floating around in that head of yours."

Her mother chuckled softly, giving her that look, the one that made it clear she knew exactly how much of a pain she could be. "Maybe one day. But I think I'll leave the storytelling to you, dear."

Cora snorted. "Yeah, well, you've got the tea-making, event-helping, and keeping-me-sane parts covered, so I guess I'll take the storytelling."

"I'm good with that."

Just then, Tessa, who'd been hanging around in the background looking like she was carefully cataloging the snacks she would sneak away for later, couldn't help herself. "Well, if *you* ever need help with your story, I'm your girl," she said with a playful grin, clearly enjoying the banter.

Cora raised an eyebrow.. "Oh really? You're gonna help me *write* a story? Last time you caught me writing you gave me hell."

"You're just such an easy target."

Before she could retort, she caught Theo's eye and excused herself to check in with him. He didn't appear as frantic as the previous day, but not completely relaxed either.

"Fairy Godmother of Logistics," Theo said as she appeared beside him, his sleeves rolled and hair ruffled from the crowd. "How's it going?"

She smirked. "The raffle box is so full, I had to sit on the lid to close it. The moonstone scrying set has three people bidding in silent increments like it's magical chess. And Lumi's cider tasting table is probably responsible for half of tonight's donations."

"Glad that ended up paying off."

"And the goal?" she asked quietly, scanning the room—locals, tourists, and witches from nearby covens mingled, drinks in hand, enchanted ornaments hanging off their coat buttons.

Theo's expression shifted, more hopeful than sure. "We're close. I won't know for sure until the auction closes. But if it holds? We're good. The store, the repairs, everything. Maybe even a decent espresso machine."

"You deserve more than a decent espresso machine, Theo."

He laughed softly, the sound frayed at the edges. "Tell that to the budget."

From the front room, a fresh wave of applause rippled through the space, followed by someone calling out for more cider. The warmth and noise of the fundraiser continued to pulse just beyond the curtain, vibrant and alive.

Theo leaned against the counter, rubbing the back of his neck. "I honestly didn't expect so many people to show. Let alone bid."

Cora smiled. "That's because you never see what this place means to everyone else. You're always too busy holding it together."

He looked at her, and for a moment, the exhaustion and worry in his eyes gave way to something gentler—grateful, unguarded. "You made tonight happen. I just kept the lights on until you walked back in."

The hush between them felt earned. Music and laughter filtered through the doorway, but here, it was just the two of them—tethered together in a moment that neither could name. It wasn't just about the bookstore anymore.

Then came Theo's voice, softer than before. "I think it's time," he said.

Cora blinked. "Time?"

"For you to share your story."

She hesitated, nerves prickling beneath the surface, but Theo gave her a nod—gentle, sure, the kind that could talk her into anything.

Out in the front room, Theo urged the crowd from playful chaos to something more attentive. One by one, children clutched their hand-decorated pages and stepped up to share their stories—tales of talking cats, moonlight princes, and sandwich kingdoms. Parents listened with soft smiles, some teary-eyed, others clearly trying not to laugh at the unexpected plot twists only kids could dream up. Each voice added to the warmth in the room, the kind of magic that wasn't conjured with spells, but with courage.

As the last young storyteller bowed to cheerful applause and returned to their seat, a gentle hush fell over the group. All eyes turned to Theo as he stood and offered a small, proud smile.

"And now," he said steadily, "we have one final story for tonight. One that's been a long time coming."

The quiet deepened as Cora stepped forward into the cozy nook, cheeks flushed and heart rattling beneath her sweater dress. Her mother and Lumi sat front and center, wearing expressions that made her feel simultaneously brave and very, very exposed.

"This is my version of *The Snow Queen,*" she said, her voice trembling slightly. "It's a little different. But I hope you enjoy it."

As she read, the world around her softened. Words tumbling from her lips as she wove the tale of Kara, the brave little girl who weathered the icy cold to meet the Snow Queen. Children leaned forward, wide-eyed. Her mother clasped her hands with proud serenity. Lumi clung to every word like it was life itself. Even Theo, across the room, watched with that quiet intensity that made her want to keep talking just so she could see that look stay on his face. With every sentence, they made her feel a sense of accomplishment she hadn't expected.

When she finished, there was genuine thunderous applause. Cora's heart swelled with joy knowing her little story left such an impact. Her heart still pounded in her chest, but she couldn't help the grin that spread across her face. As she stepped back, her mother was the first to reach her, pulling her into a hug.

"You brought it to life," Nicole whispered, teary. "It was *you*."

Lumi was next, giving her a tight hug and practically jumping up and down. "That was incredible! Seriously, I'm not just saying this; your version of *The Snow Queen* was so emotional! You made me feel like I was right there with Kara, fearless and everything. It was so real."

Cora laughed, a little embarrassed but also touched by their reactions. "Thanks, you two," she said, her cheeks flushing. "I wasn't sure how it would go over, but I'm glad you liked it."

Lumi, unable to help herself, declared it was 'selfie time' and fished out her phone for pictures, all chaotic and full of grins. She captured *everything*, including a candid of

Theo, caught mid-look, eyes on Cora like she was the only one in the room.

Cora blinked down at Lumi's phone. "He was... really looking at me like that?"

"Like you were casting a spell," Lumi teased.

She laughed—uneasy, maybe. But something warm curled inside her.

Later, as the event wound down and the last of the guests trickled out, Cora helped Theo clear the reading nook. Pillows, cocoa-stained napkins, glittery coloring pages—evidence of chaos and joy scattered across the floor like confetti after a parade. The aftermath of magic, in every sense.

"You survived," she said, nudging his shoulder with hers as she bent to scoop up a runaway crayon.

"Barely," he replied, smirking. "But we did it."

Without needing to say more they both lifted their hands in near unison, a soft pulse of magic shimmered between their fingertips. The coloring pages floated into a neat stack, napkins folding themselves and slipping into the trash bin with gentle precision. Pillows fluffed and re-aligned, and glitter lifted off the floor in a faint, golden swirl, drawn toward a waiting jar that sealed itself with a satisfied click.

Their movements were smooth, familiar. Arms brushing, fingers grazing. Like they'd done this a hundred times. Cora handed him a stack of programs, and his hand lingered a heartbeat too long, his fingers curling around hers before letting go.

"Don't think I didn't notice you doing the heavy lifting with that glitter spell," Theo said, glancing sideways at her.

Cora smirked. "Please. You owe me after nearly setting the flyers on fire this morning."

"Point taken," he said with a laugh, and the easy warmth between them settled back into place—light, unspoken, but very much there. "You have no idea what you did for this place tonight."

"You built it back up," she said, eyes meeting his. "I just...helped it shine. Helped *you* shine."

He stepped closer. "You always have, Cordelia."

There was no denying the way Theo looked at her then—like he truly saw her, not just as who she had been, but as the woman she'd become. In just three weeks, they'd fallen back into their old rhythm, but something about it had shifted. It felt deeper now, more grounded. They weren't just revisiting the past; they were stepping into who they were now. Theo still had that playful, boyish spark when he was around her, but it was layered with something steadier, something unmistakably grown-up.

Without warning, and in one swift motion, he leaned down and kissed her. Cora felt a jolt travel through her entire being at the feel of his soft lips molding perfectly against hers. The kiss was gentle yet passionate, stirring a desire for him she'd buried during their weeks together. She kissed back with just as much fervor, earning a low growl from him and a tightened grip around her waist that nearly made her knees buckle. Cora couldn't help but think back to the joke Theo made about helping her with her smut scenes, and it not being all talk.

Unfortunately for her, that wasn't the only thought that bombarded her mind.

Flashes of Avery's face barged in, sharp and unwelcome. Cora gasped, jerking away from Theo. Her hand flew to her chest as her breath hitched, the panic blooming fast and hard. She squeezed her eyes shut, willing the memory to fade, but it clung like smoke. Not now. Not here.

Her thoughts spiraled. *I can't do this. Not again.* That kiss—it hadn't been a mistake. It had meant something.

Which was exactly why it terrified her. If it broke, if they broke, she wasn't sure she'd survive the fallout. Not when she was still sifting through the wreckage of everything Avery left behind.

A gentle touch landed on her shoulders, and she flinched. Her eyes snapped open to find Theo, already pulling back, guilt flickering across his face. His hands hovered in the air like he wanted to help but wasn't sure he was allowed. And that damn frown. It twisted something in her, sharp and immediate. He looked like he thought he'd ruined everything.

But he hadn't. *I did,* Cora thought bitterly. She could still feel the heat of the kiss, her lips tingling with the memory. And she had liked it—too much. *Why does it always feel good before it falls apart?*

"What was that?" she blurted, her voice too raw, too shaken. "Theo, I told you. I can't."

She stepped back, needing space, needing air. The bookstore felt smaller suddenly, like the walls were inching closer, like she couldn't breathe with him looking at her like that. She hated this—hated how easily she could see it all slipping away. Again.

Theo's face fell. "I—I thought..." He rubbed the back of his neck, fumbling. "Cordelia, I crossed a line. I'm sorry. I didn't mean to make this harder for you. I just—" He faltered, then said quietly, "I've loved you forever."

Oh how she wished the confession swept her off her feet. Instead, Cora's mind scrambled to keep up. *Why now? Why say this now?* Her heart was barely stitched together with thread and hope. She was still bracing herself every time someone got too close, still holding pieces of herself like they might shatter if she let them go.

"This isn't what I came home to do," she said, her voice barely above a whisper. "I don't even know what I want right now."

The hope in Theo's expression drained into something more guarded. "We can forget it happened," he proposed. The forced smile he gave her made her chest ache. "If that's what you want."

"Maybe you think that's enough," Cora said, her voice rising before she could stop it. "That we've been thrown back together and it means something just because it feels familiar." Her chest tightened, heat creeping into her tone. "But that's not real. That's nostalgia. That's what Avery did, too—assumed she knew what I needed, tried to define my life for me. You're doing the same thing."

Theo blinked, stunned. "Cordelia, what in the world are you talking about?"

"I'm talking about control," she snapped. "About being with someone who decides what's best for me and doesn't ask what I actually want."

He stiffened, but didn't look away. "I'm not trying to control you. I'm not Avery. I know you're hurting. I know you need time. I'm just trying to show you that I'm here—always have been."

She wanted to believe him. Desperately. But she'd been here before. Heard promises that felt safe until they weren't. *I'm not ready to trust this. I'm not ready to trust me.*

"But that's the problem, Theo!" Her voice cracked. "You think waiting around means I owe you something."

His jaw tensed, but he didn't raise his voice. "That's not what I said."

"No," she admitted, softer now. "But that's how it feels."

Silence fell between them, heavy with what hadn't been said. She wasn't angry at him—not really. She was angry at herself for wanting it. For wanting him. For being afraid.

"I just..." She exhaled shakily, pressing a hand to her temple. "I need space. I need to figure out what this all means before I let anyone else in. I can't rush into something just because it feels good in the moment."

Theo's eyes searched hers, the frustration in his features giving way to something more morose. "Then take the time you need. I'll still be here. Friend first. Always."

Cora nodded, the ache in her chest tightening. She didn't want to walk away, but she couldn't stay in this space and pretend it didn't hurt. She turned, her steps quick and uneven, her thoughts loud and scattered. She didn't know if she was running from Theo, or from the part of herself that wanted to stay.

Chapter 25

C ora stared at the blank page, pen tapping an erratic rhythm against the paper. Her thoughts weren't just scattered; they were storm-tossed, frayed at the edges. Even her magic was back to being reactive and fidgety.

Stray curls clung to her cheeks, damp from where she'd run her fingers through her hair too many times. Her clothes didn't match—a sleep shirt under a cardigan that smelled faintly of cinnamon and missed laundry days—and the fabric kept catching static. A flicker of warmth sparked near her wrist, and she glanced down to find the cuff of her sleeve gently smoking. She pinched it out, heart skipping. That hadn't happened since she was nineteen and heartbroken over some idiot.

Pull it together, Cora. You're a storyteller now, remember?

But the words refused to show up. Her mind kept circling back like a vulture—hovering over last night. Theo's kiss. His voice, low and certain. That look, like he already knew how the story ended.

She dropped her pen, causing it to roll off her desk and stopped midair. It hovered. Wobbled like a drunk dragonfly before shooting across the room and hitting the window. The glass thankfully held, but her motivation didn't.

She blinked. "Okay. That's new." The pen fell to the ground. She didn't move to retrieve it.

Instead, she grabbed another sheet of paper, hands trembling. Her magic hummed under her skin, unbalanced, uncentered, waiting for her to name something, anything, so it could settle. She couldn't even name how she felt.

She wrote a single word: *Once.*

Then the ink bled out on its own, the letters feathering and smudging into nonsense. Cora growled, crumpled the page, and tossed it. It burst into soft green sparks midair and dissolved before it hit the floor.

"Seriously?" she muttered. "Now you're dramatic too?"

The tiny desk lamp above her flickered twice before going dark. The room seemed to exhale with her frustration. It was somehow worse than when she broke up with Avery.

"Pathetic," she muttered under her breath. "Absolutely pathetic." She was grown. She was disciplined. She was fine.

Except she wasn't. Not even close.

She stood abruptly, and the chair behind her scooted back on its own—too fast. It crashed into the floor, the force reverberating and making her lamp shake.

The silence closed back in, thick and suffocating. The worst part wasn't the kiss. It was everything that came after—the guilt, the confusion, the stupid voice in her head whispering things she wasn't ready to hear. *I'm not in love with him*, she reminded herself. *I can move on*. But deep down, she knew she couldn't.

"Damn it."

Her eyes burned with tears, chest ached, tight with things she didn't want to say aloud. Theo's voice wouldn't leave her head, that warm, earnest tone cutting through the noise. The kiss had knocked something loose in her, something she thought was locked up tight.

She buried her face in her hands. *Okay. Focus. If you can't write, then do something else. Be useful.*

Her gaze drifted toward the shelf across the room. Sitting among old drafts and half-used notebooks sat the small bracelet Theo gifted to her for Yuletide. A soft ache tugged at her chest.

Wiping her palms on her pants, she fixed the chair and moved back to her desk. Opening her laptop she typed, almost without thinking: *bookkeepers near me magical business*. The words looked ridiculous in the search bar. She hit enter anyway. Dozens of listings popped up. She scrolled past the chains and generic profiles until one caught her eye.

Alina Dorsey – Bookkeeping & Accounting for Magical Independent Businesses

Specializing in enchanted inventory, spell-imbued ledgers, and low-drama tax prep. Based in Valley Creek Hollow.

Cora blinked. Low-drama? Her face did something between a laugh and a wince.

New to town. Moved from Seattle. Friendly smile in her profile photo, messy bun, oversized glasses. She looked like someone who kept herbs in her kitchen and could catalog cursed objects without losing her cool.

Cora clicked before she could overthink it. She reached for her phone. The screen lit up with Theo's name—yesterday's missed call—before shifting to her contact list. She hesitated. Her thumb hovered, then pressed *Call* next to Alina's number. The dial tone buzzed through her. One ring. Two. Then, "Hello? This is Alina."

Cora took a breath. Her voice still came out a little too fast, a little too shaky. "Um, hi. This is Cora Sparks. I—uh, I need help. For a bookstore. It's not mine, it's—long story. But I think you're exactly who I'm looking for."

Chapter 26

C ora sat at the edge of Maple Park, on the same sun-warmed bench she used to claim during childhood summers. The playground across from her hadn't changed—the same old swings creaked with age, the same squeaky see-saw still tilted to one side. But it felt like she was watching a dream someone else had remembered for her. Kids tumbled through the park, their laughter shrill and free, while their parents sat nearby, pretending they weren't terrified of how fast everything would change.

She should've felt some comfort here. But guilt continued to press into her lungs leaving an untangled mess in her chest. Elation chased it. Desire crept in, having no business being there. And through it all, she just wanted to scream into a pillow, or disappear, or both.

One part of her wanted to act like a giddy teenager, kicking her feet and squealing about the boy she liked. The other part wanted to curl into herself and sob because—damn it—they weren't kids anymore. There was no "just hormones" excuse for this. This was real, and messy, and felt too much like stepping off a ledge.

Oh no, a thoughtful, bookish man who knows my worst habits and still cares about me wants to be more than friends. What a tragedy, she mocked herself silently. *You're absolutely drowning in problems, Cora.*

And yet, she couldn't shake the unease that maybe she'd led him on. That she'd made it worse.

"Coraaaa!"

The voice broke through her spiral like sunlight cracking through thick clouds. Lumi jogged up, her pink-streaked hair bouncing with her. But her grin faltered the moment she got a proper look at Cora.

"Hey," Lumi said, sliding onto the bench beside her. Concern drew faint lines around her eyes. "When you texted me about Theo, I thought it was good news."

"I panicked," Cora whispered. "It felt amazing... then terrifying. And now I just feel stupid."

Lumi blinked. "From what you've told me about him, he's not the type to make you feel stupid. Talk to him."

"Easier said than done," Cora muttered, eyes fixed on the monkey bars. A girl, no older than seven, swung across them with fearless ease. *Stronger than I ever was,* Cora thought bitterly. "I think it's better to stop before anyone gets hurt."

"You always assume pain is inevitable. But what if—crazy idea—it actually works out?"

"Try?" The word came out too sharp, slicing the air between them. Cora hadn't meant to snap, but there it was, raw and ugly.

The temperature around them adjusted—not enough to draw alarm, but enough to ruffle the edges of a nearby magazine and scatter leaves across the path. Lumi noticed. Her brow furrowed, but she didn't call attention to it.

Cora didn't notice. "Every time I try to get close, they leave. Theo. My dad. Avery. Why should I expect anything different now?"

Lumi's posture stiffened. Her voice, usually gentle, came clipped. "Didn't you leave, too?"

Cora turned to her, startled. "I had to. It was an opportunity. No one was cheering me on back then."

"And what about me?" Lumi's voice cracked. Her eyes shimmered. "You left, Cora. I watched you pack up and fly across the country. You left too. So don't act like you're the only one who got abandoned."

Cora recoiled. Her magic flared again, causing the bark of a nearby oak tree to darken, bruising at its roots.

She took a breath, tried to bury the burn in her throat. "That's not fair. You don't get to erase my pain just because I left."

"I'm not erasing it," Lumi snapped. "I'm pointing out that you're not the only one who's suffered. You ran, and now that you're back, you want everything to feel the same. But it's not. And maybe it never will be."

"And maybe you're still mad I didn't come back sooner," Cora shot back, unable to stop herself. "Is that it? You think I abandoned you?"

"No. I know you did."

Those words landed like a curse. Parents nearby shifted uneasily, glancing in their direction. A toddler's juice box exploded quietly in his hands. A dog refused to cross the path near them, whining.

Cora stood, not even aware she was clenching her fists until her nails dug crescent moons into her palms. Her breath came faster, uneven. The world around her pulsed faintly with every heartbeat, and she hated how the pressure built in her chest like a rising tide.

"You think I ran from everything?" she snapped. "You think I'm just some coward who bailed the second things got hard? You don't even know the full story."

Lumi stood too now, her arms crossed tightly over her chest, jaw clenched. "Then tell me!" she challenged, the words pushing past her lips like a dare. "Because from where I'm standing, all I've seen is you ghosting your entire life and acting like it's everyone else's fault when things don't go perfectly."

Cora flinched. That word—ghosting—wasn't wrong. Hypocrite. The accusation sank under her skin.

"I left because I *had* to!" she shouted. The wind responded immediately, rustling the trees above them with a force that startled the birds into flight. "I needed something else. I couldn't breathe here anymore. You don't get to act like I was just skipping town for fun."

"No," Lumi said, eyes glassy with unshed tears. "You left because it was easier than staying. Easier than asking for help. Easier than trusting anyone not to disappoint you. That's what hurts, Cora. You just...vanished. Like we, me and your mom, didn't matter."

Cora stared at her, stunned by the truth in that last line. Lumi's voice broke on the last word—not out of anger now, but heartbreak. And beneath all her defenses, Cora felt it. That slow crescendo of guilt.

A few of the other park-goers shifted uncomfortably, glancing their way. A man tugged his child off the slide, his eyes squinting as if trying to figure out what felt *off*. Another parent cast a quiet warding spell with a flick of her fingers, subtle but unmistakable.

"I know I messed up," Cora whispered, voice trembling now. "But it wasn't just me running from you. I was running from everything. Everything I thought I was supposed to be. Every way I kept failing."

Lumi's eyes widened slightly, but she didn't say anything. She waited.

And Cora's chest cracked open.

"Avery cheated on me."

Lumi's mouth parted in shock, but no sound came. Her shoulders fell slightly, like someone had popped the balloon of her anger all at once.

"I caught her," Cora went on, her voice rough, like it had scraped its way up from somewhere deep. "With someone else. I broke it off but still stayed in the city, pretending it didn't break me. But I was lying to myself, to everyone. My writing stopped. My magic got weird. I—I couldn't sleep. I kept shrinking, trying to take up less space."

She finally looked at Lumi, tears brimming now, but unshed. "So yeah. I left. Because staying made me feel like I didn't exist anymore. And I came back because I didn't know who else would even *see* me."

Lumi's own tears finally spilled, and she wiped at them with her sleeve. Lumi let out a slow, shuddering breath. Then another. On the third, her posture eased just enough to soften the sharp edge of her disappointment.

"I was mad," Lumi admitted quietly. "Not just because you left. But because you *could*. Because you *did*."

Cora's brows drew together. "Lumi..."

"I know Jax isn't..." Lumi hesitated, then pushed through. "It's like... every time I needed something real—support, presence, literally just showing up, he wasn't there. You know that. You've seen it. And I've made excuses for him for years. I guess I was angry that you chose yourself when I haven't figured out how to do that yet."

Cora swallowed hard, flashes of memory surfacing—Lumi brushing off the missed calls, the canceled plans, her too-light tone when she said *"He's just swamped. You know how work gets."* The way her voice would get brittle after, like she was trying not to care.

"I remember," Cora said gently. "I remember every time you tried to laugh it off and every time I wanted to say something but didn't know how. You don't have to prove anything by staying if it's not giving back to you" Then she smiled. "What is it you've told me? You deserve more than just the pieces he has left over."

Lumi looked down, her fingers twisting the hem of her sleeve. "I don't even know what it looks like to leave."

"You don't have to know yet," Cora said. "Just ask the question. Then ask yourself what you need and if that includes him in the picture."

Lumi looked up, meeting Cora's eyes, a flicker of something fragile and hopeful there. "It's just hard," she admitted softly. "To even imagine a different kind of life when you're used to making do with less."

Cora nodded slowly. "Trust me, I unfortunately know. But sometimes, the hardest part is giving yourself the chance to believe you deserve better. You're not alone in this."

Cora looked down at her hands, fingers sparking briefly with leftover energy—harmless, now—but the reminder of it made her close her fists again, tucking them into her sleeves.

Lumi stepped forward and touched Cora's shoulder. "You've got love here. Me. Your mom." She paused, then added, slyly, "Theo."

Cora groaned, dragging a hand over her face. "I don't even know how to look him in the eye. What if I mess it up like I always do?"

"Stop lumping him in with people who hurt you. You didn't mess up because you felt something. You left Avery because she betrayed you. That's not the same as being scared."

Cora blinked, absorbing that like it was news. Painful, but... true.

Maybe she didn't have to be fine to move forward. Maybe it was okay to be messy, to grieve, to love in pieces. She wasn't the same person who left this town, and that could be a good thing.

"So... we'll be okay?" she asked, cautiously.

Lumi smiled, wiping beneath one eye. "As soon as you text Theo to talk."

Chapter 27

The sun had dipped lower by the time Cora made it home. Her boots thudded softly against the tile as she stepped through the door, the house still and quiet around her. The kind of silence she used to crave. She tossed her keys into the ceramic bowl near the counter, but missed. They clattered to the floor. She didn't even flinch.

She exhaled slowly, resting her palms on the cool edge of the kitchen counter. Her magic, which had been pulsing under her skin all day, felt less like it was in control now. Less like it was one sharp thought away from breaking something.

She flexed her fingers, watching tiny flickers of light shimmer between them. Not wild, not reactive. Just there.

You can't keep pretending nothing's wrong, she thought. *Not with your magic. Not with your heart.*

A month ago, she would've buried this moment in busywork. Cleaned her whole space. Organized her books by theme and emotional damage. Anything to avoid feeling. But Lumi's words echoed still, sharp but honest and weeks in the making. Now that the fire between them had cooled, Cora could finally hear what she'd buried.

You can't heal if you're still pretending you're not broken.

She closed her eyes and let herself feel the ache in her chest. Not run from it. Not try to cast it out like a bad spell. Just *feel* it.

Hurrying to her room, she searched for her old grimoire in her closet—the one that had gathered dust at the bottom of a trunk beneath winter sweaters and unopened notebooks. The leather was cracked, familiar beneath her fingertips. She flipped through the pages slowly, passing old scribbled charms, childhood doodles, and tiny pressed flowers.

And then she found it, a ritual of anchoring. Something her mom had taught her when she was thirteen and overwhelmed by a school dance and a growth spurt that made her trip over everything—including her own magic. It wasn't dramatic, but a way to return to yourself. A spell written not with fancy incantations but intention.

She lit a candle, scent of lavender and thyme, before drawing a circle with salt around her and sitting cross-legged in the middle. Then, she placed her hands over her heart and closed her eyes.

"I am here," Cora whispered. "I am safe. I am not what I lost. I am still whole."

The wind didn't stir. The lights didn't flicker. Nothing exploded or caught fire. But her breath steadied. And her magic hummed gently beneath her skin—responsive, not raging. She opened her eyes and found herself smiling, just a little. It wasn't a grand epiphany. It didn't fix everything. But it was a beginning, a much steadier beginning she should've started on the solstice.

She leaned back on her palms, watching the candle flicker. She'd start small; back to basics. A little grounding every day. Journaling. Checking in. Tarot pulls.

She could finally stop running from the version of herself who needed healing, and start walking toward her instead.

Chapter 28

C ora sat on her bed, fingers nervously tracing patterns on her comforter as she heard her mom shuffling down the hallway. Lumi had been right—she had a lot of apologies to make. Theo wasn't the only one she owed an explanation to. With a mental pep talk, she stood and made her way down the hall. Her slippers scuffed against the floor as she approached her mother's room, where the woman disappeared into a pile of freshly folded linens.

"Mom?" Cora ventured cautiously. "Can we talk?"

Nicole paused, linen in hand. She didn't say anything at first, just slowly lowered the stack onto the bed and sat beside it, smoothing a wrinkle that wasn't there. She angled toward Cora, a look of knowing in her eyes as she readied herself for something heavy.

Cora sat too, tucking her legs under her and fiddling with the edge of the worn plush blanket. "I've been thinking," she started, voice hesitant, "about when I left. And about Dad. I—I need to know. Did it hurt you? When I moved away?"

She waited, eyes locked on her mother, every second of silence stretching out like a rubber band pulled to its breaking point. Finally, Nicole's gaze softened, drifting over to the window where a sliver of light from the crescent moon filtered in.

"I won't lie and say it didn't," Nicole admitted quietly. "That year... everything changed. And losing your father... it was like someone had knocked the world off its axis."

Cora bit the inside of her cheek. Of course it hurt. She'd known. She'd just been too full of her own grief to look past it.

"I thought leaving for grad school would help me get out of that grief spiral," she murmured. "I needed something new. Somewhere that didn't look like... him. But I see now it also meant I left *you*. And I didn't come back. Not really."

Nicole's hand found hers, warm and grounding. "I missed you. Every day. But your dad and I—we wanted you to live. To grow. Even if it meant doing it without us for a while."

Cora's throat tightened. The knot that had lodged itself in her chest for so long felt heavier now, but it was finally loosening. She had always thought of herself as the one carrying the heaviest burden, her grief the loudest, but now she saw something else—her mom's quiet struggle, the way she'd been left to carry on without her, too. *I didn't realize what I took from her. From both of us.* Cora blinked rapidly, trying to push back the rising wave of guilt, but it was no use. The truth had settled in, sharp and undeniable. She had left to escape, but in doing so, she'd left her own mother behind to deal with it alone.

"I didn't mean to run. But I was so afraid of being here—of being reminded. And when Avery and I got serious, and she didn't want to come visit... I let that be an excuse to stay gone."

Nicole's brows lifted slightly, but her tone was measured. "That woman did a number on you."

Cora let out a short, bitter laugh. "Yeah. She did."

"I never told you this before, but I didn't like the way you shrank yourself around her. Especially your magic. She made you quiet about it. Smaller. And you let her."

Cora winced. She hated hearing it, but she needed to. "I didn't want her to leave me. So I let pieces of myself go instead. I thought that was love. Turns out, it was just fear dressed up in nice dinners and vacation plans."

Nicole's words were so painfully similar to Lumi's, and Cora felt a flush rise up her neck. She wanted to look away, to hide from the truth, but she forced herself to stay present. *Don't run, Cora. You can't keep hiding.*

"While we're at it," Cora added, a touch accusatory, "how come you never told me Theo came back? You knew how much he meant to me."

Nicole tugged on Cora's ear, hard enough to make her hiss in protest. "You had Avery. I figured it was better to let you focus on building something new."

"I could have reached out," Cora argued, rubbing her ear once Nicole released it. "Maybe if I'd known, I wouldn't have gone so all-in with someone who barely knew me."

Nicole sighed, smoothing out Cora's hair with an affection that melted something hard inside her. "You think knowing Theo was back would've stopped you from following your pattern?"

Cora hesitated, eyes focused on the threadbare carpet. "I don't know. Maybe it would've reminded me who I was."

"I was scared, too. Scared that reconnecting with Theo would only reopen wounds you were barely holding closed. But I see now I took that choice from you."

They sat like that for a moment, still and quiet, the past finally exhaled between them. Then Nicole nudged her.

"You know," she said casually, "that young man still looks at you like his star."

Cora jerked up, heart skipping a beat at the thought of Theo. The thought of being seen, of being *looked at* with that kind of intensity, sent an unexpected flush creeping up her neck. *Stop it, don't even—why is she saying this now?* "Oh no. Don't start."

"I'm just saying. He's tall, gentle, reads books without being told to, and smells like cinnamon and intellect."

"Mom!" Cora shrieked, clutching a pillow to her chest. "You cannot talk about him like that!"

"Why not? I've been mentally planning your wedding since you were nine."

Cora groaned, flopping back onto the bed, her face buried in the pillow. It'd been ages since she felt this embarrassed.

Nicole arched a brow. "And yet, here we are. So if I told you to go kiss that man, would you?"

Cora hesitated, suddenly serious. "And what if I told *you* I panicked after the first kiss. I wanted to stay in that moment forever, and it scared the hell out of me so I ran. But now I don't want to run anymore. Yay?"

The silence stretched on for three beats, and when Cora peeked up at her mother shyly she was met with a blank but rapidly blinking expression. Then, with no warning, she stood, fetched a dry washcloth, and began swatting Cora with it like she was shooing a fly.

"Hey!" Cora yelped, batting her away with a laugh.

"Go get him!" Nicole declared between soft thwaps. "You hear me? If you don't, I will."

"Okay, okay!" Cora doubled over, laughing and dodging the gentle assault. "I'll go! Just stop hitting me with your laundry!"

"Good. Now go wash your face and pull yourself together. It's late, but it's not too late to make things right."

Cora paused for a moment, the words sinking in. *Is it too late?* Her heart beat a little faster at the thought of seeing Theo, but this time it felt different. She wasn't running.

"You're right," she muttered to herself, already heading toward the bathroom. "It's never too late."

Chapter 29

S he didn't know where he lived.

Cora stood outside for all of five minutes, letting the frigid night air brush against her shocked skin, before returning inside in defeat. She hadn't exactly thought this through, had she? All this time she'd spent with him, and she never even asked where he lived now. This was worse than when she initially forgot to ask for his number.

As she leaned against the door, phone in hand, her finger hovered over the screen, her mind racing through every possibility. She'd promised herself she wouldn't run. She couldn't keep pretending she didn't know what was right in front of her. But now, standing here with no real plan, no address, no indication of where to find him, she felt uncertainty wash over her.

That old fear crept back. What if he didn't want to see her? She didn't exactly end their last encounter on a good note, practically throwing his confession back in his face. He said he'd wait for her, but would he? It'd only been a few days, but maybe that was enough for him to cool down and realize it wasn't worth the drama.

She bit her lip and tried to suppress the flutter of panic that rose in her chest. She'd known his favorite places—the coffee shop by the lake, the record store that smelled like cedar and vinyl, his own bookstore—but she had never been inside his world, never stepped into the life he'd built when she wasn't around.

Nicole found her, giving her another few thwacks before telling her to go to bed and text him in the morning to meet. She returned to her room like she'd been punished, dragging her feet the whole way before falling face first into her bed.

Even with her magic no longer fraying at the edges, sleep was a lost cause. She lay in bed, the room dim and still, staring at the ceiling wishing it could give her answers. Every time her eyes drifted closed, the dream she'd long forgotten returned—Avery's mocking smile, that careless arm draped around someone else. Cora's breath would hitch and she'd jolt upright, the sheets tangled around her like seaweed.

By the third time, her nightstand lamp rattled. A hairline crack ran down her old ceramic mug, and a flickering bulb finally gave out with a sigh.

"Okay," she muttered, blinking back tears. "That's enough moping."

Her hand moved before her brain did, fumbling for her phone in the sheets. She stared at his contact like it might bite her. Then, she hit call.

It rang three times before his voice came through, low and rough from sleep.

"Hello?"

She panicked. Froze.

"Hello?" he said again, more alert now, and maybe a little annoyed.

"Hi." Her voice was a whisper, smaller than she wanted it to be.

"Cordelia?"

"Don't make it weird," she said, already curling in on herself with the blanket. "Sorry I woke you."

"You didn't. Couldn't sleep. I'm halfway through that mystery series you hate."

She rolled her eyes. "You mean the one where the cat solves all the crimes and no one questions it?"

"Exactly. Masterpiece."

She breathed out a soft laugh. Classic Theo. They both knew he was lying.

"You okay?" he asked.

There was space in the question—room to be honest or to lie. She chose honesty.

"Getting there."

A beat. Then he said, gently, "I'm glad you called."

It would've been easy to end the conversation there, to let it fade into awkward silence and sleep. But she couldn't do that anymore. All her confessions and heart-to-hearts and magic practice would be for nothing. She was done waiting for permission to feel better. Done treating her fear like it had final say.

"I missed your voice. Missed *you*."

When the knock came ten minutes later, light and familiar, she was already at the door.

Theo stood there in his puffer coat, hood up, a mismatched pair of socks shoved into old sneakers like he'd left in a hurry. His breath clouded in the night air.

"You came."

"You called," he replied, as if that explained everything. Maybe it did.

She stepped into him without thinking, her arms circling his waist, her face pressed against his chest. The tears came—not desperate or wild, but steady, quiet. The kind of tears that slipped out when the weight of everything she'd been holding in finally found its release.

Theo didn't say anything. He didn't need to. His arms wrapped around her instinctively, pulling her close as she trembled against him, her breath hitching every now and then. The familiar scent of his cologne—a mix of pine and rain—grounded her, a reminder that she wasn't alone in this moment. He shifted them gently, guiding her through the doorway and into the quieter space of the living room.

She didn't know how long she stood there, her body pressed against his, her head tucked beneath his chin as she let the tears fall. Her hands clutched the fabric of his shirt, holding on as if he might disappear if she let go. His heartbeat thudded steadily beneath her ear, and it was a strange comfort, steady in a way her own emotions weren't.

Theo's fingers stroked up and down her back, slow and methodical. She could feel the heat of his body through the fabric of their clothes, the way he was grounding her, keeping her present when all she wanted to do was slip away from the feelings that had been pressing on her chest for too long.

She finally pulled back, just enough to look up at him, her face flushed with emotion, her tears leaving tracks down her cheeks. "I—I'm sorry," she whispered, her voice raw but steady. She reached up to wipe her face, embarrassed by the vulnerability of it all.

"Don't," he said softly, his voice low and sure, the words gentle but firm. He cupped her face with one hand, his thumb brushing over her cheek to catch a stray tear. "You don't have to apologize for this."

Cora shook her head, but her hands were trembling slightly as she lowered them to her lap. "I dreamed about her." Her voice cracked. "Of *them* together ."

He winced. "Dreams do that. Especially the ones that still echo."

"Since when are you poetic?"

"I read books," he mocked, eyes twinkling. "Also, you're not the only one with trauma, genius."

She smirked and elbowed him lightly. "Don't get cocky."

"I would never. You'd hex me."

Cora gave him a sideways glance, teasing flickering in her eyes. "Yeah, that's the least of your problems, dork."

For a long moment, neither of them said anything. They just stood there, her head resting against his chest again, her body slowly, reluctantly relaxing against his. Theo moved slowly, guiding her over to the couch. He sat first, pulling her down beside him, then adjusting her so her head rested on his shoulder, the tears now drying.

Theo eventually broke the silence. "You've been carrying this for a while, huh?"

Cora nodded, her cheek brushing against the fabric of his shirt as she shifted slightly to look up at him. "Apparently, when you keep your feelings pent up for a long time, they can pour out in unexpected ways."

"I'll keep that in mind for my next breakdown."

Another elbow. "You're incorrigible!"

"You like it though."

His voice was light, playful, but there was a sincerity in the way he said it that made her pause for a moment. Cora shifted, turning just enough to look at him fully. Her voice steadied.

"I need to say this, and I don't want to backpedal this time." Her voice was firm, but her heart raced in a way it hadn't in a long time.

He raised his brows, waiting, the slightest curve to his lips like he already knew this conversation was coming but was willing to let her find her own way through it.

"I'm tired of pretending I don't feel something for you," she admitted, her words tumbling out in a quiet rush. "And yeah, it's terrifying. You know how I get. I'm not subtle. I panic. I throw walls up and call it strategy." She gave him a small, wry smile, as if she could almost laugh at herself. "I'm a mess, Theo."

Theo's smile softened, but he didn't look away. "I know." Those damn eyes never left hers.

She felt her stomach twist with nerves, but she pressed on, her breath evening out. "But I don't want to run from this. I think I've done enough running for ten lifetimes. And if I keep holding back, I'll regret it. I already do."

She took another deep breath. This wasn't easy. This wasn't the Cora she used to be—the one who let everything pile up and pretend it wasn't there. No, this was a new Cora, the one who chose honesty over silence. "I have feelings for you," she said again, clearer this time. "Big, inconvenient, maybe slightly explosive feelings."

His gaze never left hers. "Yeah, me too." Then, Theo grinned. "Also, big of you to admit I'm irresistible."

Cora groaned, reaching for the throw pillow behind her and smacking him with it, her cheeks flaming. "Oh my God. Don't do that." She swatted him again, more out of reflex than actual irritation.

He caught it with one hand. "Too late. It's on record."

"I take it back."

"No refunds," he replied with a grin, dimples making an appearance.

She rolled her eyes, but her smile gave her away. And when she leaned in—forehead pressed to his, hand slipping into his without hesitation—there was no panic. Just warmth. Just Cora, choosing something good.

She looked up at him. "You're kind of ruining all my excuses."

Theo gave a half-smile. "Happy to be a menace."

"I mean it. Past Cora had this whole script, you know? About why this couldn't happen. About timing, and baggage, and you deserving better, and—"

He cut her off gently. "I don't need perfect timing. I just need honesty."

She swallowed, blinking fast. "Even if it's messy?"

"Especially if it's messy."

That undid something inside her. The grief was still there, the confusion too, but now it had somewhere to go. Somewhere safe.

She exhaled slowly, a laugh caught in the end of it. "So this is what it's like? Not running?"

"Yeah. Weird, right?"

"Weird," she agreed. "But not bad."

Cora stirred against him sometime later, warm and groggy beneath the blanket he'd pulled over them. The living room was quiet, the only sound was the faint hum of the refrigerator and the soft rhythm of his heartbeat beneath her ear.

She felt him shift, just slightly, like he'd been waiting for her to wake up.

"You nodded off for a bit," he murmured, his voice low and close to her temple.

She made a sound halfway between a groan and a sigh. "Was I drooling?"

"Only a little." She could hear the grin in his voice.

"Liar."

They sat like that for a moment longer, until Cora felt the tension in his chest. Subtle, but there.

She pulled back enough to look up at him, eyes narrowed. "You're thinking about something."

Theo hesitated, then exhaled. "I checked the numbers. From the fundraiser."

Her stomach clenched a little, daring to have hope that everything turned out the way he wanted. They'd worked so hard—*he'd* worked so hard—that there needed to be good news at the end of it all.

"And?" she asked softly.

He rubbed at the back of his neck. "We didn't quite make it."

Cora's heart dropped. *Crap.* What was he going to do now? She desperately hoped he wasn't going to give up, and mentally prepared a quick pep talk for him before she caught his small smile.

"But it's okay. Really." He looked at her then, steady and sure in a way that surprised her. "We got close. Closer than I ever thought we would. And I'm not panicking. Not this time."

She blinked. "You're not?"

Theo shook his head, the corner of his mouth twitching. "It's weird. A few months ago I would've taken this as proof that the whole thing was doomed. But now?" He paused, then reached for her hand, lacing their fingers together. "Now it just feels like a setback. Not the end."

Thank goddess, she thought, still watching his face for any signs of pretending. She didn't catch any, and his voice held more conviction than weeks ago when she confronted him about the bills.

He gave a small, almost sheepish smile. "People showed up, Cordelia. For this place. For me. You did. I don't think I've ever let myself believe in that before."

Her throat tightened, but she smiled through it. "Maybe because you've never had someone annoy you into hope before."

"Yeah, loser. Maybe that's it."

Cora leaned into him again, resting her head against his chest. His arm came around her instinctively, pulling her close. There was still a gap to close, still more work ahead. But for now, neither of them felt like they were bracing for something to fall apart.

Theo's fingers brushed hers. "Hope's a weird feeling."

"Better than dread," she whispered.

He kissed the top of her head, soft and sure. "Yeah. Way better."

Chapter 30

The closet groaned when Cora yanked the door open, a rainbow of dresses swaying inside like they were bracing for judgment. She stood in front of them in leggings and an oversized sweatshirt, arms crossed, brow furrowed.

"Okay, this is war," she muttered.

Lumi appeared in the doorway with a plastic cup full of sparkling cider and a glittery smirk. "You know, most people just pick something. You're treating this like a prophecy."

Cora shot her a look but didn't argue. "I'm picking for *Theo*."

That earned a raised eyebrow, but Lumi just leaned against the doorframe ready to settle in to watch a live drama. "Oh, we're dressing for *Theo*, are we? Well, now it's serious."

"I'm not dressing for *him*," Cora clarified, cheeks already burning. "I mean, not *just* for him. It's a party. There will be people. And photos. And alcohol. And judgment."

"Uh-huh," Lumi said, sipping loudly. "And none of that explains why you've been stress-hovering in front of your closet for fifteen minutes."

Cora didn't answer. Her fingers twitched at her sides, the memory of Theo's voice curling in her mind.

"There's a thing at Briar & Barrel on New Year's. Kind of a town tradition. You know, one of those 'drink cider and pretend you're fine about the passage of time' things."

"A party?" she'd asked, skeptical.

"More like cozy chaos. Everyone shows up in layers and sequins. I think the mayor wears antlers."

He'd grinned, then hesitated, which was rare for him. "You could come. With me. If you want. No pressure. I just figured it might be less weird if we were both pretending not to be weird together."

And somehow, that had felt safer than a grand invitation. That was Theo, always giving her space to say no, while somehow making her want to say yes. And she *had* said yes.

Now, standing in front of a closet full of dresses she hadn't worn since before the grief, before Seattle, before her life had narrowed into grief and guilt and routines—she realized she wasn't just picking a dress.

She was picking a version of herself.

Lumi's voice cut through her spiral. "If you use your magic, I'm sure one of them will at least give you a little wave." Cora pouted, but the remark gave her an idea. She raised her hand slowly, fingers splayed. One by one, the dresses began to lift from the rack and floated in front of her, ready for her orders.

Lumi blinked, clearly impressed. "Well, damn. You enchanted your wardrobe."

"I needed options," Cora said, though her voice had a flicker of nerves.

"Hey." Lumi stepped closer, her expression softening beneath the usual sass. "You're nervous."

Cora hesitated. "Yeah. A little."

She wasn't sure if she meant the dress, the party, or the idea of intentionally being sexy in front of Theo.

Lumi gave a knowing smile, one hand finding Cora's shoulder. "Stop trying to predict the ending. Just go! Be present! Be sparkly! You asked the right gal to come over. Let's get you *sexified* for the night!"

Lumi dove into the floating lineup, pulling out dresses Cora had buried in the back. A sleek red dress with a daring neckline she'd never had the guts to wear, a silver sequined number that sparkled like a disco ball, and a classic little black dress that hadn't seen daylight in four years. For a split second, Cora wondered if her butt could even still fit in it.

She tried the silver sequin dress first, wrapping it around her. It zipped closed and left Cora blinking at the mirror. Too much. It was giving disco ball.

"Nope," they said in unison.

The dress undid itself and floated back. Another stepped forward—classic black, sleek and familiar. It formed to her like armor, the neckline sharp, the silhouette striking. But her mouth twisted as she looked at herself.

"Too safe," she murmured. With a soft flick of her wrist, it dissolved into a shimmer of shadow and hung itself up again.

Then came the emerald velvet.

"What about this one?" Lumi asked, picking up the deep emerald velvet dress. It had a tastefully low neckline that draped off the shoulders and would *definitely* show off her legs. "Now *this* will make Theo forget how to breathe."

Cora bit her lip, eyeing the dress with some serious doubt, but she couldn't ignore how it seemed to call her name. "But it's a lot, isn't it?"

"It's New Year's Eve. 'A lot' is the point," Lumi insisted, waggling her eyebrows for emphasis. "You want him to *see* you. Let this dress help."

Cora reached for it, and the dress reached back. The fabric wrapped around her with a hum, magic responding to her pulse. It adjusted itself as if it knew her—the neckline dipping just enough, the skirt hugging and then flowing, the off-the-shoulder sleeves clinging like ivy.

When she looked in the mirror, she didn't see someone hoping to be enough. She saw someone who already was.

Lumi whistled. "Theo's going to spontaneously combust."

Cora didn't answer right away. Her fingers moved over the velvet, then up to her shell necklace. Her thoughts immediately went to the night of the fairy tale event, the glances Theo threw her way, what he'd said. *"I've loved you since forever."* No fireworks, no performance, like it was the most natural truth in the world.

And somehow, looking at herself now, she could believe it.

Lumi stepped behind her, gently finger combing through her hair and pulling her thick curls into a high ponytail, letting a few strands fall free around her face. She then searched for more accessories, finding a tiny gold star and clipped it into place.

"Perfect," Lumi whispered.

Cora smiled faintly. "He used to chase me with frogs."

"And now he chases you with emotional intimacy. Glow up."

They laughed, and ease nestled its way back into Cora. She stepped back from the mirror, her whole stance different than when she first came home—calm, grounded, ready.

"No earrings," Lumi decided, rummaging. "We're going full celestial." She handed Cora a pair of delicate gold stars and a thick cuff bracelet.

Cora sat on the edge of the bed, smoothing the dress carefully. "Wish you were coming."

Lumi dropped down beside her. "Me too. I'd be your chaotic cheerleader." Her smile dimmed a bit. "I should've pushed harder. Back when Avery was, you know... dimming your light."

Cora looked down, turning the cuff on her wrist. "I let it happen."

She'd known it deep down—how, slowly, Avery chipped at her edges, convinced her to take up less space. But she'd let it. Until now.

"Let's call it character development," she said, her voice steadier. "I'm done hiding."

Lumi beamed. "Hell yes. And if you even *think* about shrinking yourself again, I'll glitter bomb your closet so that everything turns neon pink." Then she perked up. "Ooh! Pull a tarot card for the night."

Cora raised an eyebrow, considering the suggestion. "I usually avoid pulling before big events. Don't wanna psych myself out."

"But this is for *empowerment*," Lumi insisted dramatically, flopping back on the bed. "Let the cards hype you up!"

Cora sighed, but she was already walking over. "Fine. One card. No chaos, universe. Please."

She carefully stood up and walked to her bedside table, retrieving her tarot deck from the shelf. With a deep breath, she sat back down, shuffling the cards with practiced hands. Lumi sat perfectly still, eyes wide with anticipation.

"Okay, cards," Cora began. "I'm a bit nervous about tonight and could use some insight."

"Remember," Lumi interrupted with encouragement. "This is about empowerment!"

Cora chuckled. "Yes, empowerment. If you could lend me any wisdom and guidance for tonight, oh cards, oh Goddess, oh universe, that would be greatly appreciated."

The cards were laid out on her bed and Cora drew one card, flipping it over with a flourish. Her heart sank. There it was—The Tower.

"Oh!" Lumi's enthusiasm fizzled as she leaned in to examine the card. "Well, that's... interesting."

"Interesting?" Cora echoed, her brow furrowing as she glared at the card. The Tower depicted a shadowy silhouette of a tower being struck by lightning, flames bursting out of every window and figures tumbling down. "It's literal flaming destruction!"

"It's *transformational flaming destruction.*"

"I just wanted to kiss my almost-boyfriend and not emotionally combust tonight," Cora whined, collapsing onto her pillow, careful not to wrinkle her dress.

"Now, now, Cora, remember, it can also symbolize change," Lumi tried to salvage the situation. "You know. Big shifts. Old patterns crumbling to make room for something better"

"Wasn't the fiasco at the fairy tale event enough? Arguing with you enough?"

Lumi winced. "Fair point," she conceded, then brightened. "What if we see this as a *good* sign? The Tower can represent breaking down the old to make way for the new.

Maybe something unexpected will happen that'll completely turn your night around!"

Cora tapped her fingers against her leg, mulling it over. She was thankful Lumi remembered the meanings of the Major Arcana for situations like this, a.k.a., talking her down. Still, Cora gave her a flat look. "So you're saying I should expect the night to fall apart?"

"I'm saying something unexpected might shift everything—in a good way!" Lumi nudged her. "Embrace the chaos. This could be your cosmic glow up moment."

Cora tapped her fingers against her leg, chewing it over. "So I'm burning down my emotional baggage tower?"

"Exactly! Burn it down, queen."

Cora sighed, but there was laughter in it now. She stood, smoothing her dress one last time. "Okay. I'll embrace the chaos." She looked at herself again in the mirror, this time ready.

"Let's go burn this Tower down."

Chapter 31

Cora clutched the strap of her purse tightly, her other hand brushing against the smooth fabric of her dress. The bar party was already in full motion at her arrival. Music thumped through the floorboards, elegant enough for champagne, loud enough for bad decisions. Everyone sparkled—literally and magically. It was New

Year's Eve, after all. Glamour spells were as common as heels and highlighter.

When Theo met her at the door, he stared at her for a solid minute, mouth hanging open slightly. Which, honestly, felt fair.

The emerald gown shimmered as she moved, catching the light with every breath. Theo, in a sleek dark green suit and his signature smile, kept looking at her like she might float away if he blinked.

"Cordelia. You look..." he'd said, struggling. "I mean. You always look—okay, I'm trying not to be weird, but I'm failing spectacularly."

"Start over," she teased, cheeks already warm.

He reached for her hand and kissed it. "You look like every wish I've ever made finally answered."

Which should've been corny, but somehow wasn't.

Inside, Theo stayed close, his arm around her waist like muscle memory. They moved through the party together, collecting compliments, dodging enchanted cocktails, and making Cora feel—for the first time in a long time—*seen*. She didn't shrink. Not once.

He disappeared briefly to grab drinks, leaving her near the dance floor. Someone tripped near the photobooth, sending foam swords and tiaras flying in all directions. Cora laughed, catching a pair of heart-shaped glasses mid-air and setting them back on the table. The magic in the air made everything feel light, alive.

Then her gaze swept the crowd again and she froze. *What the **hell**?*

Avery.

She was standing just a few tables away, dressed in a chic crimson jumper that clung in all the ways Cora used to pretend not to notice. Her auburn waves were artfully loose. And beside her, like an aftershock, stood the woman she'd cheated with.

Cora's heart tripped, her breath catching in her throat. Her magic stirred, hot and uninvited, fluttering in warning. She took a breath to ground herself. Then another. Then another. But they started coming out in spurts, and she stopped before she began hyperventilating.

Theo returned with two drinks in hand and immediately caught the intensity in her posture. "What's wrong?"

She didn't answer at first. Her mouth felt dry. She didn't want to say it out loud; it would make it real. "That's... Avery."

Theo's eyes sharpened as he followed her gaze. "Do you want me to cause a scene? I can spill this with stunning dramatic flair."

Cora almost smiled. "Tempting."

Avery spotted her. And just like that, she was moving toward them, dragging the other woman along. She wore that polished but unsure smile. It was the same one she'd used the night she'd told Cora she needed "space." The same one that had followed I love yous with caveats.

"Cordelia!" Avery approached like they were old friends meeting in the produce aisle, not two people separated by betrayal and silence. Cora wished she could rip her name from her mouth. "Wow. You look..."

"Like someone who dodged a bullet?" Cora offered.

Avery blinked. "Radiant, actually."

"I know. Try not to be surprised." Cora crossed her arms. "What are you doing here?"

Was she really holding it together? Cora was impressed with her reactions so far. Anger was way better than bursting into tears.

"We were visiting friends in Philadelphia," Avery responded, gesturing vaguely. "Valley Creek Hollow just... came to mind."

Came to mind? Cora thought bitterly. "I practically begged you to visit with me and you actively refused."

Did she say that part out loud? Well, too late to take it back now.

Avery ignored it, gesturing to the woman beside her. "This is Sarah." Sarah smiled—awkward, polite, pretty. Cora's heart clenched once, then iced over.

"Nice to meet you," Cora noted, voice smooth and biting. "Though, it's hard to forget someone who helped wreck your engagement."

Sarah's smile faltered. Avery glanced between them, searching for some neutral ground.

"I didn't expect to see you tonight," she tried again.

"I live here," Cora said flatly. "Unlike you. This is my *home.*"

The word tasted strange. She'd been trying it on for weeks now, but this was the first time she'd said it aloud without question.

Avery bristled. "You didn't exactly reach out."

"I made the mistake of prioritizing you once. That won't happen again."

The silence between them stretched, brittle and sharp. She felt Theo by her side, brushing his hand against her, and she took it. Avery's eyes darted down to them and she frowned. The action made Cora laugh inside.

Avery's voice dropped lower. "So you're with him now?" She nodded toward Theo, her eyes flickering. "Did I traumatize you so much you ran to men?"

Theo stepped forward slightly, but Cora squeezed his hand and pulled him back slightly. At his glance she shook her head.

"What about you? This is clearly a witch party and yet here you are. Uninvited and unwanted."

That made her flinch back, and Cora took sick satisfaction in it. She didn't get to walk back into her life, into her *home*, and cause problems.

"You think your words still have that kind of power?" she asked.

"I didn't expect you to be so... angry," Avery said, almost like a complaint.

"Of course you didn't," Cora huffed, exasperated. "You thought I'd disappear like before. But I'm not running this time."

Avery opened her mouth, but Cora beat her to it. "I told you, 'I hope you and your mistake are happy together.'

Looks like you actually listened. Looks like it's the only thing that ever stuck with you."

Avery flinched. Sarah shrank slightly behind her, visibly regretting every second of this detour. She thought she might feel bad that the woman was caught in the crossfire. She didn't.

Cora took a slow step forward, reclaiming every moment she made herself small for the woman she used to know. She channeled each moment that happened, each moment she shrank into herself, each time her fingers itched to use the magic she stifled, and stood tall.

"This reunion?" she said coolly. "Over."

The name *Avery* lingered in the air like a curse, final and clean. Avery blinked, most likely wanting to say more, but for once, she didn't. She turned and left, Sarah trailing behind her with one last apologetic glance.

And just like that, the room seemed to breathe again. All the sounds of the party re-entered her ears. Cora realized she was trembling slightly, her magic vibrating just beneath her skin. She exhaled slowly, like she'd been holding her breath for years.

Theo was quiet for a beat. "You okay?"

"No," Cora admitted honestly. Was telling off your ex supposed to feel so exhausting? "But I'm not broken, either."

"You want to leave?"

She hesitated, then shook her head. "No. Shouldn't let it ruin the night, right?"

He gave a relieved smile. "Damn right."

They drifted to a quieter corner, near the tall windows of the bar, where the town lights stretched like constellations at their feet. The countdown began, a thunderous chorus rolling through the room.

Ten. Nine. Eight—

Cora turned to him.

Seven. Six—

"Thank you," she said softly. "For not trying to save me."

"Hey," he said, brushing a curl from her face. "You were never the one who needed saving."

Three. Two. One.

The room exploded in cheers.

Cora and Theo bumped fists—because they were still them—and then he leaned in, eyes hopeful, lips barely an inch away.

"Happy New Year, Cordelia. Can we...?"

She smiled, heart thrumming, like a spell just cast.

"Yeah. We can."

The kiss was warm and real and just a little clumsy from smiling—and when it landed, she didn't feel triumphant or vindicated.

She felt free.

Chapter 32

The morning had the audacity to be bright and loud.

Sunlight pierced through Cora's room, leading her to groan and bury her face deeper into the pillow. Her velvet dress from the night before lay in a puddle of glamour and regret at the foot of the bed, glitter clinging to it like stubborn memories. Her bonnet lay in a poor heap next to her instead of on her head where it belonged, alerting her to the fitful night she must've had.

She blinked slowly. Her head throbbed. Her emotions were still doing cartwheels. But she was alive. Barely.

A soft knock came at the door, followed by Lumi's voice, "I come bearing electrolytes."

"Kill me," Cora croaked.

"Nope. You're far too hot in that dramatic hangover chic way. Now get up, we're doing greasy carbs and bottomless coffee therapy. Theo is already downstairs."

Twenty minutes later, she found herself sandwiched in a booth at the Valley Creek Hollow Diner, wrapped in Theo's hoodie and wearing the sunglasses he'd magicked to block out "unwanted drama and sunlight." The booth smelled like butter and bacon and syrup and salvation. Her mind still buzzed with thoughts of Avery, the confrontation, and the way the entire night had veered off course. That Tower card took things way too seriously.

"And then what?" Lumi asked, wide-eyed, chin in her hand, as Theo finished describing the Tower moment as he finished half a plate of pancakes.

"She actually said 'what are you doing here,' like *I* was the surprise." Cora rolled her eyes, voice still tinged with disbelief. "I live here! I *grew up* here! My name is literally on the mailbox."

Theo snorted into his coffee. "Honestly, you handled it way better than I would've. I was about ten seconds from turning Avery into a decorative potted plant."

"Me drinking five appletinis after that is 'handling it better'?"

"Yes," Theo chirped.

Lumi leaned back, her fork hovering over a pile of scrambled eggs. "I can't believe I missed it. That would've fed me emotionally for *months.* You're telling me she showed up—with the girl she cheated on you with—and tried to guilt trip you? The *nerve.*"

"Right?" Cora tried to run a hand through her messy curls, half-flattened from sleep, but they tangled not even halfway through. *Great.* "She acted like I'd ghosted *her.* Like she didn't torch the entire relationship and then hand me the lighter."

"Classic narcissist," Lumi muttered, stabbing a piece of toast with more force than necessary. "So, what did you say? Give me the exact words. I want to tattoo them on my soul."

Cora hesitated, cheeks heating. "I said, 'this reunion? Over.'"

Lumi dropped her fork and clutched her chest, not caring about the volume of her laugh. "Cordelia Sparks. You dramatic little goddess. Did lightning strike behind you? Please tell me lightning struck behind you."

"There was definitely a flicker," Theo offered helpfully. "Also, the bar's wallpaper curled. Like, actual physical damage."

"Ohhh," Lumi groaned. "I love this for you. You finally had your villain origin moment and still came out the hero."

Cora gave a sheepish smile, stirring her coffee. "I don't know. I still feel shaky. Like part of me is waiting for Avery to pop back up and pull the rug out from under me again."

"But this time," Lumi said, pointing her butter knife at her, "you know where the tripwire is. You've got people. You've got magic. And also, you have an unreasonably hot man who wants to kiss your face at every opportunity."

Theo looked smug. "She's not wrong."

Cora glanced between the two of them—Lumi in a sleep-rumpled hoodie with sparkly nails and fierce loyalty,

Theo in his too-big flannel looking at her as he always did—and something in her settled.

She wasn't just surviving anymore. She was healing. Growing. Reclaiming the pieces that Avery tried to erase.

Lumi grinned and clapped her hands. "Okay. So you burned down the Tower. Now what? You gonna build a castle?"

Cora leaned back against the booth cushion, a slow smile spreading across her lips. "No. I think I'll build a greenhouse. Something with roots."

Theo reached under the table, linking their pinkies.

And then, of course, her phone rang, slicing through the pleasant thoughts. The name that flashed on the screen made her pause mid-sip of her coffee.

Alina Dorsey

Cora blinked and excused herself from the booth, stepping outside into the crisp afternoon air. She pressed the phone to her ear. "Hey, Alina."

"Hey, Cora! Hope this isn't a bad time?" Alina's voice was warm, with that slight Seattle polish and a hint of curiosity that always made Cora feel like she was being asked the right question at the right time.

"Not at all," Cora said, leaning back against the painted brick wall. "We just survived a night that could only be described as emotionally catastrophic, so you're actually a welcome change of pace."

Alina chuckled. "Well, I won't pry. I was actually just calling to touch base about Theo's bookstore. It's different, that's for sure. I've been knee-deep in Theo's numbers this morning, and girl, I have questions. Like, has he ever *met* a receipt printer? Or heard of folders?"

"Absolutely not. He thinks a shoebox is a perfectly valid filing system."

"That explains so much," Alina muttered. "I'll spare you the rest, but the good news is, it's fixable. Honestly, I've seen worse. The community fundraiser gave the shop a real cushion. That part? Huge. But he's going to need regular check-ins and a clear plan moving forward—especially if he wants to keep up that momentum."

"He does," Cora confirmed without hesitation. "We all do. It's more than just a shop to him. To everyone here, really. It's one of the magical cornerstones."

Alina hummed thoughtfully. "That's what I've been picking up. I've been here a few months now, and Valley

Creek Hollow has a weird way of pulling you in, doesn't it?"

"You have *no* idea."

"Most magical towns I've worked in? People talk a lot about community, but they don't always *show up* like that. What happened with Theo's shop—that's rare. That's the kind of energy worth protecting."

"You're kind of a softie under all that spreadsheet bravado, huh?" Cora teased.

"Excuse you, I'm a Capricorn. My softness is systematized," Alina replied. "Speaking of which, I'll be sending over a file I named 'The Lovers Reversed' because, frankly, the way Theo treats his ledger is borderline betrayal."

Cora laughed, a full-body kind of laugh. "You have no idea how much the store needs someone like you."

"Well, I'm glad to be part of it. Magical businesses are my thing, but this one? This one's got something different. I can tell there's a lot of heart in it. Between the community showing up and you taking charge of organizing the chaos, it's clear people care."

Cora smiled, the warmth of that recognition settling in her chest. "We do. It felt like... like if we didn't fight to save it, we'd be letting something meaningful through our fingers. But we didn't. We pulled together, and somehow, it worked."

"It's nice when things like that do," Alina replied gently. "Anyway, I'll send over some spreadsheets and projections, but I also wanted to check on *you*. You sounded... emotional, the last time we talked. I know you didn't just call me for bookkeeping help. You were carrying a lot."

Cora winced, remembering contacting Alina in a guilt-fueled panic. "I've had better months."

"Well, for what it's worth, it sounds like you're doing the hard work. And that's always the part that matters most. Showing up. Trying. I've seen a lot of magical folks who burn out because they try to carry everything on their own. You're doing it differently. That's something."

The comfort was unexpected, but oh so needed after the night she had. "Thank you."

"No pressure, but when Theo's ready, I'd love to sit down and talk about a plan for the shop. Maybe something a little longer-term. He seems like he could use some structure, and I think you might need a project that's not quite so emotional."

Cora laughed, sharp and unfiltered. "God, yes. Please. Give me something with clean rows and color-coded tabs."

"Say the word, and I'll make a whole spreadsheet color palette just for you," Alina teased.

"That sounds deeply soothing."

They confirmed a day next week to meet in person at the bookstore, and when the call ended, Cora threw a fist in the air in triumph. She was helpful. She accomplished something. Things were working out.

She stood there for a beat longer, letting the breeze calm her nerves, then glanced back toward the diner window. Theo caught her eye and smiled again.

For once, she let herself believe that she could bloom.

Chapter 33

The afternoon sun painted the streets of the town in yellow hues. Snow from the previous night, which thankfully began to fall once Cora was already in bed, left everything dusted in white. Cora and Theo walked side by side toward her house, the crunch of snow beneath their boots the only sound between them. Now, in the quiet of the day, the events of last night made themselves apparent at the edges of her mind.

She glanced at Theo, his hands stuffed in his pockets, his breath fogging in the cold air. The way he walked, slower than usual, made her feel like she could breathe a little easier. As she'd learned throughout December, there was no need to rush. She was still getting used to that idea; life not being a series of near-emergencies.

"You know," she started, her voice quieter than she'd intended, "I thought the hardest part would be last night, but waking up today...it feels like it all just *settled* into me."

Theo nodded, his eyes meeting hers briefly. "That's a good sign, right?"

"I think so. I feel like I've been holding my breath for months, trying to get through the day without cracking, and last night—everything with Avery—I guess I didn't expect it to hit me like it did."

They continued walking, the silence between them no longer awkward but comfortable. Cora's breath came in little clouds, and for a moment, she felt her mind drift back to Avery, to everything she had tried to avoid thinking about. The way her ex had always lived rent-free in her head, rearranging the furniture and muttering critiques. Even after everything ended.

"I think I hated her more than I realized," Cora admitted, her voice soft like she was still sorting through the feelings. "She... she took up so much space in my head, you know? I kept trying to make myself smaller, just to survive the relationship. Shrink down, let the pieces of her fit into the cracks of my life. But last night? I didn't feel small standing in front of her. I was just *done*."

Theo's steps slowed, and when he spoke, his voice was careful. "That sounds like the bravest thing I've ever heard, Cordelia."

She turned to face him, catching the sincerity in his eyes. The moment stretched, her heart beating a little faster as she let herself feel what he said. Was it brave? Maybe. Or maybe she was just tired. Tired of letting fear narrate her life. "I didn't expect it to feel like this," she admitted. "Like I could actually be okay, maybe even better."

Theo didn't say anything for a moment, just nodded. They kept walking, and he let Cora speak her thoughts and feelings as she processed them in real time.

"I can't believe I let myself be that honest," Cora continued. "But there's this feeling, like I'm not constantly trying

to hide who I am anymore. With you, at least. I think—"
She hesitated, her breath catching, but she pressed on. "I
think I'm finally starting to choose. Instead of running
away from everything. From... *her.*"

Theo stopped walking then, turning to face her completely. His gaze didn't waver, and she noted that same
tenderness in him that he'd always had ever since they
reunited.

She tilted her head to look up at him. "You know, if
you'd told me two months ago that I'd have a meltdown
at a New Year's party, banish my ex, and then end up
eating French toast with you and Lumi in the same twen-
ty-four-hour window, I would've hexed you for even sug-
gesting it."

Theo grinned, the familiar warmth in his smile. "And
now look at you. Emotionally wrecked and well-fed."

"I'm thriving," she said, deadpan. And weirdly, she kind
of meant it.

Theo's hand slipped up to brush a curl from her forehead. "Can I kiss you?"

Cora paused, letting the heat rise to her cold cheeks,
then nodded. "Please."

The kiss was soft, not the kind that ignites fireworks, but the kind that builds something steady. It was warm, slow, safe. When it ended, Cora kept her forehead pressed to his, her smile small but real. Not a performance. Not a shield. Just hers.

"Hey," she whispered, her voice barely above a breath. "I think I want to see where this goes."

Theo's breath hitched just slightly. "Yeah?"

"If you're still up for it."

His hands traced down to hers, entwining their fingers before lifting them to kiss each knuckle. "Oh, I am."

They stood for a few moments despite the cold, oblivious to the world around them. Cora leaned back slightly, her lips still curved in a soft smile she didn't try to hide. For once, she didn't feel like she had to manage the moment—didn't feel the impulse to narrate it in her head or make a joke to deflect sincerity. She finally felt steady in her own skin.

There had been so many times before when the idea of this, of anything real with Theo, felt like a trap door waiting to swing open. She'd kept it at arm's length, told herself she wasn't ready, that she was better on her own, that needing someone meant losing pieces of herself again.

But this didn't feel like losing anything. It felt like gaining room. Like she could still be wholly herself and make space for someone else. She hadn't expected that.

And now, standing here, with his fingers warm around hers and her breath fogging quietly in the cold, she wasn't afraid of what might come next. Not because she was sure of it—but because she wasn't trying to outrun it anymore.

Then, her brain, never one to leave silence untouched, remembered something.

"Oh, by the way," Cora broke the quiet. "I found you an accountant."

Theo's eyes widened, surprise flickering behind his glasses. "An accountant? Did you—did you just magic one up?"

Cora laughed. "No, I didn't *magic* one up, but close. Her name's Alina Dorsey. She moved here from Seattle a few months ago, set up shop above the tailor's. She specializes in magical businesses."

Theo looked at her, blinking slowly, his expression torn. "I'm flattered and alarmed at the same time. But... you actually found someone?"

"Yeah, I think you'll like her," Cora said, pulling out her phone and finding Alina's website before handing it to him. "She's smart, detail-oriented, and she's worked with creative types who'd rather face an angry dragon than look at numbers. I set up a meeting with you for next week."

Theo scrolled through the website, his brow furrowing. "This is... thorough. And she does way more than I've ever put together. She even included a sample monthly report template to buy."

"Told you. She knows her stuff. And I'm serious when I say you need help that doesn't involve you and a shoebox full of receipts."

He met her gaze with a quiet gratitude. "You didn't have to do this."

"I know," she shrugged, brushing another curl from her face. "But I wanted to. I like the idea of this place sticking around. I like the idea of you letting people help. And I think you'll like her. She's got a direct and quirky way of speaking, and you won't have to pretend you understand everything."

Theo's lips curled into a small, thoughtful smile. "You know, I keep wondering when I'm going to wake up and realize this whole fundraiser was a fever dream. Or that Mrs. Averly didn't really walk out of the snow and hand me a bag of miracles."

"It's not a dream, Theo. This is real. People want this place to thrive. You just have to let them help."

They finally reached her house, and Theo paused in front of her, giving her a look that was both playful and sincere. "You keep showing up exactly when I need you."

Cora's smile faltered for a moment, unsure but touched. "Maybe I like showing up. Or maybe I'm just here for the free tea."

"I'm going to start charging you rent if you keep showing up like this."

"Fine, fine," she said, grinning up at him. "You can make it up to me by telling me where you live. I'm still super embarrassed I didn't know this whole time."

Theo raised an eyebrow. "I could just take you there instead."

Oh, he was good.

Cora rolled her eyes, but didn't protest when he reached for her hand again. Some answers, apparently, were better walked toward than spoken.

As they approached the bookstore, a figure caught Cora's eye standing at the door. Wrapped in layers of indigo wool with a lacquered cane hooked over her arm and a small, neatly wrapped box in hand stood Mrs. Pemberly—the town's most reclusive elder witch, looking like a portrait from another time.

Theo's brows rose. "What the—"

Mrs. Pemberly turned sharply as if she'd known they were coming the whole time. "I detest public spectacle," she said crisply—no greeting, no smile. "But I heard about the fundraiser. Thought I'd bring this directly."

She handed Theo the box without ceremony. He opened it, revealing a thick envelope and a note written in looping, elegant script. Cora watched his expression shift—first confusion, then disbelief.

"A donation?" he asked.

Mrs. Pemberly's mouth curved ever so slightly. "Call it an investment. I've seen how you care for this place since Hargrove's retirement. Magic like that doesn't come cheap—or often."

And just like that, she turned and disappeared down the snowy street, cane tapping softly, the ends of her scarf fluttering behind her.

Theo stared at the envelope. "That's more than enough."

Cora touched his arm lightly. "You did it."

He looked up, a flicker of awe still in his expression. "Not alone. You made the event happen *and* got me an accountant. I just kept the lights on."

They stepped inside together, the bookstore quiet and cool in its stillness. Theo set the box on the counter and sat down behind it, the envelope still half-open in his hand. Cora perched on the arm of the nearby chair, watching as he pulled out his laptop and typed in a few numbers, tallying things up.

After a moment, he let out a soft breath. "We were short. Before this."

Cora leaned forward. "But now?"

He nodded slowly, almost in disbelief. "Now we're covered. Not just barely—*covered.*"

Cora's lips parted, surprise blooming into something soft and weightless in her chest.

"I keep wondering when I'm going to wake up and realize this was all a fever dream," Theo said, looking up at her. "Like... she didn't really walk out of the snow and hand me a box full of miracles."

Cora smiled. "It's not a dream. This is real, Theo. People want this place to thrive. You just have to let them help."

He leaned back, his eyes warm. "You're amazing, you know that?"

She shrugged while blushing, brushing a curl behind her ear. "You could stand to say it more."

He rolled his eyes playfully, then shut his laptop. "Alright, let's give you the grand tour of my place."

Cora raised an eyebrow. "Oh, so now you're just going to kidnap me?"

"I'm escorting you," he said, grinning. "Very romantic. Very legal."

Chapter 34

"Cordelia?"

Cora froze mid-step, the name slicing through the evening air like a splinter. Her stomach twisted—low and immediate. Not today. Not *her* again.

She turned slowly, already bracing. Avery sat hunched on a bench near the circle of Logan Square, arms wrapped around herself, sleeves pulled over her hands. Her hair had slipped from its usual curated perfection, curling messily around her jaw. No makeup. Eyes rimmed with exhaustion. She looked deflated. *Good*.

For a long second, neither of them moved. The town square around them buzzed faintly with tourists and locals, Cora, able to tell the difference by the people attempting to cross onto Vine. Couldn't she just get to Lumi in peace? She was so close, so close, to Sabrina's. She wondered if the universe was trying to be poetic, or just cruel.

Avery finally stood, slow and cautious. "Hey."

Cora didn't reply. She wasn't frozen with fear, just tired. It surprised her, how little heat rose in her chest. No flood of panic or shame. Just the cool, still knowledge that she'd already survived the worst part.

"I didn't expect to see you," Avery admitted, glancing around the square. "But... this is your home."

Cora nodded once. "Yeah. It is."

There had been a time when hearing Avery's voice would've unraveled her. When she would've second-guessed every boundary, every truth she'd fought to name. But now, standing here, Cora was rooted. She'd stepped fully into the version of herself who no longer bent to make others more comfortable.

Avery took a tentative step forward. Her voice cracked. "I know I hurt you. I came to say I'm sorry."

"You cheated on me."

Avery flinched. "I know. There's no excuse. I was selfish. Scared."

"You asked me to build a life with you," Cora noted. "And I gave up pieces of myself trying to make that happen."

Cora's words landed like stone. Not cruel. Not cold. Just the truth, finally spoken aloud in full daylight. It didn't feel like a weapon in her mouth anymore. Just a fact. The one that had shaped the last two years of her life.

She'd twisted herself in knots for so long trying to decode Avery's reasons—trying to carry both their hurts, wondering what she'd done wrong. And now, Avery was naming it herself. Finally.

She remembered the nights spent in that apartment in Seattle, editing herself down to the safest version—less stubborn, less magical, less *her*. She'd thought compromise was the cost of love. That being hard to love was her fault.

Avery looked down, her hands clenching the fabric of her sleeves. "I wasn't ready. And instead of admitting that, I blamed you for everything I wasn't." Her voice trembled.

"I was wrong. And I came all the way here, to the home you spoke so fondly of that I couldn't give the time of day, to tell you that."

"There's nothing between me and Sarah," Avery added quickly. "I let you think there was, but it wasn't like that. She helped me after you left. That's all."

There was something fragile in Avery's eyes now—raw, but not performative. Maybe this wasn't about winning Cora back. Maybe it really was just what it looked like—someone trying to pick up shards she'd scattered.

Cora felt a flicker of heat rise at the mention of the other woman. The familiar ache of being compared, replaced, misunderstood. But it didn't stick. Not this time. Instead, her jaw tightened. She felt her magic stir under her skin, wild and unamused, just like it had the night she walked out on Avery. Cora drew in a slow breath and pressed the heat back down. She wasn't going to let it write this scene for her.

"I'm not interested in your damage control," she said, quiet but firm.

Avery nodded slowly, guilt softening the angles of her face. "Right."

"I don't forgive you." Cora let the words settle in her mouth. They didn't taste bitter. "I might never. But I'm done holding this."

Avery blinked, taken aback by the gentleness beneath the sharpness. That part surprised even Cora, how it felt once she said it. Light. Not healed, but released. Refusing to carry the wreckage of that relationship. Who knew embracing even the messiest of feelings could actually help.

Cora turned, her coat sweeping around her legs as she walked away. But behind her, Avery spoke again, quieter this time. "Wait, Cordelia. Could we... ever be friends again?"

Cora paused, glancing over her shoulder. The question landed awkwardly, not knowing where it belonged. She searched Avery's face, wondering if it was hope or habit asking. Maybe both.

"Don't call me Cordelia," she answered. "It's Cora."

Then she turned and walked away, her heels clicking with each step—measured, unshaken, like punctuation. Not an ellipsis. A full stop.

And as the wind carried the last of Avery's presence away, Cora didn't feel like she was leaving something behind.

She felt like she was walking into the life she'd already started building.

By the time she reached the restaurant, her hands had gone cold from thinking her coat pockets would be enough, but she didn't really mind. The warmth blooming in her chest felt like enough. A peace that came not from fixing something, but from finally letting it stay broken.

Inside, they were seated at the far table, with Lumi staying wrapped in one of her signature oversized scarves. She opted for ordering a drink where the photo looked aggressively pink. Cora chose a blueberry lavender lemonade.

"You're late," Lumi said pointedly, raising an eyebrow even when they received their sugary drinks. "I was about to file a missing person's report."

"I had an ex-fiancé sighting," Cora sighed.

Lumi's cup paused midair. "Seriously?"

Cora nodded, shrugging out of her coat. "On a bench. Looking like a ghost of holidays past."

Lumi winced. "Yikes. Did she cry? Did you *make* her cry?"

"Almost. In that really dry, emotionally mature way. She gave me the whole 'I'm sorry' thing and decided to mention she's not dating the woman she cheated with."

"Just what you needed to hear," Lumi said with an eye roll. "She definitely only said that to make herself feel better. You okay?"

Cora hesitated, not because she wasn't, but because it was still new. "I think so," she said finally. "I told her I don't forgive her. And that I'm done holding it. Which sounds very dramatic in hindsight, but honestly? It felt like clearing the last cobweb out of my brain."

Lumi leaned back, visibly impressed. "Damn, look at you. Dropping truth bombs and setting emotional boundaries in the same sentence."

"I know." Cora smiled, just a little. "It's unsettling."

"So now that you've closed the ghost-of-ex-fiancé chapter, what comes next?"

Cora took a sip, thought about Theo, and the slow, steady warmth of his hand in hers. About how she'd spent so much time trying to figure out who she was without Avery, and now, how strange and beautiful it felt to finally know.

She smiled again. "I think I finally get to find out."

Chapter 35

Later that night, Cora stood barefoot in her room, the lights dimmed to a soft glow. The scent of rosemary and orange peel wafted through the space, smoke curling from the small ceramic dish on the floor. A circle of salt outlined a portion of the floorboards, containing the ritual.

She exhaled slowly and reached for the two cords she'd set aside earlier—one gold, one deep indigo, the colors she'd once used for binding spells, back when she believed in shared futures. Back when she believed *Avery* was her future.

She tied the cords loosely around a sprig of dried lavender, symbolic and a little poetic, which felt on-brand for her, even if she hated to admit it.

"I release what is no longer mine to hold," she muttered. "I release what never should've been mine to carry."

She paused. The silence in the room was alive and waiting.

"I release you, Avery. From my memory, from my worry, from the space I kept making in myself for you."

The scissors glinted in the candlelight—silver, well-used, the same pair she'd inherited from her grandmother. She took a breath and cut the cords clean through.

The threads fell in two pieces onto the small dish beside the smoking herbs. No flash of magic. No surge of power. Just the sound of release.

And still, it altered something in her.

She sat back on her heels and let the stillness settle in. For a long moment, she just breathed. She thought she might feel grief. Or regret. But mostly, she just felt light. Tired, maybe, but in a good way. Like after a long walk that took you farther than expected, only to bring you somewhere better.

She snorted, wiped her hands on her leggings, and stood. Then, a soft knock tapped at the doorframe, reminding her she'd sent a text for post-spellwork company.

Theo leaned there with his usual casual slouch, a little tousled, eyes soft. "Hey. You good?"

She looked at him, really looked, and felt that small shift again. Not like something was beginning. Like something had landed.

"Yeah," she said, and the word felt like a truth instead of an answer. "I think I am."

He stepped inside and sat beside her on the edge of the bed. "You did it, didn't you?" he asked gently.

She gestured to the cords still on the floor, and the burned lavender sprig. "I let her go."

It was the kind of statement that once would've been a performance, something she said to convince herself. But now, it sat easy on her chest. She turned toward him, fingers brushing his, and he caught her hand like he always had—with care.

Her voice caught. "Theo..."

He didn't speak, just waited, thumb tracing quiet shapes along her knuckles.

"I love you," she admitted, the words clearer than she expected. "I think I've loved you for a while. But I didn't know how to say it. Or I thought if I said it out loud, it'd vanish."

She used to believe she was too much. Too sharp, too weird, too uncertain. She'd twisted herself into someone more palatable before, and it had almost broken her. But with Theo, she hadn't needed to bend. She could bring her whole self, and still be held.

"You don't have to say it unless you're ready," he murmured. "But I've been waiting for you to."

She chuckled softly. "It's not that I wasn't ready. I just didn't trust myself not to break the good thing."

He tilted her chin, meeting her eyes with that same steady warmth. "You're more than enough, Cordelia. I don't need perfect. Just you. Snark, magic, emotional hedging included."

She blinked, then smiled through it. "You're really committing to this emotionally mature boyfriend thing."

"Terrifying, isn't it?"

"Truly. I was banking on you being a cryptic forest hermit."

"Still a possibility. But now I come with feelings."

She shook her head, laughing into his shoulder as he pulled her closer, his heartbeat steady against her cheek. The same room that had once felt too quiet now held warmth, movement, presence. And she wanted it all.

"I'm scared," she admitted.

He didn't flinch. "Me too."

"I'm scared I'll mess this up. That I'm too much. Or not enough. Or just a walking complication."

"You *are* a walking complication," he said, nudging her. "But you're also my favorite person."

She smiled, brushing her thumb across the back of his hand. "I love you."

His gaze softened, like she'd handed him something fragile and priceless all at once. "I love you too. And not just because you found me an accountant."

"Oh, right, *that*." She laughed against his chest. "Do you know how hard it is to find someone who understands enchanted inventory and quarterly taxes?"

"Clearly harder than falling in love with you."

"You're getting *way* too good at this," she muttered.

"Oh, I know," he said, smug now. "I'm unbearable."

Theo leaned back on one elbow, watching her like she was his favorite thing to look at. "So, now that we've confessed our feelings and had a vulnerable emotional breakthrough, what's next? Shared bank account? Matching broomsticks charmed to actually fly?"

"Don't push your luck."

"I'm just saying. I make a mean Sunday breakfast. Could be a package deal."

Cora leaned into him, warm and loose-limbed. "You're lucky I like you. Even if you are a mushroom-in-your-omelet kind of guy."

"Oh no, the ultimate red flag."

She groaned, flopping onto her back jokingly. "I'm in love with a mushroom apologist. This is my life now."

"Yep. You're doomed."

But Cora didn't feel doomed. Not even close. She remembered how lost she'd felt walking back into this house for the first time—unsure, angry at herself for hoping it could be different. But now? She wasn't trying to reclaim some old version of her life.

They lay back, tangled in each other and in no rush to untangle. The windowpane rattled gently with wind outside, but it only made the room feel cozier.

"You know," she murmured, "when I came back, I thought I was just escaping. But I think I was actually starting something. Even if I didn't know it yet."

Theo kissed her cheek. "You've been writing your next chapter this whole time. I just showed up halfway through."

"Well, I'm keeping you in the epilogue."

"I'll try not to ruin it with too many puns."

Cora reached for the blanket and tugged it over them, her voice barely a murmur. "If you start snoring, I'm putting a silencing charm on your face."

Theo hummed, eyes already drifting shut. "Worth it."

As the candlelight dimmed to a final flicker, Cora let herself drift. She may be able to figure out her thirties after all.

Chapter 36

The cemetery sat just outside of Valley Creek Hollow, tucked between brittle oaks and a field gone silver with frost. January had settled in fully—gray skies, frozen earth, a hush in the air that seemed too delicate to disturb.

They walked the winding path in silence—Cora, her mother, and Theo trailing just behind. The sound of boots crunching on frozen grass was the only thing that accompanied them.

Cora had offered to come alone. Her mother had refused.

"I think it's time," Nicole had said that morning, her voice even but laced with something older than grief. "We can't keep honoring him only in private."

So they came together. And Theo—Theo had understood with a glance. He didn't ask questions, just brought hot chocolate and drove, offering the collectedness Cora didn't know she'd need until she had it.

The grave was the same, but the sight of it still gave her a jolt, as if grief had quietly frozen in her chest and was just now beginning to thaw.

JAMES SPARKS, Beloved Father. Coach. Collector of Terrible Jokes.

Nicole stepped forward first. She knelt beside the headstone with the kind of graceful, grounded reverence Cora had watched her use for years during their household rituals—when lighting a candle for protection or drawing sigils in chalk during a new moon.

From her coat pocket, Nicole pulled out a small glass vial. She uncorked it and poured the contents—a mixture of rosemary, lavender, and dried apple blossom—into the grass beneath the stone. Then, softly, she whispered something under her breath. A charm for peace. A calling home.

She placed one gloved hand on the stone, closed her eyes, and stayed like that for a long moment.

Cora didn't move until her mother did.

Nicole stood slowly and turned to her, eyes a little red but calm. "Go ahead, sweetheart," she said gently. "He's missed you."

Cora knelt, the cold biting at her knees, even through her jeans. In her hands, she carried a small bunch of yellow snapdragons—her father's favorite. She laid them at the base of the stone, brushing a thin crust of frost away.

"Hi, Dad," she said quietly. "It's been a minute. Well, more than a minute."

She paused, closing her eyes as she breathed in and let out a shaky breath. The last time she was here she told him about meeting Avery. That felt like lifetimes away now.

"I'm back in town. For real this time. And I'm—" she paused, swallowing, "—I'm trying. To build something again. To not run."

She reached into her own coat pocket and withdrew a slip of paper, folded twice. A letter, inked with a spell of remembrance. She'd written it the night before at her kitchen table, a candle burning beside her, salt scattered across the threshold.

She tucked the letter beneath the snapdragons.

"I think I finally understand what you meant when you said grief doesn't mean something's broken. Just changed."

Behind her, she felt Theo's presence—close but not crowding. And beside him, her mother, arms folded against the cold, gaze turned skyward.

"I miss you," she whispered. "But I think I can carry it now. And I'm not doing it alone anymore."

She let out a breath, white in the air, and glanced over her shoulder to where Theo stood with his hands in his pockets, trying to pretend he wasn't watching.

"I wish you could meet him. I mean, you *knew* him, technically," she said with a soft laugh. "But he's not the quiet kid who chased me with frogs anymore. He's—" she hesitated, then smiled. "He's someone good. He makes me laugh. He makes me feel like I'm allowed to take up space."

Her fingers trailed across the top of the gravestone, brushing away a few stray flecks of frost.

"And just so you know," she added, voice lighter now, "if mom was planning our wedding when I was nine, I sincerely hope *you* weren't sketching blueprints for the backyard reception. That would be mildly alarming."

The wind stirred, and a small gust brushed through the snapdragons like a whisper.

She glanced toward Nicole, who caught her eye with a knowing smile.

"You two always did think you were being subtle," Cora added under her breath, then softened. "I still remember that night you let us camp in the backyard. Me and Theo in one tent, you and Mom in the other, pretending not to listen while we made up stories and talked about what our magic might look like someday. You let us stay up way too late. And when we ran out of marshmallows, you conjured more with that smug grin like it was no big deal."

Her throat tightened, but she pushed through it, letting the memory hold her up.

"I think you'd like who he's become. I think you'd be proud of who I'm becoming, too. Or—I hope you would."

She paused. "I want to build something real this time. Not just survive it. And I think... I think Theo's part of that. If you're watching, maybe nudge him toward a good ring size or something."

Cora laughed softly, wiping one corner of her eye.

"Anyway. Just wanted you to know."

She stood slowly, brushing off her knees, and laid her hand flat against the stone one last time.

"Thanks," she whispered. "For the good parts of me. For the magic that still works, even when it hurts."

When she turned, Theo offered her his coat. She didn't need it, but she took it anyway, wrapping herself in the cedar and cinnamon warmth of him.

Nicole stepped forward again and linked her arm with Cora's. "You did good, darling."

Cora let her head rest briefly against her mother's shoulder. "You too. Very impressive restraint on not crying louder than me."

Nicole sniffed, eyes still red. "Please. I'm saving that for when you two get married."

Great. She'd heard.

For a moment, they stood together—three people connected by love, loss, and the kind of magic that threads through generations like quiet candlelight.

The wind shifted, a soft breeze rolled down from the trees, rustling the leaves they hadn't cleared. The snapdragons trembled, just slightly. Cora smiled at the way they stood defiant against the frost.

They started walking back to the car, the sky softening to that late-winter shade of lavender that always made Cora feel nostalgic for things she hadn't lost yet.

As they neared the car, Nicole reached into her pocket and handed Cora a small bundle—sage wrapped with black thread and a sprig of thyme. "Hang this above the door," she said. "For grounding. And for new beginnings."

Cora looked at her, emotions swimming just behind her eyes. "Thanks, Mom."

Nicole kissed her cheek and gave her hand one last squeeze. "And don't think I didn't see you and Theo looking all cozy by the snapdragons. Your father would've had a *field day* with that."

Cora snorted. "Please, he'd already be planning a double wedding with Lumi just to mess with us."

"I miss his chaos," Nicole said with a wistful smile. "He kept my hexes interesting."

Nicole climbed into the back seat as Theo approached. He hadn't spoken much since they arrived. But once Nicole was in the car, he turned to Cora before climbing in the driver's seat.

"You okay?" he asked.

"Yeah," she said, surprised to find she meant it. "I think I am."

Theo reached over and brushed a bit of leaf from her scarf. "Your mom is definitely invested now."

Cora raised an eyebrow. "She's reserving complete approval until you can cook a roast chicken with nothing but intention and a salt circle."

Theo gave a dramatic sigh. "Guess I'd better practice my poultry magic."

As they drove away from the cemetery, Cora glanced in the rearview mirror once more. The snapdragons looked absurdly bright in the frost.

And for the first time in a long time, she didn't feel like a visitor in her own life.

She felt home.

Epilogue

C ora didn't expect the moment to feel quite like this.

She sat cross-legged on the floor of her living room, the aftermath of their Samhain gathering strewn around her—empty cider cups, a blanket of orange and burgundy leaves Lumi had "borrowed" from the park, half-melted candles that still smelled like clove and sweet woodsmoke. The windows were cracked open just enough for the chill to sneak in, but inside, the air was warm, humming with candlelight and contentment.

Lumi was vibrating beside her. "OPEN IT. You're going to make me combust. This is actual medical distress."

Cora rolled her eyes, but smiled as she reached for the box. Her fingers hovered over it, hesitant. This wasn't just a box. It was a moment. The kind you didn't get twice. Well, hopefully she would get it more than once, but this is the *first* time. It's different.

She glanced at Lumi, who was still humming with excitement — and new freedom, too, now that her complicated thing with Jax was finally behind her.

It had started almost by accident—her writing that ridiculous novella during sleepless nights and long afternoons tucked in the bookstore. But Theo had read it and immediately declared it 'the exact right kind of ridiculous.' Lumi had begged for more chapters. And somehow, it had grown into an actual book. A real, published thing. And now... now the author copies were here.

She sliced open the tape and folded the flaps back. The room stilled.

Inside, stacked neatly, were her books. *Her* books. The covers shimmered slightly under the soft light—gold foil catching the curves of the title: *Brewing Up Mr. Right*. Zemina stood proud on the cover, wild hair and sharp grin, surrounded by swirling leaves and magic.

"Holy shit," Cora breathed, and Lumi immediately grabbed one.

"It's so pretty I want to eat it," Lumi said, hugging the book to her chest. "I mean, is it weird to cry over font choice? Because this font is giving me actual emotions. I need to sniff it, cry over it, annotate the spicy scenes—"

"Absolutely not annotating the spicy scenes," Cora laughed as she pulled out the top copy.

Theo crouched behind her, a soft smile tugging at the corners of his mouth. "Told you it'd be good."

Cora turned the book in her hands, her thumb brushing over the edge of the spine. She opened it to the dedication:

For Mom, Lumi and Theo—my light, my chaos, and my calm. Thank you for helping me write the best version of myself.

Theo's hand found her shoulder and squeezed gently.

"I still can't believe it's real," she said.

Theo leaned down so his chin brushed her shoulder. "You earned it. Every page."

Just then, Cora's mom walked in from the kitchen, carrying a tray of her famous cider. "I hope no one's summoning anything else in this house tonight."

"Only overwhelming pride," Lumi said dramatically, waving the book in the air. "Your daughter is a published romance author."

Cora's mom smiled, but her eyes were already misting. "I know. I read it twice."

"*Wait,*" Cora said, narrowing her eyes. "How? It just came out."

"I may have borrowed your proof copy a few weeks ago. It was excellent, honey. A little steamy, but I skipped those pages." She paused, then added slyly, "Well, most of them."

Theo coughed into his mug, and Cora groaned. "Please don't discuss my sex scenes with my mother."

Nicole just patted her on the head like she was five. "Too late. I've already recommended it to all of my customers and my book club. Gloria from down the street thinks Theo looks like your cover model."

"Oh my gods," Cora muttered, shoving her face into a pillow.

Theo grinned. "Do I get royalties if they base the next one on me?"

"Only if you stop trying to reorganize my event calendar," Cora shot back. "Just because I'm your planner doesn't mean you get to take advantage."

He just nudged her knee with his. "I love a feisty woman."

Nicole settled onto the couch, cider in hand, watching her daughter with a fondness that made Cora's throat tighten.

"You know," Nicole said softly, "your dad would've been proud, too."

Cora stilled.

Nicole reached over, brushed a curl off her daughter's forehead. "He used to say you'd write stories that would make people feel seen. Agreed with me about that kind of magic in you."

Cora blinked rapidly. "He also said I'd probably end up writing about dragons and dating apps."

"Well," Nicole said, smiling over the rim of her mug, "he wasn't wrong."

Theo raised his hand. "I'd read that."

"And he'd be bragging to everyone who would listen," Nicole added. "Probably trying to get your book into Little League goodie bags."

They all laughed, and the emotion softened just enough to feel safe again.

It was strange. When she'd first come home, the future felt like fog. But then Valley Creek Hollow felt like hers again, and the bookstore gave her a new sense of purpose.

With Alina's sharp mind and meticulous spreadsheets, the store wasn't just surviving—it was thriving. Alina had even suggested quarterly themed pop-ups, which somehow made budget meetings... fun? Cora still wasn't sure what sorcery that was, and Theo was equally terrified. After sitting down with them both, Alina had the suggestion that Cora work at the store, too, drawing up projections and PowerPoints on how she'd get paid. Theo didn't argue.

"You're really good at this," he'd said, somewhere between impressed and mildly panicked as he looked at Alina's preparedness. "Want to help me run future events?"

That partnership had grown like the rest of them—quietly, with room to breathe. They made a surprisingly good team—Cora brought the structure, Theo brought the heart. And somewhere along the way, she'd stopped wondering if she belonged in her own story.

Now, her name was on a book. Her story was out there.

Lumi nudged her with an elbow. "Okay, but when is the release party? I'm already designing the cookie table in my mind. I'm thinking pumpkin-shaped sugar cookies, edible glitter, champagne punch, themed candles—"

"We're still doing it at Sticks and Stones, right?" Theo asked, flipping through the pages. "I've already got a wait-list."

"Apparently, half the town is showing up. Including some surprising names." He raised an eyebrow and handed her his phone.

Cora read the screen and froze. At the top of the pre-order list was: *Avery Chen.* Underneath it, a message: *I'm proud of you.*

The words didn't hit like a punch. But there was a feeling there, a ripple, unexpected but not devastating.

Lumi peeked at the screen and made a face. "Seriously? She *pre-ordered*?"

Cora exhaled slowly. "I guess she's watching from a distance now. That's fine. I'm not carrying it anymore."

Theo, still by her side, gave her hand a quick squeeze. "She's not on the RSVP list. Just so you know."

"I wasn't worried." And she meant it.

Lumi wrapped her in a quick side hug. "Good. Because this party is for you. Not for past drama. For *your* book. Your story. Your happy ending."

Cora smiled, a real, deep one, and looked down at the glossy cover in her hands.

"Not an ending," she said. "More like a sequel."

Theo bumped her shoulder. "Do I get to be a recurring character?"

"You're contractually obligated."

"I knew this relationship came with fine print."

"And glitter," Lumi added, holding up a bag. "So much glitter."

Cora glanced around the room—the candles, the cider—and smiled. "Maybe. Depends if my mother survives the steamy parts next time."

"No promises," her mom said, already thumbing through the book again. "But I'll be proud, no matter what."

They all laughed, and for a moment, the world shrank down to this room, this circle, this warmth. Cora leaned her head against Theo's shoulder, book in her lap, Lumi chattering excitedly about release day playlists, and her mother excitedly re-reading her work. The future still stretched ahead, unknown but not empty anymore. It felt like magic. The kind she'd made for herself.

And if the sequel involved Nicole's overzealous holiday planning, Theo's mushroom omeletes, and Lumi threatening to bedazzle the bookstore sign. Well, Cora was ready for it. The shop was thriving, her mother was proudly telling anyone who'd listen that her daughter was a published author—and that Theo was 'very tall and helpful'—and Cora? She was finally living a story she didn't need to rewrite.

About the Author

Lily A. Larkspur is a cozy witchy romance author who writes love stories steeped in magic, moonlight, and just the right amount of emotional baggage. By day, she's a mere mortal. By night, she's spinning tales where spells get tangled with feelings, cats offer commentary, and fictional crushes feel a little too real. Lily's stories blend slow-burning romance with mystical vibes—ideal for anyone who's ever pulled a tarot card for clarity, cried during an anime intro, or screamed as a form of self-care. When she's not writing, you can find her whispering to her bamboo, feeding every cat she comes across, rewatching her favorite K-dramas, or hosting her one-witch coven (open to cats, snacks, and soft blankets).